EMPIRE OF THE CHOLAS

Siddharth N. Vijayaraghavan is an author, musician and anthropologist-in-training. Born in India and educated in Singapore and India, Siddharth is currently completing his Master's (Integrated) degree in English Studies at the Department of Humanities and Social Sciences, IIT Madras, and a Diploma in Carnatic Music at the Swami Haridhos Giri School of Music, Narada Gana Sabha. *The Ascent* is Siddharth's first novel.

EMPIRE OF THE CHOLAS

SIDDHARTH N. VIJAYARAGHAVAN

Published by
Rupa Publications India Pvt. Ltd 2024
7/16, Ansari Road, Daryaganj
New Delhi 110002

Sales centres:
Bengaluru Chennai
Hyderabad Jaipur Kathmandu
Kolkata Mumbai Prayagraj

Copyright © Siddharth N. Vijayaraghavan 2024
Illustrations courtesy: Vishnu Prasad

This is a work of fiction. Names, characters, places and incidents are either the product of the author's imagination or are used fictitiously and any resemblance to any actual person, living or dead, events or locales is entirely coincidental.

All rights reserved.
No part of this publication may be reproduced, transmitted, or stored in a retrieval system, in any form or by any means, electronic, mechanical, photocopying, recording or otherwise, without the prior permission of the publisher.

P-ISBN: 978-93-5702-876-9
E-ISBN: 978-93-5702-701-4

First impression 2024

10 9 8 7 6 5 4 3 2 1

The moral right of the author has been asserted.

Printed in India

This book is sold subject to the condition that it shall not, by way of trade or otherwise, be lent, resold, hired out, or otherwise circulated, without the publisher's prior consent, in any form of binding or cover other than that in which it is published.

Foreword

The Cholas, one of the best-known dynasties of India, were a small power, ruling from a place named Uraiyur (near present-day Thiruchirapalli in Tamil Nadu) from *c.* 3rd century BCE up to the 9th century CE. It was during the reign of King Vijayalaya in the 9th century CE that the capital was shifted to Thanjavur, and from then onwards, this dynasty grew from power to greater power. The Cholas are best remembered today for their contribution to temple architecture and sculpture, but their inscriptions reveal that the emperors of this dynasty were great conquerors and excellent administrators too.

This book, a work of fiction, written by Siddharth Vijayaraghavan, a college student, highlights these dimensions brilliantly. He has, as is very clear, an excellent grasp of the nuances of Chola history. This novel is set in the reign of Raja Raja Chola I (985-1014 CE), one of the greatest emperors of India who has ably assisted his son, Prince Rajendra, the heir (yuvaraja) to the throne. The Cholas had a mighty navy and Rajendra Chola bore the well-known title *Kadaramkondan*, as he had defeated the Sailendra king of the Srivijaya dynasty which ruled over Indonesia and parts of Malaysia. The author has brought to light the naval might of the Cholas.

Bringing in various characters, both real and fictitious, Siddharth beautifully weaves a story of power, vengeance, romance and administration of those times. The best-known temple of the Cholas is the famous Brihadeeswara temple in Thanjavur, which is a UNESCO World Heritage Site. Details about how this temple was initially planned, the architects who designed it, how the work was executed, and many other aspects find a place in this book. Each of the characters here, whether historical or fictitious, will appear real to the reader, as the author has brought out the essence of those bygone times.

At a time when youngsters show virtually no interest in history, especially of South India, it is indeed very commendable that a youngster, who has mostly had his education outside India, should show a phenomenal interest in this subject and write a novel which showcases the Chola Empire in all its glory. Starting from the very first page, it has been written in a racy style, and I found it quite difficult to put it down till I had reached the end.

I foresee Siddharth Vijayaraghavan, whom I have known since he was a school student, writing many more such books and I have absolutely no doubt that they will be well received. When that happens, there will be no person happier and prouder than me. We need more such youngsters taking India's glorious history forward.

Chennai

Chithra Madhavan
28 April 2024

Author's Note

So where does one start a story? To quote Julie Andrews from *The Sound of Music*, a good place to start would be 'the very beginning, a very good place to start'. But really, where is the beginning of this story? The story of my writing this book was rather unusual, non-linear even. This story shall thus begin with the storyteller. For me, the story of *Empire of the Cholas* does not begin a thousand years ago but instead in December 2014, when my family and I travelled to the verdant Kaveri delta region to visit the temples. For an irrepressible 13-year-old, it was a dream come true—a long train journey, watching seemingly foreign villages whizz past me into blurs of brown and beige against a green landscape, lots of long drives and visiting new places. Being a history buff even then, I voraciously read up on the history of the region and kept looking for historical facts and narrating it—much to my poor mother's and grandmother's exasperation—everywhere. The 13-year-old me imagined the unfamiliar environs I was in as a repository of a great, dramatic past that I was getting to watch later, akin to the sets of one of those garish Tamil TV serials I used to consume voraciously. Being a bibliophile also meant that we made stops at each of these temples' bookstores with an unfailing religiosity to pick up books on the history of the temple and its surroundings.

As we saw the Brihadeeswara Temple in Thanjavur, an oddity in the north face of the temple caught my eye—a man in a bowler hat? In the middle of Thanjavur, Tamil Nadu, in the eleventh century? How did that even work? My mind ran amok with the possibilities, starting from the very outlandish 'was he an alien' and 'was there time travel involved'. Probably, Emperor Raja Raja Chola had a secret twin with a misshapen mushroom head separated at birth, of whom he had very faint memories which materialized in the form of this sculpture! But as I read the history of the temple, I realized that the truth was in fact closer to reality and far murkier, more unclear even. The obsession over the strange European sculpture continued in one corner of my mind.

In another corner of my mind existed a different kind of wonderment—the Great Living Chola Temples themselves. In this picturesque Kaveri region of South India stand three grand, awe-inspiring temples—of which I visited all three during my December 2014 trip—constructed by the medieval Tamil kings who exercised suzerainty over this region for almost half a millennium. These temples, visited by millions of both domestic and international tourists every year, represent and showcase the rich architectural, artistic, cultural, aesthetic and intellectual heritage of not only the region but also of Tamil Nadu itself.

The first constituent of the troika is the Brihadeeswara Temple or Rajarajeswaram Kovil of Thanjavur, built by Emperor Raja Raja Chola I between 1004 and 1010 CE. It is an imposing temple with its highest point at an impressive 216 ft, surrounded by a moat and constructed using granite, an oddity in the undulating land around Thanjavur. It is also colloquially known as the Big Temple or Periya Kovil. To me, the most fascinating feature of the *vimanam* (spire over the inner sanctum) of the temple is the sculpture of a face bearing European features and attire, which, in my novella, is the character of Vellaiappan, a close associate of the Chakravarthy or the Emperor.

The second of the troika is the Brihadeeswara Temple at Gangaikonda Cholapuram, which was a city built by Raja Raja Chola's son and successor, Rajendra Chola, in approximately 1022 CE. The temple was a centrepiece of the city once commemorative of Rajendra Chola's military successes. It is now the largest edifice in a small village in the Ariyalur district of Tamil Nadu. Its vimanam is fairly tall at 182 ft, but not as tall as the one in Thanjavur. The temple itself is sometimes regarded as the female counterpart to the Periya Kovil.

And the final temple of this troika is the Airavateeshwarar Kovil in the village Darasuram, just about 3 km away from Kumbakonam. It was constructed by Raja Raja Chola II in the twelfth century, almost a hundred years after the construction of the Periya Kovil. It was built in stark contrast with its period in history, when the once magnificent Chola Kingdom was plagued by wars and was set on a path of decline. Yet, this temple is arguably the most unique and beautiful of the troika, its most striking feature being the musical steps leading to the temple itself.

One of the most intriguing parts of the temples' histories is the contrast between period, location and architecture. These temples were conceived of, planned and constructed in medieval Tamil Nadu, where only rudimentary technologies existed. And yet, vimanams of such height and temples of such size, grandeur and perfection were built. The temples are all located in the Kaveri delta region—an undulating, green stretch of land without a single hill—and yet, the temples are all built out of stone—granite, to be more precise. The construction of the Kovils wouldn't have been an easy exercise.

And thus, these two conversations coagulated in my mind;

I realized there lay a story here, in these Great Living Chola Temples, and that needed to be narrated to the world. Even more significantly, I realized while writing the book that the story that needed to be told was not of the temples' construction but rather of those who constructed the temples—in other words, the human efforts and emotions that went into the construction. I had an issue with the way history was written and studied as an unemotional narrative of forces majeures that seemed to be so alienated from the emotions of the people involved. We must face it; the actors of human history were humans, with their own joys and passions, strengths and weaknesses, likes and dislikes, foibles and failings. To ignore that and merely study the outcomes of the said issues, to me, was problematic to a great degree. This is also why I wrote the book—to enliven the characters that hitherto only existed as paper tigers, to immortalize my interpretation of who these epoch makers, like Raja Raja Chola, Kundavai and Rajendra Chola, were as humans.

Of course, as this is a work of historical fiction, I have taken liberties in the creation and depiction of characters. The entire family of Roeland Crape, including Angayarkanni, Kayalvizhi and Aniruddhan, as well as the kingdom and the rulers of Sepang are products of my imagination. I'd like to think that these people did live in the real-life parallel of my book's universe, except they lacked a voice to tell their story. Through this book, I hope to not only tell their story, but also raise their importance to a level that I feel they deserve.

As I wrote this book, these characters and the temple itself, seemed to grow up, through a pliant childhood, to a rebellious teenage phase where nothing seemed to work and no one seemed to listen to me, to finally a more mature adult phase where I developed a rapport with them. The way the temple has been depicted or these characters have been written may be fictional to other people, but to me, every one of these characters is a person I have lived with, conversed and partaken of food with. They didn't become these people overnight; indeed, as my mother can well attest, it took a lot of screaming, crying, shaking my fist at the laptop screen, and much more drama. But today, they are people with a beautiful story, they are ones I relate to, and I hope you find them and their stories relatable as well.

Characters

Chola Dynasty

Raja Raja Chola/ Arulmozhi Varman	Chakravarthy (Emperor) of the Chola Empire
Kundavai Pirattiyar	Sister of Raja Raja Chola, married to Vandiyathevan
Rajendra Chola	Raja Raja Chola's son and the Crown Prince
Illavarasi Kundavai	Raja Raja Chola's daughter
Vandiyathevan	Kundavai's husband and the Chola army's *senathipathi*

Court of Raja Raja Chola

Aniruddha Brahmarayar	Prime Minister of Chola Nadu
Chezhian*	Chief of the Kudandhai Kottam
Dandanayakan	A Brahmin general in the Chola army

Vellaiappan's family

Subbiah*	A fisherman and pearl hunter
Angayarkanni*	Subbiah's only daughter and the wife of Vellaiappan
Vellaiappan/Roeland Crape	Angayarkanni's husband and a Chola minister

Aniruddhan*	Son of Angayarkanni and Vellaiappan
Kayalvizhi*	Daughter of Angayarkanni and Vellaiappan

Royalty of Sepang

Aryapriya*	Governor of Kadaram
Abhinava*	King of Sepang, Aryapriya's older half-brother

Vengi Dynasty

Shaktivarman	Heir apparent to Maharaja Danarnava
Vimaladityan	Maharaja Danarnava's younger son

Other Characters

Alagiya Nayaki	A cowherdess
Chidambara Vaidhyar*	Physician, living in Poompuhar
Karpagavalli*	A *nakkan* or professional dancer
Kunjara Malla Peruntachchar aka Raja Raja Peruntachchar	The architect of Rajarajeswaram, aka Periya Kovil
Sivanandam*	A musician and Karpagavalli's partner
Sivakozhundu Pathar*	A jeweller in Thanjai and Subbiah's cousin
Thirupurasundari ammai*	Sivakozhundu Pathar's wife

---

*Fictional characters

Prologue

Dusk began to set over the city of Thanjavur, the capital of Chola Nadu. Balancing multiple earthen pots over her head with the adroitness of a far more experienced woman, the young, bony girl walked down the dusty road leading from the central markets to her small house on the edge of the village. The day had not gone particularly well for her—not only had she been unable to sell all the *mor* that she had made for the day but a young child had also, rather callously, aimed his slingshot at a mud pot she had bought recently. To make things worse, when she hauled the child to his home and complained about the kid's misdemeanours to his parents, rather than apologizing for the kid's mistake, the parents very condescendingly suggested that she should have guarded her wares better. 'Perhaps you should invest in brass pots, young lady, so they can't be broken by children so easily'—these were the words of the parents, dripping with an air of superiority as though their family was incapable of doing any wrong. Now she had to dig into her family's already dwindling savings to buy a new pot. The kids needed to be fed, parents-in-law needed to be tended to, and feed had to be bought for the cows. The worst part? She only had 24 hours a day to do all of this, *and* sleep, *and* eat, *and* take care of herself!

Leaving the pots in the adjoining cowshed, she entered her home. The setting sun had cast a variety of shadows over the house, making it seem eerie and deserted. She quickly bathed in the well in the backyard and draped herself in an old, tattered brown saree. She forcefully coaxed her frizzy hair into a tight bun and tied it with a bit of old cotton strip—she didn't even have the time to shampoo her tresses with *seeyakai podi*, so her hair had become a knotted, obdurate mass. *As though her children's obduracy wasn't enough!* She entered the kitchen, and began converting the leftover lunch into dinner. As the pot began to boil, she heard the door open and her in-laws come in from the temple. Her mother-in-law offered her some fresh jasmines strung together, which she smilingly accepted and wrapped around her hair. Her children too returned home. Small talk ensued, and soon, a meagre dinner was served. The children made a face about the same thing for lunch being retrofitted into dinner. Her father-in-law threatened the children with violence. All was well. After the in-laws and the children went to bed, she retreated to the cowshed to tend to the cows and prepare the pots for the next day. Unmindful of her weariness, the cows—like her children—mooed with joy at seeing her. She gently caressed them. The solitary oil lamp was suspended high over the thatched floor of the cowshed, illuminating the space dully. The only shadow was her solitary human frame.

Hers was a crowded and lonely existence. Her husband was a low-ranking foot soldier in the Chola army, which meant that he was inevitably fighting in some war or the other and was seldom home. Her kids missed their father, and so did she. Relationships with her in-laws appeared close to an outsider, but she knew of their disapproval and disdain for her, for she dared to sell buttermilk in the markets. Her parents, friends and family lived in the faraway village of Thirusengattankudi, where she was born and raised. She hadn't seen them in ages, having last met them when she had visited her parents' home for the delivery of her younger child. The loneliness ate into her heart as she swept, mopped and cleaned the entire cowshed, in utter, all-encompassing silence that seemed to suffocate her. She knew that once she slept, the events of this day would repeat themselves endlessly, over tomorrow, the day after tomorrow, the day after that, and after that, and so on and so forth. At least, she could take some solace in the consistency and predictability of her life.

Yet, she, Alagiya Nayaki, a simple buttermilk vendor in Thanjavur, dared to dream. As she lay in the large room next to her sleeping children, dozing off while staring at the roof whose gaps needed to be fixed as soon as possible before the next rainy season, Alagiya Nayaki dreamt. Instead of the bland, unplaceable shade of grey that coloured the dreams of most people, Alagiya Nayaki dreamt in vivid colour of the history of an entire nation seemingly far, far away.

In her dreams, she saw the younger brother of the crown prince suddenly and unexpectedly thrust into becoming the king. She saw him rising to the challenge spectacularly, by not only expanding his empire's power but by also becoming a ruler whose every decision ensured that each and every one of his subjects was happy, well-fed, and had the potentiality for a fulfilled life. She saw a man as white as a jasmine, washing up on the seashore and rising to be a trusted lieutenant of the king, making himself a part of his new adopted nation by marrying into it. She witnessed the king sailing across the seven seas, ensuring his people living across the globe were never under the threat of mighty despots, tyrants and bigots. She saw a benevolent deity Emperuman who blessed the king in his efforts to render his nation prosperous, and she saw a king who sought to thank Emperuman for His guidance and His blessings in each endeavour of his. She saw the entire nation swing into action to build a monument in reverence, which seemed to be so tall that its peak paid obeisance to the gods in the sky.

Amongst this varied scenery, she saw herself in the mix, at every scene. She wasn't alone—no—she was part of something far larger than herself. She saw herself giving her all, whatever she could do, to this nation, to this monument, to this king. She saw herself finally not being alienated but instead being an integral part of the nation—included, wanted, valued. She saw herself merging into the monument and becoming someone who won't be forgotten, who won't be taken for granted, who'd be forever remembered, heard and cherished.

And then she woke up, right at the first crow of the rooster next door. She stared once again at her broken ceiling and the tiny water drops that clinged at its edges, holding on for dear life. She let out a long sigh and began preparing for the day ahead.

1

'Nagapattinam. With the Bay of Bengal lapping up against its white beaches, Nagapattinam truly shone as a pearl of the Tamil country. It was a busy trading port where multiple nations converged and conversed amidst its antediluvian port and warehouses. It was a centre of learning, with the Kayarohana Temple, Soundararaja Perumal Temple and the Chudamani Vihara attracting Shaivite, Vaishnavite and Buddhist scholars from Chola Nadu and the distant lands across the Bay of Bengal alike. Afforested with palmyra trees, which sheltered the throngs who descended upon its busy markets from the relentless tropical heat and the ever-looming threat of cyclones, Nagapattinam was the crucible of possibility, the cradle of hopes—the city where anything seemed possible.'

AD 980, Margazhi
A village near Nagapattinam

The sun rose on the eastern horizon, casting a golden pink glow over the sea, the paddy fields and the coconut groves adjoining the ancient port city of Nagapattinam. A cool, gentle breeze created seemingly infinite ripples on the rivers and canals flowing into the sea. The early morning sunrays and the gentle breeze transformed the verdant coconut fronds into a swaying symphony of emerald green.

Birds had begun to shrug off their sleep and chirp merrily as they set about their daily chores. Waves of the cold seawater gently caressed the sylvan shores of Nagapattinam. It was a peerless visual, auditory and olfactory feast.

Sixteen-year-old Angayarkanni, a beautiful and reclusive fisherwoman, stepped out of her humble yet immaculate two-storey abode, draped in a dark blue saree. Angayarkanni's small round face was beautifully framed by her luxurious waist-length ebony hair. Her hazel eyes outlined by dark eyelashes offered a sharp contrast to her bronze complexion. Her nose was as sharp as the edge of the knife of the Yemeni traders who frequented Nagapattinam. Her firmly closed full lips reflected her decisive and introverted nature.

Angayarkanni hailed from a family of pearl divers and fishermen who had previously lived in Pandya Nadu. The family's skills in fishing for exquisite pearls and large hauls of the choicest fish had endeared them to the Pandya royalty. The family was more affluent than most of their kin. Angayarkanni's father, Subbiah, was not only an expert pearl diver but also a reputed pearl merchant. He had relocated from Pandya Nadu to Nagapattinam in Chola Nadu, which was then flourishing under the reign of Utthama Chola[1] and his able nephew and deputy, Arulmozhi Varman. Subbiah's decision to relocate to Nagapattinam turned out to be a sagacious one, as his clientele soon expanded to include the Chola royalty, affluent families of the Chola kingdom, traders from Arabia, China, Sriwijaya, Champa and Angkor, and the Swahili traders of Mombasa.

Subbiah's wife, Valliammal, had passed away when she was just twenty-five, leaving behind a son, Ponniah, and a

---

[1] Utthama Chola reigned from 970 CE to 985 CE.

daughter, Angayarkanni. Angayarkanni was just an infant when her mother had died. When Ponniah was seventeen and Angayarkanni was ten, Subbiah moved to Nagapattinam along with Angayarkanni to expand his business interests there, while Ponniah continued to manage the family's business interests in Pandya Nadu. Ponniah, who was seven years older than Angayarkanni, continued to live at Korkai in Pandya Nadu. He and his wife Ambika, after their marriage, had been overseeing their family's pearl and fishing businesses. The couple had a seven-year-old daughter named Devyani.

Subbiah brought up Angayarkanni, showering immense love and affection on her. Angayarkanni was equally loving towards him. The duo lived in an adventure-filled world of their own. As Angayarkanni grew up with just her father for company most of the time, she savoured solitude. Subbiah trained her in not just fishing but also in pearl diving. Angayarkanni accompanied Subbiah on his pearl-hunting expeditions at Korkai and Nagapattinam. The fishing community, aghast at a young girl being trained in deep-sea diving, protested vehemently. They stopped short of excommunicating the family, courtesy the family's close ties with the Pandya and Chola royalty and Subbiah's philanthropic ways. Subbiah chose to ignore his community's disapproval.

That morning, Angayarkanni skilfully manoeuvred her boat out into the sea after praying to Kadal Thai, the Sea Mother, for her safety and for a large haul of fish. This was the tradition among the fisherfolk of those times. When she reached mid-sea, she cast her net and waited patiently. Barely one *nazhigai* after she cast the net, she sensed it becoming taut. She pulled up the net to find a huge haul of squids.

Angayarkanni was thrilled. She looked forward to handing over the catch to one of her father's employees for selling in the market and returning home to cook a delicious, hot meal for her father.

Though Angayarkanni generally made ragi porridge along with some *karuvadu* (dried fish) and sliced onions for her father's lunch, she was happy whenever she had an opportunity to serve him a freshly prepared meal. *Today must be my lucky day!* she thought. Little did Angayarkanni realize that it was indeed her lucky day on other counts too. As she shored up the haul, she saw a peculiar sight. A pink mass more than six feet long, swathed in blue silk and attached to what seemed to be a wooden plank, was bobbing up and down in the sea. Angayarkanni would have normally ignored the occurrence, but something within urged her to row towards the mysterious object. What was it? Was it the wreckage of an ill-fated merchant ship? Was it some treasure?

It was neither.

A barely conscious, white-skinned young man was clinging onto the wooden plank precariously. Angayarkanni was already rowing the boat with a large haul of fish. She knew that she would not be able to haul this tall, well-built man single-handedly. Angayarkanni decided to blow her conch, an instrument all fisherfolk possessed, to send a signal to others for assistance. Fisherfolk of those times always carried conches with them. They had a set of signals, which they conveyed with the blowing of the conch. This was used to transmit several messages like a potential haul that was too large for one boat to handle, impending natural disasters, the presence of predators, and appeals for assistance.

A couple of sturdy fishermen who were in a nearby boat rushed to her aid. Angayarkanni pointed out to them the unconscious man clinging precariously to the plank of wood, and the fishermen immediately jumped into the sea and hauled the foreigner into Angayarkanni's boat. One of them then got into Angayarkanni's boat to assist her with rowing the boat to the shore.

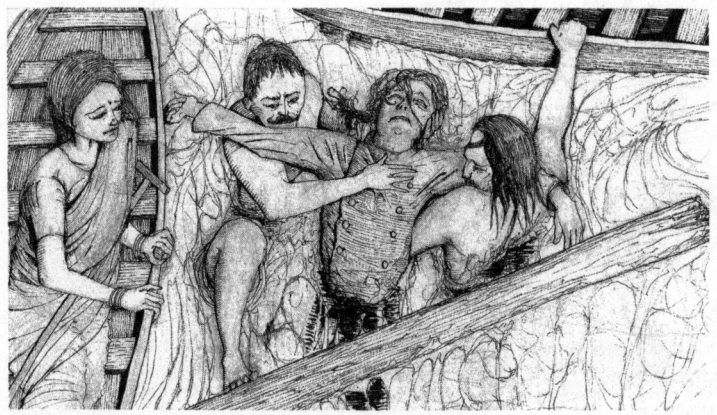

Once they reached the shore, the fisherfolk carried the man to Angayarkanni's house. Subbiah rushed out of the house on hearing a noisy procession approaching. When Angayarkanni hurriedly narrated the incident to her father, he immediately made way for the motley crew to carry the stranger into his house and sent for the *vaidhyar* to treat him. The unconscious stranger was laid down on a mat and Subbiah began pumping his chest to expel the sea water he had swallowed in copious quantities. By the time the renowned Chidambara Vaidhyar of Nagapattinam reached Subbiah's house, the stranger was already babbling incoherently.

Chidambara Vaidhyar examined the stranger's pulse and assured the onlookers that all was well with him. The vaidhyar felt that the stranger was probably a survivor of an ill-fated ship and the protracted time spent floating in the high seas had rendered him delirious. He administered a few herbal medicines and gave Angayarkanni instructions on nursing the sick man, before taking leave of the family.

2

Angayarkanni diligently tended to the unconscious stranger. For the first fortnight after he was rescued, he streamed in and out of consciousness. She regularly administered the prescribed medicines to the stranger, fed him rice and ragi porridge, and arranged for one of her father's men to bathe him in warm water every day. During this period, Angayarkanni—the beloved daughter of Kadal Thai—stopped fishing, which had been her passion since she was thirteen. She sat by the stranger's bedside day and night, attending to his needs.

One night, Subbiah walked into the stranger's room to find Angayarkanni slumped over the side of his mat, clutching a palmyra fan. The stranger too slept peacefully, his body drenched in sweat from an unusually warm Panguni evening. Subbiah froze; this was evidently not the gawky, awkward ten-year-old whom he had taught how to fish, who would swap her 'ta' with 'da' so often while speaking that Subbiah also began speaking like her, and who would make a sour face whenever she was served bitter gourds, which she wholeheartedly abhorred. She had blossomed into a woman. What kind of a woman she was, Subbiah didn't know for sure, but this was definitely not the petulant tantrum thrower she used to be. That conversation would have to wait, for Subbiah being the father that he was, cradled her gently in his arms, tiptoed across the courtyard into her quarters, and lay her on her bed. Just as Subbiah covered his daughter with a muslin blanket, his daughter began stirring, crumpling her eyelids into the sockets wearily, and stretching her arms into the mudbrick wall behind her. '*Appa,*' she slurred, 'How long have I been asleep?'

'I don't know, *kuzhandai*. But it must have been quite a few nazhigais; you were sound asleep in that stranger's room when I carried you here'.

'I fell asleep? There? And you had to carry me? Appa, you really do not need to do this. I am an adult woman! You've seen me fish!'

'Whatever it may be, we can talk about it in the morning. First, sleep properly. You need to rest.'

'Appa...' started Angayarkanni, only to be cut off by Subbiah insist, 'Angayarkanni, sleep.'

And sleep she did, but a new life sprung into existence while she slept. She dreamt of the stranger and his confused grin during his initial moments of consciousness. She dreamt of his strong, muscular arms, wrapped around him while he slept, cradling his self through a lonely, nebulous night. Most of all, she swum in the dreamworld through the stranger's eyes—a startlingly light shade of an indescribable hue, full of a sparkling wit, kindness and vulnerability. She dreamt of a day when her soul would unite with his and expand her twofold. She had not spoken a word to the man, but she still dreamt of a life of ecstasy, companionship and commitment.

During one of his conscious phases, the stranger told Angayarkanni that his name was Roeland Crape. She and Roeland Crape enjoyed conversing, though they were unable to comprehend each other. She found it difficult to pronounce his name and addressed him as Vellaiappan, which literally meant the light-skinned one. Vellaiappan is also how he gradually came to be called by others. As Vellaiappan recuperated, the reclusive angler and the mysterious foreigner spent most of their waking hours together.

Vellaiappan was no master of mime, but he managed to convey to Angayarkanni about his desire to learn Tamil. Hence, a Moorish trader, Subbiah's good friend, was asked to teach Vellaiappan Tamil and to act as an interlocutor between Vellaiappan and Subbiah's family. However, Vellaiappan did encounter difficulties in learning. The Moorish trader was slightly hard of hearing, and thus misinterpreted Vellaiappan's statements to Angayarkanni, with hilarious consequences. The conversations between Angayarkanni and Vellaiappan were stilted with misunderstandings, misinterpretations and mirth.

Yet, Angayarkanni and Vellaiappan became inseparable.

Through a narrow steel-barred window in Vellaiappan's room, he observed Angayarkanni hunched over the garden in the blazing heat of the day, her dark hair shining like fine silk, as she watered the vegetable patches unassisted. Immediately, Vellaiappan tore a small piece of his bed sheet, and, using an old quill he found in his room, he began drawing what he could see from beyond the window. When the Moorish trader called on their house again, Vellaiappan presented his drawing to Angayarkanni, and used the Moorish trader to delineate the various aspects of it. Angayarkanni discussed the drawing with Subbiah. The latter, excited by its ideas, immediately gave Vellaiappan a free rein over his garden.

A month later, the garden was unrecognizable. From the back of the house ran a system of waterways dug into the soil, transporting water across the garden into small pools. The excess water was thereafter transported into a pool amidst coconut trees and the once swampy garden transformed into a verdant grassy meadow, abounding with a variety of sweet-smelling jasmines, hibiscuses, roses and several other flowers.

'Vellaiappan! See what you have done to the garden!' said Angayarkanni one breezy evening as she cooked the day's dinner.

'What do you mean by "see what you've done"? The garden is flowering! Look at the lady's fingers, brinjals and the plantains flourishing! The flowers—jasmine, hibiscus and atthi—are growing in profusion!' retorted an amused Vellaiappan.

'Yes! You devised a method to reuse the water used in the household to irrigate the garden. You will soon beautify the *koodam* that will leave the dwellers and the visitors to this house spellbound! You will ensure that this house resembles a palace from your faraway homeland,' retorted Angayarkanni, caustically hoping to engage the foreigner in verbal sparring.

'Angayarkanni, dear, dear Angayarkanni,' replied Vellaiappan, gently enunciating the first 'a' in her name. 'Now that I am in this beautiful, bountiful Chola Nadu, I shall serve this land. After my ship was wrecked, I was adrift and thought I would die. It was you and the denizens of your land who rescued me, nursed me back to health and nourished me. I might be a Yavana, yes, but I desire to be a son of this land. And to that end, I shall do what it takes for the people of this land to accept me.'

Neither Vellaiappan nor Angayarkanni noticed Subbiah standing at the entrance of the kitchen, listening intently to this conversation.

As Vellaiappan recovered, he became increasingly curious about the new land he now lived in. At his request, Angayarkanni and Vellaiappan set off at the crack of dawn on most days to explore the exotic Nagapattinam, its various nooks and crannies, its idiosyncrasies and its charms. He realized that he was getting enchanted with Nagapattinam; he also realized that his fascination was not restricted to the city.

One day, as twilight set in, Vellaiappan and Angayarkanni sailed in a boat to witness the sunset. The duo gazed into the city, its gardens, temples, markets, monasteries, schools and houses being lit up in an ethereal orange halo as the sun descended behind it. The stars began appearing in the sky, like diamonds studded in a rainbow-like silk gown. Vellaiappan found himself gazing at Angayarkanni as she looked up at the sky with starry eyes.

Angayarkanni turned around and asked, 'Vellaiappa! Why are you gazing upon me like one who is possessed?'

Vellaiappan hoarsely whispered, 'I am gazing upon the brightest star in my horizon'.

Suddenly, there was silence, as Vellaiappan and Angayarkanni locked themselves in a passionate embrace, so much so that the boat they were travelling in capsized, dunking the two unceremoniously into the ocean. All the duo did was laugh with each other as the sun disappeared behind the horizon.

As they walked back home against the setting sun, clouds of worry began to shroud the newfound lovers. What would Subbiah say? Until now, Angayarkanni and Subbiah had shared a completely transparent relationship. Suddenly, she felt hesitant about confiding her feelings for Vellaiappan to Subbiah, who until then had fulfilled every wish of his daughter. She was, after all, the apple of his eye—perfect and peerless in all respects. But falling in love with a foreigner of unknown antecedents? Had she gone too far?

As she drowned helplessly in this tempestuous sea of

thoughts, Vellaiappan gently remarked, 'Angayarkanni, he's your father. No matter what you say or do, he will love you. Just be upfront with him.'

Angayarkanni blinked cluelessly and then said, 'Well, we don't have any other alternative. He is likely to disapprove of our relationship. But we are going to be forthright with him.'

Subbiah was in the front porch of the house, playing *paramapadam* with a few neighbours as Angayarkanni and Vellaiappan turned into the street. As Subbiah cast the die, one of his neighbours cheekily pointed out, 'Subbiah, every day I see your daughter walking around with this foreigner who is staying at your house. Always inseparable! Just like Shakuntala and Dushyanta. I hope she does not have to undergo the hardships Shakuntala had to!'

While the coterie burst into laughter, Subbiah remained silent. The couple greeted those sitting on the porch and walked into the house. After the neighbours left, Angayarkanni coyly approached her father and stated, 'Appa, I need to talk to you. Alone.'

Subbiah ushered Angayarkanni into the kitchen. The moonlight streaming in through a window illuminated the various silver and brass vessels, stacked neatly one atop the other, into incandescent diamond and golden hues that irradiated the room. The room was filled with an awkward emptiness, as Subbiah intently looked into Angayarkanni's fear-laden eyes. Unable to tolerate the all-consuming silence, Angayarkanni nervously gulped down her fears and blurted out, 'Appa, I am in love with Vellaiappan and I want to marry him.'

Subbiah continued staring, saying nothing. Deep within him, however, a miasmic fire was beginning to consume his thoughts. For one, he was angry—*how could she fall in love with this foreigner? Who are his parents? What is his pedigree? Did she deign to enquire into that? What will the neighbours say? The community? This cannot go on, I made a mistake,* thought Subbiah, while staring at Angayarkanni. *I should have never taught her to fish and be her own person in the first place,* he ruminated. Despite that, he gulped his fire, and walked out of the room, heading to his chamber to sleep.

The war without words continued for a week. Subbiah spoke to no one; he ate not a morsel of food, nor did he drink a drop of water from the well at home. Angayarkanni and Vellaiappan looked on hopelessly as Subbiah saw them as shards of glass from a window long broken. Initially, Angayarkanni and Vellaiappan resolved to let Subbiah be by himself, thinking he was struggling to accept their relationship. But the silence was more painful than any hurtful words Subbiah could have possibly uttered.

Thus, one afternoon, when her father had shunned her preparation of his favourite *meen kozhambu*, Angayarkanni approached him and said, 'Appa, you've not spoken anything for a week to anyone. This silence is killing us. Please, say something'.

'The silence is killing us, you say,' replied Subbiah caustically.

Angayarkanni bit her tongue.

'Listen to me. That alien is our guest, so I am not evicting him from our home. I have sent word to your brother in Korkai to look for a groom for you there. I will ensure that you are married by the end of the next Chithirai month and will live in Pandya Nadu. No one needs to know about this indiscreet dalliance you have engaged in. If you insist on contravening my wishes, then I shall throw that foreigner out of our home. Let's see how long he survives in Nagapattinam after antagonizing me—'

'But Appa...' interjected Angayarkanni.

Subbiah left the room abruptly.

As Angayarkanni drowned helplessly in the depths of sorrow and desperation, she received help from unexpected quarters.

Subbiah was not only an accomplished pearl hunter but also an informer to Aniruddha Brahmarayar, the exalted prime minister of Chola Nadu. In fact, there was a secret passageway unknown to even Angayarkanni that connected their house to the royal guest house at Nagapattinam. Aniruddha Brahmarayar and Arulmozhi Varman frequently used this tunnel to step out incognito and conduct reconnaissance of the country.

Aniruddha Brahmarayar was already impressed with Vellaiappan's skills and the method he had devised to irrigate the trees and plants at Subbiah's house. He enquired about Vellaiappan's well-being whenever he met Subbiah. It was during one such instance that Subbiah mentioned his disapproval of the romance that had blossomed between Vellaiappan and Angayarkanni.

Aniruddha Brahmarayar, who was an astute judge of human character and who had known Angayarkanni since childhood, stepped in. He advised, 'Subbiah, Angayarkanni loves you too deeply to disobey you. You may be successful in preventing her from marrying Vellaiappan. But being a headstrong girl, she will not marry any other man. Besides, it will be difficult to find a suitable man for Angayarkanni, someone who will match her intellect and skills.'

A somewhat mollified Subbiah said, 'Sire, I have other concerns too. Roeland does not belong to this country, let alone my community. I have anyway antagonized my people in the past by teaching Angayarkanni fishing and pearl hunting. Now if I get her married to a casteless stranger, won't they ostracize me? Moreover, how can we be sure that Roeland is not already married? He has not given us anything more than the most basic details about his life before his arrival in our country. What if it turns out that he has taken advantage of our generosity? What if my only daughter decides to travel to a foreign country?

Aniruddhar smiled as he replied, 'Subbiah, while inter-community marriages are uncommon, they are not non-existent. Isn't Kundavai Pirattiyar happily married to Vandiyathevar?' Aniruddhar was referring to the Chakravarthy's brother-in-law, the husband of his older sister. When two hearts bond, caste and social standing do not matter. Vellaiappan appears to be an honourable man from what I have observed and heard of him. Let me speak to him. If he has never been married and promises to live in Chola Nadu henceforth, will you happily consent to this wedding?'

'Of course, Ayya!' replied Subbiah earnestly.

Aniruddhar then spoke to Vellaiappan, who swore by the Holy Trinity that he was unmarried and promised to live in Chola Nadu forever after marrying Angayarkanni. When Aniruddhar conveyed this to Subbiah, he happily agreed to the match and started planning for the wedding. Angayarkanni's brother, Ponniah, initially protested, though he kept his reservations to himself once he came to know that the wedding was being held under the auspices of the all-powerful Aniruddha Brahmarayar.

Angayarkanni and Vellaiappan were married at the majestic Shiva temple in Nagapattinam. Their marriage celebrations, unlike the simple Parayar weddings, were lavish. The temple was bedecked with festoons of mango leaves and rows of jasmines, hibiscuses, chrysanthemums, and other flowers. The scent of fresh jasmine mingled with the fragrance of food that was being cooked in the vast outdoor kitchen built for the purpose. At the centre of it all, various priests propitiated Agni, the fire god, by feeding vast quantities of ghee into the flame, so that the union would be blessed. The entire town's hoi polloi had descended into the precincts of the temple for the wedding. The fabulously wealthy traders and nobles attended the ceremony to bless this couple. Emissaries of the Chola and Pandya kings conveyed the royal families' blessings and showered the couple with expensive gifts. Kundavai Pirattiyar, who used to buy pearls regularly from Subbiah, gifted Angayarkanni with a beautiful red-and-gold brocade silk wedding saree, gold jewellery and, most importantly, the *thirumangalyam*. Aniruddha Brahmarayar gifted Vellaiappan an equisite white-and-gold zari *veshti* and *angavastram* and sponsored the wedding feast, to which all Nagapattinam residents were invited.

However, Angayarkanni and Vellaiappan were oblivious to all the gaiety and merriment that surrounded them. They had eyes only for each other. They joyously looked forward to the blissful future that awaited them.

3

Aniruddha Brahmarayar wasn't entirely altruistic in mediating Angayarkanni's marriage with Roeland Crape, who had now become Vellaiappan. The wise prime minister of the Chola kingdom recognized in Roeland Crape an extremely skilful engineer who possessed the rare talent of using available resources to develop effective and sustainable structures. These skills were well in excess of what was available even in Chola Nadu—obviously, this strange, foreign man had travelled across the world, taking the best of the world's knowledge like a honeybee seeking nectar in flowers. Vellaiappan's idea of irrigating Subbiah's garden—an idea utterly alien to Bharata Kandam until that point—by recycling water deeply impressed him.

This, coupled with the foreigner's congenial nature, prompted Aniruddha Brahmarayar to secure the Chola emperor Utthama Chola's approval for Roeland Crape to reside permanently in Chola Nadu. Utthama Chola provided Roeland Crape a copper plate on which was inscribed the royal decree that Roeland Crape had the right to reside permanently in the Chola kingdom and enjoy all the rights the Chola citizens possessed, barring enlisting for the army. He was free to pursue any job and had to pay all taxes and levies.

Vellaiappan was happy, now that he had secured the sovereign's approval to live permanently in Chola Nadu. The idea of living with Angayarkanni and Subbiah in their house gave him a lot of satisfaction. Subbiah and Angayarkanni were exhilarated. But Vellaiappan was concerned that he was unemployed and wondered what he ought to do for a livelihood. One day, Aniruddha Brahmarayar summoned Vellaiappan to his residence. Vellaiappan was filled with excitement and trepidation. He was now more fluent in Tamil than when he had first met the prime minister. The elderly Moorish trader–*dubash* had been the interpreter for the two men during their first meeting.

'I hope that all is well, Vellaiappan?' asked Aniruddha Brahmarayar.

'Aiyya, by your grace, Angayarkanni and I are leading a blissful life,' replied Vellaiappan.

'I presume you've received the royal decree.'

'Yes, aiyya. Thank you so much for that. If not for the decree, I would not have been able to uphold my promise to my father-in-law and live in the bountiful Chola Nadu with Angayarkanni.'

'Now that the bountiful Chola Nadu has given away one of her daughters in marriage to you, shouldn't you also contribute to Chola Nadu's development?'

'What can I do for Chola Nadu's development?' asked Vellaiappan curiously.

'Dedicate your talents to the state's welfare.'

'I don't understand!'

'I observed your skills in recycling water to irrigate Subbiah's garden. It would be good if you could use your skills to ensure that water is justly distributed amongst the various *kottam*s of Chola Nadu.'

'How can I achieve this single-handedly?

'You won't. I have asked the Chief of Thiruvarur Kottam

to grant you an audience tomorrow. Take this royal insignia and decree with you and present them to him. He will tell you about the water situation and the challenges in the kottam. You can then devise a plan to ensure uninterrupted water supply to the kottam, secure the approval of the chief of the kottam, the *dhanadhikari* and myself, and then implement it.'

'Aiyya, thank you so much. I was disturbed by my idleness, and now you have provided me with the opportunity of a lifetime.'

'I am happy that this venture excites you, Vellaiappan. I hope you rise up to the challenge and live up to the trust the Emperor has reposed in you.'

Roeland Crape arrived at the Thiruvarur Fort early the following morning, but was not met with the warm welcome that he was anticipating. For one, the guards at the gates of the fort completely looked through him; when he drew their attention by walking as close to their faces as he humanly could and spoke in a raised volume, they acknowledged his presence. Upon seeing the royal insignia, however, they concluded that this strange foreigner was a criminal who was attempting to infiltrate one of the wealthiest kottams in the land through forgery. If it did not so happen that the chief of the kottam happened to ride out of the gates at that very moment, Roeland Crape would have been imprisoned or worse.

'Ignore those small-minded guards, Vellaiappan,' said the affable chief. 'They can barely tell our Emperuman in procession as the mendicant Bhikshatana from an actual beggar or street urchin. Not everyone can easily appreciate the intricacy of a goldsmith's work as they would with a clay bangle being sold adozen in the markets of the small towns of this land, Vellaiappan; and before doubts creep into your mind, let me also clarify that you are the best work of the goldsmith—at least, if Aniruddha Brahmarayar is to be believed.' The chief let out a throaty laugh, as Vellaiappan squirmed in his place while forcing a smile, still shaken after the perilous encounter at the gate.

The chief of the kottam welcomed him warmly and briefed him on the water-related challenges the kottam faced. As the Kaveri was a rain-fed river, the area was flooded during the monsoon. On the other hand, during years of scanty rains, the farmers faced water scarcity and, consequently, unemployment. The harvest was also poor when monsoons failed.

Vellaiappan travelled the length and breadth of the kottam, understanding its terrain, cropping pattern, the access agricultural lands had to rivers, canals, ponds and wells, and the available active and dormant sources of water storage. He then devised an efficient and cost-effective plan for equitable water storage and distribution that included optimal usage of existing sources of water supply and building new canals and wells. He secured the necessary approvals and implemented it successfully over a period of two years.

Vellaiappan then took the chief of the kottam, the dhanadhikari and Aniruddha Brahmarayar for a survey of the kottam. As the four travelled in a carriage during peak summer, they observed that the kottam was considerably greener than before. The granaries were well-stocked. Most importantly, Vellaiappan's irrigation scheme had not disrupted the water supply to the kottams surrounding Thiruvarur.

When Arulmozhi Varman, the able heir apparent of Utthama Chola, and Aniruddhar travelled incognito, they understood that the citizens in Thiruvarur were delighted with the uninterrupted water supply, and that the chiefs and citizens of the other kottams were keen to replicate the Thiruvarur irrigation model. Vellaiappan was soon promoted to devise an irrigation scheme for the whole of Chola Nadu.

Bounty abounded in Vellaiappan's personal life too. Despite the initial friction between Vellaiappan and Subbiah, they had become good friends. Angayarkanni and Vellaiappan's relationship with Subbiah was one characterized by love, respect and symbiotic need. Subbiah's pearl business continued to flourish, and the family had become considerably more affluent. More domestic helpers were employed and this resulted in Angayarkanni spending more time helping her father with his pearl business. Two years into the marriage, Angayarkanni and Vellaiappan had their first child, whom they named Aniruddhan, after the venerable Aniruddha Brahmarayar.

Three years later, Angayarkanni realized that she was pregnant again. The entire family including Aniruddhan was thrilled. Aniruddhan was an energetic and cheerful kid who rolled in the mud, played games with other kids, massaged his grandfather's legs as the latter related stories and talked incessantly. Happiness reigned supreme in their lives.

Angayarkanni's second delivery was more difficult than her first, but the pain was worth it. She delivered a beautiful baby girl who inherited Vellaiappan's pale skin along with her mother's hazel-coloured eyes and ebony hair.

Four-year-old Aniruddhan flung open a window to announce the good news to his grandfather Subbiah, who was in the courtyard. But his tender voice was drowned by the sharp notes of the curved horn and drum beats. The herald accompanied by the royal drummer announced:

'Hear Ye! Hear Ye!

'A new era has dawned! A new era has dawned

'Our benevolent and gracious ruler Utthama Chola has reached the feet of God!

'Our new king will be crowned!

'Our new king will be crowned!

'All Hail Raja Raja Chola, our new king!'

Was it mere coincidence that the ascension of one of the most renowned Chola emperors and the birth of Kayalvizhi, whose fate was intimately intertwined with that of the Chola dynasty, occurred at the same time?

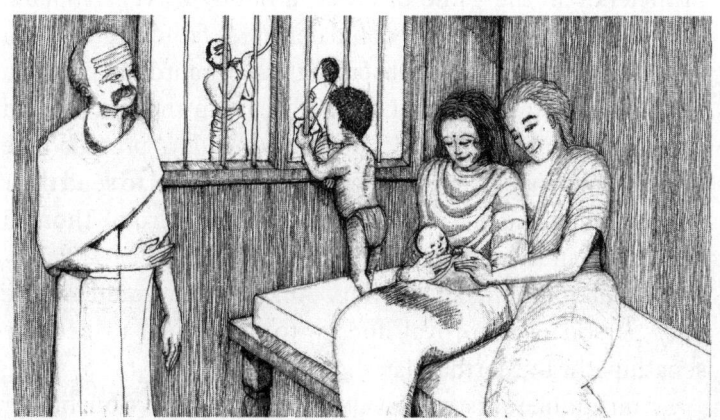

4

It had been apparent from a very young age that Aniruddhan, the son of Vellaiappan and Angayarkanni, was endowed with a razor-sharp mind. Despite his youth, he quickly gained proficiency in the game of chess, a hobby of Vellaiappan's. Before he turned seven, he could defeat his father from whom he had learnt the game. Observing his extraordinary skill in strategizing, Angayarkanni and Vellaiappan thought he had enough potential to head an army one day, provided he underwent proper training. Hence, they decided to send their son to Marthandan, a reputed senathipathi from Thondai Mandalam in the north, where the scions of the royal family were sent for military training. Aniruddhan would be the only person of non-royal lineage to be trained to become senathipathi in Marthandan's *gurukulam*.

Aniruddhan's sister, Kayalvizhi, too, was no slouch. Her privileged position meant that, unlike other girls of her age, she learnt a variety of skills. In addition to learning warcraft and statecraft from her father, she also learnt how to be a good wife from her mother as the recipes of the community were passed down to her meticulously, one by one. Her father taught her how to ride horses, how to wield a sword, and how to read the few handwritten manuscripts written in the Yavana Basha of his youth, at the Royal Library of Thiruvarur. Just by observing the court's vaidhyars in action, she built up an enviable knowledge in medicine. From discussions between her father and the court's astrologer, she was able to understand the essence of mathematics, geometry and *jyotisha*. As her parents watched her learn the subtleties of such varied bodies of knowledge at a pace that left them breathless in awe, they pondered, what more could they do to engage their daughter?

Despite her mastery over such varied bodies of knowledge, Kayalvizhi's passion lay in music. Drawn to the sounds of the *melakkaarars* who performed during the temple *utsavams*, she was struck by the magnetic quality of the music, its movements and how it captivated an audience into a trance. Of course, only *devadasi*s—women married to the Lord— could perform in public, but she learnt to sing as well for her own gratification. Her mother approved, for it meant she would be able to charm prospective suitors, but Kayalvizhi learnt it for she yearned to sing. Singing, for her, was her freedom, her creative outlet, her very raison d'etre. As was custom, she learnt the veena too as an accompaniment to her singing, and quickly became adroit in that instrument as well. She would visit temples regularly and imbibe the newly unearthed Thevaram hymns sung as part of worship. Similarly, she'd religiously attend poetry recitations of Sangam-era poets in a house in the neighbourhood and learn to sing those poems too. The music around her seeped into her skin, mingled with her blood and became part of her being. She was acknowledged by her teachers as the brightest student they had the privilege to teach—the most passionate *vidushi* they had ever encountered.

As for Aniruddhan, education at Marthandan's gurukulam was an extended feast of stimulation for the body, mind and soul alike. The older disciples of Marthandan followed a multi-disciplinary approach to impart training to the younger students. Archery, mathematics, politics, jurisprudence, espionage, oration, writing, languages, astronomy, theology, and many more areas of knowledge were covered by them. Though most of the students of the gurukulam were scions of royal families, they were expected to do many menial chores such as collecting firewood and dried leaves, drawing water from the well and filling the open tanks to help in cooking. This holistic education that Marthandan gave to his students, made them shine like lustrous diamonds.

Yet, all other diamonds seemed to be merely dull pebbles in a muddy brook, compared to the two *sishya*s of Marthandan, the two solitaires—Vellaiappan's son Aniruddhan and the Chakravarthy's son and heir apparent, Rajendra Chola, the *ilavarasan*. Apart from being the best, Aniruddhan and Rajendra were the best of friends.

Even then, there was a subtle difference between the two bosom pals, with Vellaiappan's son proving to be the brighter one than the son of the Chakravarthy. But then, there existed no discord between the duo. Yet, when the Chakravarthy and the rest of the Chola clan periodically visited their wards at the gurukulam, it was Aniruddhan whom they lavished their attention on. To them, Aniruddhan provided a breath of fresh air, like a whiff of musk. In every debate, duel and discourse Marthandan organized when the royal family visited, the gangly Aniruddhan stood head and shoulders above the ilavarasan. The attention showered on Aniruddhan roused a feeling of isolation in the ilavarasan.

That Aniruddhan displayed wisdom beyond his age, made him the cynosure of all the courtiers. Like the fragrance of the burning camphor, his prowess attracted the visiting Chakravarthy and other dignitaries. The 'outsider' thus occupied centre stage, pushing the ilavarasan to oblivion, unwittingly.

While most failed to notice Rajendra, the ilavarasan, Kundavai Pirattiyar, the beloved elder sister of the Chakravarthy who was Rajendra's aunt, lavished her attention on him. She was one of the most powerful women in Chola Nadu and was interested in the welfare of the people as much as of the Chakravarthy. Renowned for her political acumen, she was an advisor to the Chakravarthy. She was fair and generous. Her strong will was evident from her marrying the man of her choice, Vandiyathevan, a penniless royal. She and her husband were close to Aditya Karikalan, the erstwhile heir apparent, whose mysterious death paved way for the current Chakravarthy's ascension to the throne. A number of universities, libraries and hospitals across the Chola Nadu benefitted from her philanthropy. Her sharp intellect, dazzling looks and generous outlook made her as popular as her illustrious brother. If only Kundavai Pirattiyar were a man...

Kundavai Pirattiyar was also an influential mentor to the young princes and princesses of the royal family. Amongst the princesses she mentored was her niece, the daughter of Raja Raja Chola, Kundavai. The younger Kundavai had not only inherited her name from her aunt but also her intelligence and obduracy. While her siblings and cousins listened to whatever their parents and their tutors told them, young Kundavai questioned them incessantly. Not used to the inquisitive child, the tutors attempted to silence her, which made young Kundavai even more difficult to teach. By the end of a month, she had chased away three of the royal family's most senior and respected tutors, as they were unable to take the young girl's incessant questioning or her argumentative nature. The girl, bored by the slow pace of her tutors, threw tantrums with an unfailing regularity, which drove the ladies-in-waiting to despair. Kundavai Pirattiyar observed the roguery of her younger namesake and decided to step in, for seeing her was holding up a mirror to her own childhood antics. Despite her official duties and the vast number of institutions she patronized, she took it upon herself to personally educate her niece. She first relieved all the young princess's tutors of their duties, and personally brought her along wherever she went. Just the act of touring the vast Chola Empire with her aunt kindled a spark of curiosity in the young girl, who had with her a mentor eager to feed into that curiosity. Beneath all these layers of obduracy and argumentativeness, Kundavai discovered, there was an insightful, inquisitive, yet angularly intelligent girl, who was tired of her separation from her brother, Ilavarasan Rajendra. Kundavai Pirattiyar began taking her niece along with her to the gurukulam of Marthandan on a regular basis to meet her brother and alleviate the aching loneliness in her soul.

Kundavai Pirratiyar could also sense the young prince's alienation and the hurt he felt on account of being ignored in Aniruddhan's presence. Whenever she would arrive from Thanjavur, she ensured that she brought along ilavarasan's favourite sweets like *adhirsam*, a deep-fried jaggery pancake, and *thattai*, deep-fried discs made from rice flour. She made it a point to talk about ilavarasan's achievements and brilliance to her family members. Whenever she visited Marthandan's gurukulam, she ensured that Rajendra was the centre of all her attention.

Yet, a morsel cannot satisfy a hungry man!

It was during those difficult times, when neglect hurt him, that the ilavarasan found a friend in Kayalvizhi, the sister of Aniruddhan.

Kayalvizhi had a very unusual appearance for a woman in Chola Nadu. From her father's European roots, she had inherited high cheekbones and from her mother, the hazel eyes. She towered over most of her contemporaries, sticking out like a tall coconut tree in the middle of a paddy field. Moreover, she was far more intelligent than her father, more dexterous than her mother, and more sagacious than her maternal grandfather. Yet, the world she inhabited shunned her for her unusual appearance, her piercing intelligence and her mixed background. Her sole confidante and partner-in-crime in Thiruvarur was the *ilavarasi*, Kundavai. The two young girls brought out a different side in each other—Kundavai made Kayalvizhi more decisive and brave about fighting for what she believed in, and Kayalvizhi, for her part, made her friend appreciate the subtleties of arguments, to introspect instead of acting in haste, and to turn inwards and question her long-held beliefs.

Whenever Kayalvizhi visited the gurukulam, she would

gravitate towards the ilavarasan. Kayalvizhi brought the ilavarasan not just the latest manuscripts of Tamil poems from Thanjavur and Nagapattinam, but also the latest gossip. The young ilavarasan too appreciated her qualities. He, in turn, would entertain her with the stories of the great warriors he had read about or some juicy gossip about the royals at the gurukulam.

Thus, the two young seekers of knowledge would sit down under the banyan tree, exchanging notes, sharing camaraderie and developing a bond.

Observing their friendship blossom, their doting elders, Angayarkanni and Kundavai Pirattiyar, were reminded of their own romances, which made them smile wistfully at the brooding adolescents following in their footsteps. They had found long-lasting joy in their love for 'unsuitable' men, which had later aided them in their pursuit of success and happiness. Yet, they were able to retain their identities, their individualities, their passions, their souls, unlike the female citizens of Chola Nadu who sacrificed everything for the prosperity and happiness of their families. The joie de vivre that the ladies exuded was to attain new heights in the reign of the new Chakravarthy.

5

What makes an emperor great?

What determines whether a human whose very name connotes frailty, whose preoccupations are puerile and petty, is made *by* history, or *makes* history?

Scholars across time, across disciplines, across theoretical preoccupation and predilection, have been united in their attempts to construct, and indeed deconstruct, this 'theory of epoch-makers'. It is also telling that they have been united in their inability to put this into existence and thus reify it into a single phrase, a single tuneful musical note amongst an unaccordable cacophony of undiscernible frequencies.

And yet, epoch-makers continue to make epochs, whether scholars are there to watch them or not. They speak, and they speak with a clarion voice that resounds across time and space—not through words but through actions.

And thus spake, or rather acted, the young Arulmozhi Varman, well before he could speak or even act. Sometime a long time ago, during the reign of Parantaka I, the royal family comprising Sundara Chola and his queens were making their way down the Kaveri in the royal flotilla, when something happened; no one on the boat was entirely sure of the sequence of events. A child in the royal entourage began wailing and crying, and the mother, Sembiyan Mahadevi, set him down on a wooden plank. As the wet nurse was going to pick the infant up, all of a sudden, there was some kind of a swill in the river, causing water to invade the flotilla.

Next thing they knew, the baby went missing.

The parents were distraught. The numerous courtiers, the servants, were all distraught; not only was the loss of an infant of royal lineage foreboding of potentially more disastrous events, but the baby in particular was loveable, rarely kicking up a fuss, dazzling all who passed by him with his toothless smile.

There was nothing that could be done. The flotilla made its way down to the nearest jetty. As they approached land, they saw a large crowd gathered on the bank. The wet nurse made her way down the gangway of the boat, towards the crowd. Before she could make any enquiries about whether a child could have possibly washed ashore, through a narrow parting of the crowd, she could see the silken swaddle in which the babe had been swathed last.

The wet nurse was stunned. She made her way to Sundara Chola and told him of this. A wave of relief swept over the royal coterie embanked on the Kaveri. Sundara Chola and his wife, Sembiyan Mahadevi, made their way to the gathering, where they announced their presence, and collected the baby. As they were comforting the baby, the village chieftain approached them.

'Ayya! If you may so deign to hear me speak!'

'What is it, Ayya?'

'The circumstances related to your child's appearance were most remarkable. From the middle of the river, seemingly, some farmers sighted a beautiful young woman walking on the water, the infant in hand. We all gathered on the shores to see her. When she landed on the shore, she told us—in the sweetest tone that one could even dream of hearing—that as the baby drowned, she saved him and that you, the family, will arrive to reclaim their infant. And thereafter, she was gone into the same nothingness she had emerged from, before we could press her anymore! This baby is divinely ordained by the goddess Kaveri herself, Ayya. Please worship this child as we will continue to do'.

And thus, Raja Raja Chola—Arulmozhi Varman, as he was called then—was born, not in the royal bedchambers as history books narrate but instead on the banks of the river that nourished his land. As a veritable son of the soil. As The Beloved of the Golden-Hued. As Ponniyin Selvan.

Sundara Chola was blessed with two valorous sons— Aditya Karikalan and Arulmozhi Varman—and one sharp daughter—Kundavai. Though Aditya Karikalan was the heir apparent and the siblings loved each other deeply, Kundavai, from a very young age, believed that Arulmozhi Varman was destined to become a great emperor. Astrologers pointing out that the conch insignia on Arulmozhi Varman's palms presaged his ascent to the throne strengthened Kundavai's conviction. It was this belief that prompted Kundavai to convince Sundara Chola to appoint the seventeen-year-old Arulmozhi Varman as *thalapathi* to the forces that were dispatched to Eelam in Sinhala Desa to put an end to the civil war that had erupted after the death of King Sena III.

Arulmozhi Varman brought the civil war to an end, taking care not to cause any harm to the citizens of the emerald isle. The Sinhala citizens and influential *bikshu*s were so captivated by the brave and dashing Arulmozhi Varman that bikshus of a powerful *vihara* wanted to coronate him as the king of Sinhala Desa. Arulmozhi Varman, realizing that this monastery was just one of the influential viharas in Sinhala Desa and that his acceptance of their offer may result in civil riots erupting again, declined. His love for Chola Nadu, and inability to stay away from it for long, might have prompted him not to ascend the Sinhala throne.

Tragedy struck Sundara Chola's family soon after Arulmozhi Varman returned from Eelam. Aditya Karikalan was mysteriously assassinated. A few conspirators—Soman Sambavan, Ravidasan and Parameswaran—loyalists of the Pandya king Veera Pandian—were captured and their properties were confiscated. Aditya Karikalan had decapitated Veera Pandian at the end of a bloody war between the Cholas and Pandyas. The mastermind behind the assassination was never discovered.

Sundara Chola passed away four years after Aditya Karikalan's tragic demise. Sundara Chola's cousin Utthama Chola succeeded him to the throne and reigned for another decade and a half, with Arulmozhi Varman as his co-ruler. When the virtuous Utthama Chola passed away, Arulmozhi, the beloved of the people and Ponni alike, ascended the throne. The passage of time and the ascension of her younger sibling to the throne mollified Kundavai. The nation moved on from Aditya Karikalan's death and rejoiced. At the majestic stairs leading to Nataraja's shrine in the imposing Chidambaram temple, where all Chola rulers were coronated, Arulmozhi Varman stepped aside at the last moment and insisted that his uncle Utthama Chola be crowned emperor. Utthama Chola, who was only a few years older than Arulmozhi Varman, was virtuous and devout. Though the citizens respected him, he was not a warrior and hence not anointed co-ruler to Sundara Chola. Arulmozhi Varman argued that Utthama Chola, who was older to him, ought to ascend the throne by virtue of being one of Sundara Chola's predecessors Gandaraditya Chola's son. Arulmozhi Varman averred that his heart lay in defending Chola Nadu and building temples and monasteries that rivalled those in Sinhala Nadu in grandeur and scale. This action made Arulmozhi Varman a demi-god in the eyes of the Chola citizens.

Utthama Chola's reign, though peaceful, lasted for just five years. He was ably assisted by his co-ruler and heir apparent, Arulmozhi Varman. After Utthama Chola's untimely demise, the citizens and nobility of Chola Nadu unanimously voiced their desire that Arulmozhi Varman ascend the throne. Much blood had been shed and several warriors had lost their lives in their bids to rule nations. Arulmozhi Varman had demurred on taking the throne twice, and he had prevailed. And yet, when the forces of history conspired to place the crown unto his head a third time, the people forced him into the limelight.

The Chola royals, nobility and citizens congregated for the second time in five years at the Chidambaram temple. The grand *pattabishegam* of Arulmozhi Varman ensured a smooth transition of power after Utthama Chola's death. Royalty from across Bharata Kandam and beyond attended this lavish ceremony. Even the Pandya king, a sworn enemy of the Cholas, sent an emissary to represent him at the ceremony. Representatives and royalty from Champa, Angkor, the Rashtrakuta Kingdom, Rajputana, Pratihara, the Hindu Shahis, Malabar and even from faraway Socotra, who were the trading partners of the Cholas, joined the festivities. After the ceremony, the new king was ushered into the sanctum of the dynasty's deity, Chidambaram Natarajaswamy, and conferred with the title 'Raja Raja Chola', the King of Kings.

Raja Raja Chola's reign began with a roar. His vision for a vast and powerful Chola Nadu became apparent when he addressed his courtiers after the coronation festivities ended. He declared, 'For far too long, we have lived in peaceful coexistence with our neighbours, be it the Pandyas, or the Sinhalas in Eelam, or those Chera kings in Kerala Desa. But our friendship, our guileless generosity has become an opportunity for them to piggyback on us and interfere in our internal affairs. It shall happen no more. Ably supported by the brave Chola armies, my elder brother, the brave Aditya Karikalan, vanquished Pandya Nadu. I brought an end to the civil strife in Eelam. It is necessary that the mighty Cheras become our vassals for peace to prevail in Dakshina Bharata. The Kulasekhara Bhaskara Ravi, who is said to be the moon itself inspiring the oceans of his people to rise in glory, shall be eclipsed by the blazing Chakravarthy, Raja Raja Chola!'

'How will we do it, Chakravarthy? How shall we eclipse the Cheras?' asked a minister, his voice breaking through the cheers echoing through the chambers of the court.

The Chakravarthy's lips curled upwards smugly. He had seen that question coming. 'By destroying Kandalur Salai,' he said.

The echoing cheers were now replaced by an echoing, deafening silence. What else is to be expected? The very name struck fear into the hearts of every warrior in Dakshina Bharata. Located in the heart of Chera Desa, Kandalur Salai was a university of sorts, like the magnificent ones which once thrived in Takshashila and Nalanda, except it imparted knowledge of the art of war, instead of the *itihasa* or *mimasa*. The gurus who taught at Kandalur were the finest generals and soldiers that the Chera nation had produced, as well as soldiers from Cheena Desa and the distant foreign lands of the West specially invited by the Chera suzerain to impart the knowledge of warcraft to the next generation of leaders. The soldiers protecting Kandalur were amongst the most skilled and experienced alive. The destruction of Kandalur would be akin to cutting off the poison-secreting glands of a viper, for the Chera nation would struggle to rise to prominence again.

The new Chakravarthy had made up his mind. He was going to kill the dragon by aiming for its jugular. He was going to conquer Kandalur, come hell or high water.

And thus the expedition began. Due to the impenetrable mountains between Kandalur and Chola Nadu, it was decided that Kandalur would be seized by sea. The vast shipyards of Nagapattinam swung into action, transforming the quiet beaches on the outskirts of the town into an ocean of brown, as shipwrights worked tirelessly around the clock to build up the Chola navy for its latest feat. The foot soldiers of Chola Nadu were trained to row boats in naval combat at gurukulams across Chola Nadu. Realizing that the Pandyas and the Sinhalas were not too amicable with Chola Nadu, the Chakravarthy reached out eastwards, to the emperors of Jawadwipa and Cheena Desa, securing favourable trade deals for the import of steel swords and fuelwood for ships, as well as mercenaries to provide additional manpower. The entire nation seemed to be readying itself for a conflict with the enthusiasm of a bride dressing herself for her wedding.

When it rained arrows, it was a veritable deluge. Ships brimming with Chola soldiers, with the Chakravarthy himself leading the forces, left the shores of Nagapattinam under the cover of night. Avoiding the usual sea routes taken by other ships, as well as the coast entirely, the fleet sailed swiftly through the treacherous waters around the Sinhala island, before gradually curving towards the coast near Kandalur. Swift Arab dhows equipped with long-range flamethrowers, a recent innovation by the *senacharya*s, were able to sink the measly few ships that did survive. While the unsuspecting Chera forces were sleeping, the entire force of the Chola army descended upon Kandalur, stage by stage, defeating the layers of defense. By the time dawn broke, Kandalur was nothing but a smouldering wreck.

Meanwhile, Raja Raja Chola's brother-in-law, Vandiyathevan, led the armies across the narrow passes in the mountains bordering the Palakkad region, launching a full-on attack on the capital and the southern region of Chera Nadu. Before the year closed, the Cheras were vanquished and the Chola tiger flag flew high above the Padmanabhaswamy temple in Thiruvananthapuram, whose underground vaults were known to hold vast quantities of gold. The Kulasekhara tried to raise his head again and again from his base in the northern end of Kerala Desa, but time and time again, the Chola army crushed the Kulasekhara, and conquered Kerala country as a whole.

The Chakravarthy had done the impossible. He had obliterated Kandalur Salai.

Raja Raja Chola ordered that the gurus who taught in

Kandalur be captured and brought on the ships back to Chola Nadu. These gurus were hosted in the finest mansions of Thiruvarur, fed and feted, and, under the stewardship of senathipathi Marthandan, a new gurukulam was set up in the northern reaches of Chola Nadu with these captured gurus of Kandalur. This gurukulam would be where, the Chakravarthy decreed, the future generation of Chola Nadu would be educated and groomed for leadership.

The salai in Kandalur, which may have had a hand in Aditya Karikalan's assassination, was destroyed. But the knowledge it imparted would strengthen several rulers of the Chola Empire.

6

Years before his coronation, Raja Raja Chola married Vanathi, a Chola general's daughter and a companion to his sister Kundavai Pirattiyar. Subsequently he married many noble ladies in Tamizhagam, such as Lokamahadevi and Cholamahadevi, to cement political alliances. These alliances brought him handsome dowries, including extensive granite quarries, meadows, agricultural lands and hamlets of strategic importance, along with the loyalty of several chieftains. Lokamahadevi was a powerful woman who commanded the respect of not only her husband's own court but also those distant courts, such as that of the emperor of Srivijaya Empire, far to the east. Hailing from the arid regions of central Tamizhagam, she had a keen interest in agriculture. Lokamahadevi found a willing partner in Vellaiappan, now a senior courtier, to discuss ways to improve the harvests of Chola Nadu and to ensure that hunger was eradicated.

Raja Raja Chola was a perceptive diplomat. In 1003 CE, he had annexed the regions of Gangapadi, Nolambapadi and Tadigaipadi, ruled by feudatories of Ganga Nadu, with his characteristic panache. He victoriously waged wars against the Chalukyas, the sworn enemies of Tamizhagam, and married a Chalukya princess to seal the post-war treaty with the Chalukyas. Starting with the daring obliteration of Kandalur Salai, Raja Raja Chola won the Cheras in multiple wars, after which the latter accepted his suzerainty. Nevertheless, Raja

Raja Chola treated his vassal kings with respect and, later in his reign, helped the Chera king defeat the pirates in the Arabian Sea. His capture of Vengi in the Telugu nation established Chola supremacy in Dakshina Bharata.

The next project he embarked on was the irrigation of the arid Arcot region. Once part of Pallava Nadu, the existing irrigation systems were built during the reign of the great 'Mamalla' Narasimha Varma Pallavan in seventh century CE. By the time Raja Raja Chola ascended the throne, the three-century-old irrigation systems were decrepit, causing crop failure and much grief to the farmers. The king wanted to change this. He allotted ample grants to the project and appointed Vellaiappan and his minister of agriculture to set the irrigation systems right. Vellaiappan, by then, was a senior minister in the emperor's court and was residing in Thanjavur itself. The emperor had also instructed Lokamahadevi and Rajendra to assist Vellaiappan in his endeavours.

Vellaiappan and his hand-picked team designed a system of rainwater canals and reservoirs, rainwater tanks and valves to solve this pressing problem. He realized that lack of maintenance was the reason for the dilapidation of the advanced Pallava irrigation systems. Vellaiappan immediately procured several tons of cast iron to create efficient valves to regulate the flow of water to the fields. The consequent reduction in famines improved lives in Arcot, turning the arid lands into fertile grounds. Assisting him were his son Aniruddhan and Crown Prince Rajendra. The agricultural ministry under Vellaiappan also renovated the Kallanai, a stone dam constructed by Karikala Chola nearly a millennium ago. The entire Chola court was struck with awe that a foreigner, from a land so far away that even their best cartographers could not determine its exact location, had enabled this exponential increase in grain production and eliminated the possibility of any famine for years to come. In gratitude to the Gods for bringing them Vellaiappan and prosperity to Chola Nadu, Lokamahadevi consecrated her very own temple, Lokamahadevishwaram, near her parental home of Vandavasi.

Raja Raja Chola constantly strove to improve bilateral trade and was a good negotiator. So, when the Cholas and the merchant body of Zanzibar failed to amicably conclude a trade deal, he personally invited the emissaries to his court and negotiated with them, securing a lucrative deal for the empire. Realizing the importance of trade, he issued an edict announcing that a new Mercantile Civil Service would be established. Raja Raja Chola invited the foremost maritime engineers of the day to craft one of the most sophisticated mercantile navies of the day. This modern new fleet was based in the southern ports of Nagapattinam and Arikamedu.

At the same time, Raja Raja Chola was acutely aware of his own mortality and the potential disarray after his death. Thus, he began training his son Rajendra, fresh out of Marthandan's gurukulam under the guidance of the gurus of the Kandalur Salai, in the art of statecraft. Every day in the week, the leading scholars of Chola Nadu would come together and teach Rajendra the nuances of various aspects of statecraft, especially the arts of diplomacy and espionage. Raja Raja Chola also began sending out emissaries to neighbouring kingdoms, scouting for brides for Rajendra to marry and forge alliances. Rajendra, in the meanwhile, already had his eye on a certain daughter of a minister of agriculture, a friend from his days in the gurukulam. If only he knew whether she reciprocated his feelings...

7

Dweller of Blessed Vennai Nallur,
Lord of the Arul Thurai Shrine,
Is it fair to turn me away, your slave,
Who called you 'Pittha'—the possessed?

As the sonorous tones of the wandering minstrel began to resonate across the court, the Chakravarthy was spellbound, stupefied. What beautiful poetry enveloped in such graceful melody! As the minstrel began to expand more and more upon the lyrics, twisting the melody along one word first and then tagging additional words, one by one, to create additional layers of meaning, the Chakravarthy and the rest of the court were awestruck. How could one poem birth so many from within itself? How could a dialogue exist within each word of the text of four lines, maybe a score of words, so perfectly chosen?

As the minstrel drew to the close of his performance, the court sat in absolute silence, unwilling to disrupt the rarified atmosphere created. Finding the words from within himself, the Chakravarthy managed to say, 'Ayya! What a beautiful, beautiful rendition, but pray, please do tell us, who is the blessed soul who wrote these words?'

'*Arasey!* The soul who wrote these words is none other than our Emperuman, who dwells in each and every one of our hearts. It is said that Emperuman blessed these words through a man of great beauty, so beauteous his name was Sundarar—the beautiful. Not unlike your father, arasey. This Sundarar, along with two other great saints—Tirunavukkarasar and Manickavasagar—are said to have been the unique vessels of His grace that enabled them to honour him in this splendid manner.'

'Are you aware of more of these verses, Ayya?'

'But alas, Chakravarthy, it is here that I become woefully inadequate. It is said that these verses were popular across Tamizhagam once upon a time, but due to the vagaries of time, we have lost many of these. I was blessed enough to be taught this by my now deceased grandmother on her deathbed, as a precious heirloom that I was entrusted with. Yet, of what consequence is a diamond shrouded from light? I have made it my mission to propagate this solitary gem as widely as my limited capabilities permit me to. I apologize for my inability to shed further light on this matter.'

The Chakravarthy nodded, honoured the minstrel and retreated to his chamber. And yet the minstrel's melody gripped his entire being. His mind could not escape the possibilities those four lines, couched in simple, elegant language, conveyed. He could not sleep, for the visions he had awake obviated the need for sleep to bring him dreams. He strolled around the terrace of his palace that overlooked the Kaveri. Illuminated by a waxing moon, the primordial river, which was in spate, transformed into a stream of molten silver, blazing its banks with iridescent hues. As the Chakravarthy witnessed the moon rise and set, and then witnessed the sun rise, an idea germinated in his mind.

The next day, the court convened. While ministers animatedly discussed matters of the state, the Chakravarthy, uncharacteristically and wordlessly, watched. Rising at the end of his ministers' deliberations, the Chakravarthy announced:

'Dear courtiers, fellow citizens of Chola Nadu, there is no question that the words of the bard yesterday have left space in our minds and hearts for little else; such are their impact. If the words of the bard are indeed true—and I believe them to be, for his reverence and humility were palpable from every note he sung—there are more of these hymns, laying asunder across our beautiful land, away from prying eyes, the devotion of these great men being unknown to the world at large. It is our moral duty, as rulers of this land, to discover these hymns and ensure that their meaning and melody are propagated across Chola Nadu and beyond. I thus dedicate the tax revenues collected from 10 villages towards this endeavour. I trust that all of you will support this initiative.'

The court acquisced, albeit unsurely, taken aback by the suddenness and the import of the announcements. The Chakravarthy made his way to the royal chambers and was greeted by his esteemed sister, Kundavai Pirattiyar.

'*Akka*! To what do I owe the pleasure of your company?'

'The pleasure of your sudden proclamation in the court today, *Thambi*.'

The Chakravarthy looked confused. 'What do you mean, Akka?'

'There is absolutely no doubt that these songs will outlive those composed before or after. I, in esteemed gatherings of scholars, have heard hushed references to the existence of these songs. But along with those hushed references are assertions of the fact that these are lost texts. Is it not a futile endeavour? Aren't there better ways to honour our Lord—something far more tangible, something far more achievable, than this futile quest?'

The Chakravarthy smiled. The conversations he had played out in his mind, strolling that moonlit night along the terrace of his royal abode, had entered the realm of reality.

'Akka, I am not denying it is a difficult endeavour. I do not even aim to deny that it may ultimately be in vain. But, at the end of the day, why do we do this? Do we do this to gratify our own individual hubris, to feed our egos? No! We serve Him because serving Him, in itself, is a blessing. And in serving Him in this manner, by ensuring His utterances, through the blessed tongues of His devotees, spread across the land and beyond, or even trying to achieve that magnificent goal, are we not achieving something of value?'

Kundavai Pirattiyar's expression softened, but she still looked unimpressed.

The Chakravarthy continued, 'There is another reason for this decision, Akka—for what unites our land better, more strongly, than devotion to the Almighty? Our land is diverse and prone to division. We strengthen our land by spreading the fragrance of *Shiva bhakti*, devotion to the Lord, and creating a culture of *bhakti*, devotion, Akka. Culture unites our land. Culture builds our nation. And as rulers, we have an obligation to unify our population and instill hope.'

Kundavai Pirattiyar still looked unimpressed. She smiled wryly. 'All said and done, you do speak well, Thambi,' she scoffed.

The Chakravarthy smiled too. 'I do more than speak, Akka. You will see. My Lord, upon whom I have reposed so much faith, will surely not let go of His devotee's hand. He will reveal the bounty of His words. He will make the nation stronger, more cohesive, more united. And I, His instrument, will comply with His will. *Ellam Sivan Seyal*, Akka; He is the

Cause and Effect. And He will cause and effect nothing but positivity upon our blessed empire, on our people.'

'I thought that the murky waters of statecraft would diminish your idealism, Thambi, but I can see my fears were misplaced there. Let's hope, with His grace, that I am proven wrong once more,' said Kundavai Pirattiyar as she took her leave.

'A sivanadiyar is here to see you, arasey.'

'Not today. There are too many urgent matters to be attended to. Just ensure that he's put up in one of the guest chambers in our palace; feed him. He may speak to me tomorrow or the day after.' The Chakravarthy paused. 'Did he tell you what matter necessitates this audience?'

'Arasey, he says he that he possesses information about the Thevaram texts.'

The Chakravarthy's attention was piqued. 'Send him to me immediately,' he instructed the guard.

Into the Chakravarthy's well-appointed retiring chamber, located off the royal court where the nobles met, walked a tonsured, young sivanadiyar, clad in ochre robes with strings of *rudraksha* beads fastened around his neck and wrist and *vibhuti* smeared on his forehead. As the mid-afternoon sun cast itself across the chamber, his face shone brightly—partly because he was so young that his smooth, bronzed skin naturally reflected the light, and also because there was something divine about his countenance, as though the light of enlightenment emanated from within him.

The Chakravarthy prostrated in front of the ascetic, whose face remained impassive. The Chakravarthy felt impelled to sit at the feet of the sivanadiyar, wash his feet and pay obeisance to him. The monk broke his silence stating, 'Arasey! My name is Nambiyandar Nambi. My family has been serving Emperuman for generations upon generations. One day, in my dream, Emperuman Himself appeared and disclosed that behind the dancing Nataraja idol in the Chidambaram temple there is a hand-sign marking the location of a secret chamber that only the four thousand Dikshitars (Saivite priests hailing from Chidambaram) descended from those hand-picked by Emperuman know of. Within the chamber, there exist thousands of hymns by Sundarar, by Manickavasagar, by Tirunavukkarasar—there are one lakh and four thousand hymns in totality. I heard of your mission for the search of the Thevaram couplets, and I felt it was my duty to tell you about the words strung together in His honour. I would be remiss if I didn't make my way to you to tell you of this, so I left my village at the dead of night and have been walking ever since.'

The Chakravarthy sat silently, contemplating the words of Nambi Andar. He looked at the young, earnest eyes of the lad, blazing in quiet determination. He observed the glow and the quiet authority in his face, the certitude it exuded.

He motioned to the guard, saying, 'This sivanadiyar and I need to travel to Chidambaram this evening. Make the necessary arrangements including a palanquin for him.'

The royal retinue led by the Chakravarthy and Nambi Andar Nambi set off from Thanjavur at the crack of dusk, travelling the royal thoroughfare to Chidambaram. Through the night journey, neither the Chakravarthy nor Nambi Andar uttered a word. None broke the journey to partake of dinner. They instead stared outside as the argentine seas on the horizon shifted, seemingly springing up from the ground with the same alacrity as they retreated into the earth. The entourage faced no obstacles as it traversed dark forests. In fact, the twinkling stars augmented the illuminated torches carried by the foot soldiers, transforming night to twilight. The royal entourage travelled day and night for three days with the foot soldiers being replaced twice daily. Emissaries had conveyed to the village chieftans beforehand the Chakravarthy's desire to reach Chidambaram at the earliest. As dawn broke on the fourth day, the trees flanking the highway gave way to Chidambaram.

The Chakravarthy and Nambi Andar stepped outside the carriage as dawn began to break and took a breath of the salty sea air that hung over the town. At a distance from the Nataraja temple, at the fingers of the mangroves reaching into the town's centre, young fishermen and fisherwomen returned from their expeditions in the mangroves of Pichavaram on whose shores the town was. In the distance, chimneys from the houses in the residential districts began to smoke up, casting dark, fragrant plumes from wood stoves into the brightening morning skies. A crow cawed languorously. Freshly picked flowers and camphor being sold outside made the air heady and fragrant.

The Chakravarthy, in the robes of a commoner, and Nambi Andar bathed at the temple tank, stepped into the temple and paid obeisance to the deity of Nataraja. As they stepped outside the sanctum sanctorum, they wandered around the precincts of the temple.

And there, in a dusty corner of the temple, they spotted a stone carving of a hand symbol standing out. Piqued, the two men followed in the direction pointed by the hand symbol. A cavernous hall led them to an ancient wooden door. The steel lock on it, wrapped in muslin and stamped on with turmeric and vermillion, was new. A small shrine seemed to surround the door. An elderly priest approached the duo.

Nambi Andar spoke up. 'Ayya! What lies behind this door? Why is it locked?'

The priest replied, '"What lies behind this door" it seems! Young boy! Go play somewhere else. The secrets behind this door are well beyond your ken.'

'Would it be above my ken, *swami*?' asked the Chakravarthy as his angavastram slid off his shoulder, exposing his ring that bore the Chola insignia.

The priest quivered. Regaining his composure, the priest said, 'Arasey! It does not matter if you are prince or pauper; even if the Lord himself demands the opening of this door, we have been instructed to keep it closed to all prying eyes.'

'Then who would you open it for, swami?'

'Let the three men who wrote about the treasures contained within the doors come to the door. Only if those men themselves come, would we be able to break open the locks.' Through the dimly lit chamber, it was evident that the priest was smirking.

The two men walked away from the chamber, the slump in their shoulders remaining even as they emerged into the sunlight. Having lunch in the royal palace in Chidambaram, the day was whittled away with the Chakravarthy tending to matters of the state and the young Nambi Andar deep in meditation.

The evening arrived, and with that, the anticipation of having to depart. 'Let us at least stay for the *utsava murthy* circumambulating the town. It would not be right for us to reject His grace,' the Chakravarthy told Nambi Andar.

Hearing this, Nambi Andar smiled.

'Why are you smiling, swami?'

'The utsava murthy coming around the town at sundown

is to signify that He is travelling the town to see His divine subjects. That doesn't mean that He ceases pervading every atom of creation, maintenance and destruction. And yet, when He arrives in this utsava murthy, it is as though He exists only at that particular point in space and in time.'

Realization dawned upon the Chakravarthy. The two men smiled at each other. Their task was cut out for them.

The next week, a small ebullient procession made its way to the temple at Chidambaram. Mounted on a fresh bamboo palanquin, three bronze idols made their way into the rear of the temple, into the cavern. Following them were the Chakravarthy and Nambi Andar, walking with their heads held high and shoulders erect.

The elderly priest was stupefied at the unexpected procession. The Chakravarthy and Nambi Andar walked to the head of the procession. 'You said you needed the men who wrote those works. Lo and behold! They have been manifested in front of you.'

Indeed, at that moment it appeared that the gazes of the lifelike statues of Manickavasagar, Tirunavukkarasar and Sundarar instructed the elderly priest to open the door of the chamber.

The events that ensued occurred at a frenetic pace.

A locksmith apparated. The lock was smashed. Several dikshitars and courtiers congregated. While the gathering conversed in hushed tones as the locksmith was at his task, it fell silent the instant the lock broke. The locksmith collected the fragments of the broken lock and his tools, and stepped aside. Those assembled held their breath as an elderly dikshitar placed two illuminated lamps on either side of the door, lit a piece of camphor on a silver *tambalam*, performed the *arthi* and used a bunch of neem leaves to sprinkle water from a silver pitcher on the doorstep and the door.

The dikshitar stepped aside, making way for the Chakravarthy to open the door. Raja Raja Chola firmly pushed the two wooden doors that slowly creaked open, but not completely. The Chakravarthy then signalled to the chief of his retinue, a sturdy warrior, who came to the fore. He and the Chakravarthy energetically pushed open one door each to reveal a dusty chamber enveloped in darkness.

A few dikshitars carrying illuminated lanterns ushered the congregation into the chamber. A few people sneezed; but no one remarked that the sneezes were inauspicious. Suspense and expectation of a momentous discovery had rendered the congregation mute. As those assembled got used to the dimness of the chamber, they observed a set of old, wooden shelves containing what seemed to be old palm-leaf manuscripts. Water had seeped through the ceiling. The floor was caked with mud and filth. Nambi Andar entered the room and touched a palm leaf at random. The leaf disintegrated at touch.

'Termites, Arasey.'

The congregation appeared crestfallen. Soon they wordlessly started examining the shelves and started collecting those manuscripts that had survived the ravages of time. The task took around two days to complete.

'Time is impartial, but our Lord will not forsake His true devotees. The Almighty has endowed humankind with the Thevarams it requires to lead an honourable life and has appropriated those verses He deems unnecessary. Bring the surviving manuscripts to the Royal Library in Thanjavur. Scholars at the *patashala*s of Thanjai, Kanchi and Madurai will transcscribe the Thevarams the Almighty has bestowed upon us. Musicians will set them to tune. Priests at the numerous Shiva temples across Tamizhagam will chant the Thevarams and propagate these divine verses among the population,' the Chakravarthy pronounced.

Nambi Andar nodded his head in assent. At that moment, united by that common cause, everything around them dissolved except the heady determination to impart the knowledge and music of the Thevarams to the future generations.

8

With the progress of time, Prince Rajendra shot upwards like a bamboo tree, growing into a tall, strapping young man. He had his father's dark, piercing eyes. The denizens of Chola Nadu looked up to this ambitious and idealistic young man, whose charisma earned him a great deal of popularity. Unbeknownst to him, a bevy of maidens, including Kayalvizhi, the daughter of the agriculture minister, Vellaiappan, were besotted with him. Rajendra had inherited his father's short temper too, which came to a head in crucial moments of his life, especially when there was some profoundly disturbing news from Kadaram, a prominent trading province of the kingdom of Sepang.

Kadaram was an island that lay across the Vanga Sagaram, what is now known as the Bay of Bengal. This narrow, triangular peninsula was ruled by a dynasty that hailed from the heartland of the peninsula. Kadaram's strategic location had enabled it to flourish as a crucial trading port in the trade route between Cheena Desa and Bharata Kandam. Their kings had mostly allowed the province to be administered as a semi-autonomous city-state ruled by an elected merchant council. The new king of Sepang rescinded Kadaram's autonomy and installed a military governor, Aryapriya. This led to a series of increasingly violent persecutions against the minority Tamil elite.

As an overseer of trade in the region and the provider

of security to merchants from Tamizhagam in general and Chola Nadu in particular, the Chakravarthy felt compelled to intervene.

His son, however, begged to differ.

Upon hearing about the preparations for an expedition to reinstate the merchant council, Rajendra Chola, the ilavarasan, stormed into his father's court angrily, and asked, 'Appa! I have just heard very disturbing news! Apparently, the Tiger Fleet is going to set sail to Kadaram? Please tell me it is just a baseless rumour, Appa!' His eyes flashed with red-hot flames of fury.

The Chakravarthy looked on calmly, and responded, 'Ilavarasey, it is not a rumour anymore. It is absolutely necessary that we send our fleet to Kadaram to defend those hapless merchants. As a protector of our people and of mercantile freedom and security in the region, we must intervene.' His dark eyes burrowed into the fire in his son's eyes.

The still angry Rajendra, realizing the setting, replied, 'But arasey! We have just had our best harvest in so many years! The price of grain is lower than ever! And we are barely able to confine all our gold in the royal coffers for the first time in so many years! It is absolutely ill-advised to send a fleet to protect foreigners, isn't it, arasey?!'

The Chakravarthy responded, 'Commerce and the state of the treasury is just one aspect of governing a nation. Our brethren are being persecuted, and we must protect them. In fact, Emperuman has augmented our wealth at this crucial juncture to protect our merchants and also expand Chola Nadu. This is the best time to invade. Chola Nadu has had a bountiful harvest. Our coffers are overflowing, and our brave army is raring to go. If not now, Ilavarasey, when will we launch the invasion?'

Rajendra didn't respond.

'Moreover,' continued the Chakravarthy, 'what constitutes Chola Nadu? Does it end at the seas embracing Dakshina Bharata? The northern extremes of Chalukya country? Or the southern tip of Eezham? No, my dear son, no! Our nation resides not in the Kaveri River coursing through our land and every inch of it but in the people it nourishes. These sons and daughters of the golden-hued Ponni River live not only along its shores but also beyond it, in the empire of the Sriwijaya, the empire of the Champa, the empires of Cheena Desa and so many more. They are as much our people as anyone living in Thanjavur or Thiruvarur, Ilavarasey, understand that! You can take the people out of Chola Desa, but you can never, ever take the Chola Desa out of the heart of its people. The people of Kadaram are no different. They might be *sreshti*s, merchants, who left our land long ago, but the temples and *vaidyashalai*s of our empire are made rich by their gold. Why do you think our wealth is measured in massive palams, instead of the smaller kalanjus? It is because of these sreshtis! When they are in need of our help, we provide it, and we provide it in every way possible.'

Aniruddha Brahmarayar, wishing to avert a father–son showdown in public, interjected, 'Arasey! Both you and ilavarasan are united in your concern for Chola Nadu's well-being. I urge you to allow the ilavarasan to read the missives sent by Kedaram's sreshtis. It is my humble opinion that he will agree with you after reading the missives.'

The fearless ilavarasan's retort flew back at the minister, swift as a flaming arrow: 'Respected minister! I have learnt from you that one ought not to decide on an issue based on incomplete information. While I am deeply concerned for our sreshtis, it is not wise to despatch our forces to Kadaram based on their woes—real or imagined.'

The ministers and nobles stood stone-faced, fearing an imminent tempest.

Pat came the reply from Aniruddha Brahmarayar, 'Ilavarasey! I wish you had heeded another counsel of mine—that armies may be used to wage wars and broker peace. When your illustrious father was an illavarsan and thalapathi of the Chola forces in Eelam, he commanded our forces to assist the Sinhalas and Tamils of Eelam in building temples and viharams. I beseech you to read our sreshtis' epistles. I am sure you will concur with the Chakravarthy that despatching an army to Kadaram is of utmost importance. If the sreshtis are indeed tyrannized, our army will give a fitting response to Kadaram's ruler. If the concerns of the sreshtis turn out to be overblown or unfounded, we may leave a small contingent behind to assuage them and charge them a fee for providing them security. This will also enrich our treasury.'

Ilavarasan Rajendra's tongue was tied.

Aniruddha Brahmarayar continued, 'Oppression is cancerous by nature. It may only affect a small part of our body now, but, if left untreated, it will spread at the blink of an eye and wreak havoc on our existence. Similarly, if we let our brethren across the Kalinga Sagaram rot under oppression, there will come a time when we too will be condemned to their fate. If we are so strong and prosperous now, those traders played no mean role. Their wares fill our markets, their donations fill our temples, their jobs fill the stomachs of so many of our brethren that they are part of our nation. If we abandon them now, we will be condemned to a lifetime of poverty, wretchedness and misery.'

The Chakravarthy interjected by saying, 'Ilavarasey! I

understand your view, for I too once possessed your passions untampered by the cooling effects of wisdom. While they might have immigrated long ago, when our great ancestor Parantakan ruled Tamizhagam, and while they might have married into the families of those foreigners who inhabited those alien lands, they too are Tamizh. Our identities—being a Chola, a Pallava, a Chera, a Tamil, an alien—are not our identities but are merely roles that we play on this stage of life. We assume them and discard them rapidly, play multiple roles at the same time, and, when asleep, play none. Even our names, our regal titles, are not who we are but are merely the roles that we play on a day-to-day basis. At the end of the day, what unites us, beyond our tribal instincts, is our fundamental humanity, that we see each other not as beasts but as members of the same species. Our scholars consider this to be a higher order of intuition that binds our senses together, a "sixth intelligence". You, Ilavarasey, must exercise this faculty of yours. Our shastras require us Kshatriyas to protect these members of our clan who suffer at the hands of an alien in a faraway land. Play not just the role of an ilavarasan but also the role of a human. Empathize with the pain your fellow humans are suffering and try to alleviate their pain.'

The ilavarasan opened his mouth in response, but couldn't find the words to respond with. Instead, he stammered, 'Arasey, aiyya, I will head to the correspondence chamber and read the missives sent by our sreshtis. I wish to acquaint myself with our sreshtis' troubles. Arasey, if you deem fit, please send me to Kadaram, so I can play a part in saving our brethren.'

The Chakravarthy looked into his son's eyes, the older man's eyes looking curiously into a replica of his own eyes that glistened with desperation and ambition, just as his own eyes had, years ago.

But the Chakravarthy paused and contemplated for some time. The court eyed the father-son duo askance.

After about a nazhigai, the Chakravarthy announced, his booming voice resonating across his court, 'Summon Senathipathi Vandiyathevar at the earliest! I need to inform him of the appointment of Ilavarasan Rajendra and Minister Vellaiappan's son, Aniruddhan, as *anipathi*s for the Kadaram expedition.'

The distant shores of Kadaram, almost a lifetime away, danced like a temple dancer, before the eyes of the quasi-delirious ilavarasan.

9

The Tamil population had been hitherto concentrated around the Kadaram province of the Shailendra realm, while a significant population did exist in and around villages towards the south, in the Peenangam region. Generations of intermarrying meant that the Tamil population had familial ties with the native Sepangese, the Angkorese and the Chinese—descendants of traders who had migrated aeons ago. The Shailendra kings, though ethnically Sepangese, did have significant Tamil ancestry; in fact, it was rumoured that the present Shailendra king, Abhinava Shailendra, had been born to a Tamil concubine of the previous Shailendra king Nilakanta Shailendra.

Chakravarthy Raja Raja Chola saw this as a test of the country's sense of justice and military might and dearly wished that Kadaram and its adjoining areas be liberated from the despotic king. The Chola naval force embarked to invade Kadaram led by Vandiyathevan as the senathipathi, and Ilavarasan Rajendra and Aniruddhan as anipathis.

It was not because Vandiyathevan was the Chakravarthy's brother-in-law that he led the Tiger forces. Indeed, from his youth, he had consolidated his stature as a brilliant military strategist and an even more astute political strategist. A member of the Vana clan, which once ruled the land before the era of Chola supremacy, Vandiyathevan had swiftly and surely consolidated his position in the firmament of Chola royalty. One of the most skilled generals in the army of Aditya Karikalan, he became close to the current Chakravarthy as the duo led the Chola invasion of Eelam. He, belonging to a minor vassal clan, married Kundavai, the love of his life, and the Chakravarthy's beloved elder sister, before gaining for himself and his clan proximity to the Chakravarthy, who increasingly relied on Vandiyathevan's military expertise for consolidating the might of the Chola realm.

However, there was the matter of determining the path of invasion. The route between the Chola realm and the Southeast was a busy trading corridor, which meant that the large military vessels of the Tiger Navy sailing towards the Southeast would have been easily discernible. Hence, it was decided that they would sail during the off-season of the monsoon, taking a less-used and roundabout route. The finest astrologists of the Chola Empire were convened with its anipathis and the senathipathis, to determine the optimal path towards Kadaram. After consulting the traditional *panchangam*s, which determined the movement of the stars and the moon and thus the currents of the seas, a path was selected and a date was duly chosen to launch the expedition.

To further compound the element of surprise, Vandiyathevan split the fleet into smaller forces and set sail to Sepang, the coastal capital of Kadaram, in a covert manner. This, and the sensitive nature of the operation, meant that the traditional pujas that would have otherwise been performed for all the soldiers as they departed, were dispensed with. Thus, one humid morning, about 150 soldiers assembled in an isolated corner of a military harbour on the outskirts of the town of Arikamedu. A few *ganapathigal,* sworn to secrecy under threat of punishment, propitiated Ganapthi,

Muruga, Emperuman and Durga to ensure that their support was earned.

As the ship sailed away, the Chakravarthy stood on the shore, surrounded by none but his sister Kundavai Pirattiyar and a trusted bodyguard. Kundavai noticed the Chakravarthy's pensive expression—his brows knotted in a way that she knew intimately to be one of worry. She entwined her fingers with his, and squeezed his hands firmly.

The Chakravarthy's expression eased.

Recognizing the need to collect espionage intelligence from Sepang, Vandiyathevan had instructed his mole in the court of Aryapriya to send word of the defences in Kadaram to Java Dwipa, where the Chola forces were scheduled to halt and devise their strategy to invade Kadaram. Vandiyathevan was eager to reach the tropical shores of Sepang and urged his sailors to sail faster to capitalize on favourable monsoon winds. It was his first major overseas expedition in a long time, and a large-scale one at that. Not only did his fleet consist of multiple catamarans indigenous to Tamizhagam, there were also numerous junks from Cheena Desa, their masts towering over every other ship in the vicinity, and Arab Dhoonis, small, swift ships carrying the supplies for the trip. The variety in the fleet was a product of the Chakravarthy's foresight; recognizing the advances in naval technology elsewhere in the world, ship-building experts were invited to Chola Nadu. They worked on modernizing the Chola fleet, so it could embark on long expeditions such as this one. The tiny dhows were loaded with massive cotton bags containing a variety of dried meats preserved in rich spice blends and pickles of various vegetables. Bags of rice in these dhows co-existed with the large sacks of swords and spears for terrestrial combat. The catamarans and ships themselves carried these too, but the Chakravarthy anticipated a long and protracted siege of Kadaram, and hence the need to ensure adequate supplies. The ships headed east, first for the friendly Srivijaya Empire in Java Dwipa.

The Srivijaya emperor had married a distant cousin of the Chakravarthy, and thus, there was a strong alliance between Chola Nadu and Java Dwipa. Both Chakravarthy Raja Raja Chola and the Srivijaya emperor had endowed land and gold for the renovation and expansion of a Buddhist viharam in Nagapattinam—the Choodamani Viharam. Raja Raja Chola's endowment was in memory of his father, the late Chakravarthy Sundara Chola. The bikshus of Choodamani Viharam had frequently travelled overseas to propagate Gautama Buddha's teachings. The itinerant bikshus had collected maps and literature native to the nations they visited and meticulously preserved these at the library of Choodamani Viharam. One of the nations the bikshus frequented was Kadaram. The maps, religious and political treatises the bikshus had brought back from Kadaram proved to be invaluable to the Chola forces.

Having replenished supplies at Java Dwipa and stocked the ships' catapults with the incendiary material to power the flamethrowers, the ships departed at sunset, sailing eastwards towards Sepang. The journey was overnight, but it was the most crucial part of the voyage due to the imminent threat of naval patrols from the king of Sepang. The mole in the court of Aryapriya had already communicated to the Chola forces the route taken by the naval patrols. Vandiyathevan meticulously planned the Chola fleet's route accordingly. Even if one sentry caught a glimpse of the Chola armada, the war would have broken out earlier than planned, and rivers of blood would feed into the murky oceans.

Not a soul in the ship slept a wink, as they watched the nazhigais elapse like fine sand through loose fingers. A couple of nazhigais before sunrise, word was sent to Vandiyathevan that no sentries of the Sepangese had been spotted.

'Don't celebrate now,' said the sleep-deprived Vandiyathevan, the dim flames illuminating his body's scars from years of warfare he had engaged in for the greatness of the Chola Empire. 'Celebrate when we have conquered Kadaram. Celebrate when we rescue our people from their tyranny. Till then, sleep as much as you can. Our voyage may be drawing to a close, but we have a long, long journey still ahead of us.'

Finally, just after the crack of dawn, the Sepang coastline came into view. The city lay ahead, its graceful harbour lying in the azure seas, the stone jetties devoid of any activity.

'First, we conquer,' said a restless Vandiyathevan, 'and then, we may enjoy Sepang's bounties at leisure.'

The ships dropped their anchors at a safe distance from the harbour, near a shoal of rocks which provided cover from the eyes of the sentries. This particular blind spot of the lighthouse had been identified—thanks to a map in the library of the Choodamani Viharam—and verified through a communique from the mole. Within a few minutes of them dropping their anchors, the mole himself, an elderly Angkorian man whose full lips and beaked nose made him look more bird than human, boarded Vandiyathevan's ship from his weathered coracle. Word had been sent to the Tamil households that an invasion was imminent, and families had begun to evacuate the city into the jungles that freckled the edges of the city. The mole also presented a recent military survey map of Kadarapattinam that detailed the defences of the city.

Wordlessly, Vandiyathevan summoned Aniruddhan, who

stood at the corner of the room, to inspect the map. Rajendra looked on, but a beckoning glance from Aniruddhan indicated that he too was to inspect the map. Yet, while Rajendra still took his time to inspect the map, Aniruddhan had already formulated a plan; his eyes began to twinkle, his lips began to reveal a smile and the thousands of ideas that it contained within it.

Seeing this, Vandiyathevan motioned him to speak. Aniruddhan smiled widely—eagerly—his teeth shimmering like a row of pearls in the abyss of an ocean. Excitedly gesticulating across the map, he illustrated:

'Ayya! From the maps our ally has provided, we can see that there exist weaknesses in the defences—and not just small weaknesses but glaring ones—at every cardinal and ordinal direction surrounding the city. This presents a multitude of opportunities. I am reminded of the great Kautilya of Uttara Bharata who advised that the Mauryan emperor Chandragupta take Magadha from all directions, surprising and stunning the enemy.

'Kadarapattinam is flanked by tropical jungles and scrub that lead into a city which we, thanks to our intelligence services, have intimate knowledge about. If we take this opportunity of the last *jamam* of the night to disperse and assemble across the city, at the break of dawn we can launch attacks and take the city from all directions. They are not expecting us, so they will not have the time to gather their forces to mount any form of a meaningful defence—at least, that is what I anticipate. And we make our way to the centre, to the hill where the palace is. If my calculations are correct, we will reach the centre around sundown,' Aniruddhan concluded, rather anti-climactically, and turned to Vandiyathevan.

Vandiyathevan gave his assent.

From the large ships were lowered small coracles full of soldiers down into the inky black sea. Guided by the favourable tides of a sun yet to rise, the coracles made their way swiftly and surely to the coast, cutting through a sea eager to greet them. They landed on beaches across the coast, abandoning their vessels to embark on foot. The soldiers slipped into the nebulous, dark jungle that flanked the beaches. Lit by torches, they made their way to the points—indicated by Aniruddhan—overlooking the city at its edges, waiting, looking upwards for a sign from above.

The torches they kept lit diminished with the rising sun, and immediately, on cue, the invasion began. The soldiers launched forth into the city, sleeping through its own liberation in the throes of dawn. Cries of '*Vetri Vel! Veera Vel!*' invoking the spear of Muruga, echoed through the streets, waking up the sentries. Kadarapattinam's harbour, one of the largest and most important in the region, decked with ships and wares from across the world, remained a silent spectator to the hordes of Chola troops rushing forth with their swords and maces, taking over the city.

Yet, as they began to invade the city, they found a conspicuous lack of opposition. The sentry posts across the borders of the city were deserted—and not even looking like they'd been deserted in a hurry, but with the doors carefully locked and the interiors neatly arranged and maintained. This was an army that had mutinied, that had collectively forsook its paymaster—a paymaster it had recognized to be unjust.

Aniruddhan, who led the advance from the coast into the city, did not seem to be delighted by the lack of military resistance. Turning to his aide-de-camp, he whispered, 'Don't mistake this absence for a complete absence. It is extremely likely that they have caught wind of our invasion and that they have rallied in the fort. Remain vigilant.'

In a normal coastal city, the buzz of the harbour would have matched the cries of the marketplace, where traders would be setting up shop for the day. There would be a few early-bird housewives who would have come to pick the best of the vegetables before other women could lay their hands on them. In this place, juicy gossip was bound to be exchanged among all present, accompanied by subdued sniggering, meaningful glances and long sighs. These simple pleasures were denied to the citizens ever since the predominantly Chettiar shops were banned from the market.

The grandiose shops, constructed as per Pandya style, popular in Tamizhagam, were now bereft of both people and merchandise. Not only the market but also many other mansions on the way to the palace of the governor, Aryapriya Shailendra, were being razed to make way for army barracks and watch towers. The governor had little taste for mansions. Fearing a naval invasion, he wanted watch towers to warn him in time and an army to protect him from the invaders.

If only he could foresee the Chola army's invasion!

Neither Aryapriya nor the Cholas could feel the pulse of the public. The governor was unpopular. He had, after all, gotten rid of the traders, destroyed mansions, and had even dared to impose draconian laws on those who retained. They knew that soon enough crude loud-mouthed soldiers employed by the governor would occupy the barracks and start looting them. The citizens were scared that the unruly soldiers might even occupy civilian houses and force themselves on the women.

Indeed, no one had anticipated the silent, unheard-of confederacy between invaders and the invaded that had formed out of nowhere. A dissatisfied citizenry, a mutinious defending force and an invading force powered by its own righteous willpower had somehow conspired to connive a bloodless invasion. Most of the citizenry had escaped into the woods, having caught wind of the attack. The few who did remain in their homes watched the spectacle silently from their wide verandahs.

Aniruddhan strode into the empty city hall, located not far from the harbour, in the commercial core of the city. Surrounded by a public garden containing many fruit-bearing trees, the city hall had once been a sign of the independence of Kadarapattinam, hosting an elected council of merchants who governed the city with little interference from above—that is, until the racist, avaricious Aryapriya was appointed the governor of Kadarapattinam. Aryapriya dissolved the council, had the members executed for trumped-up charges of high treason, and also had the city hall shuttered while planning its demolition. As Aniruddhan attempted to break the brass locks of the building, a couple of soldiers emerged from the woodworks, brandishing their spears at Aniruddhan. Prepared for this, Aniruddhan unsheathed his sword and killed the soldiers even before they could attack him. The soldiers fell to his feet, their bronzed skins embellished with a bright red line that adorned their neck like a ruby choker. A couple of soldiers walked behind him, lighting the torches as they climbed onto the top of the tower.

A sight began to emerge—the flagpost in the centre of the city, one of the tallest in the world, saw the death of the Shailendra scorpion and the emergence of a Chola tiger whose blazed yellow bestrode a sky where luscious pink reigned.

Soon, the pink gave way for a baby blue, which gave way to the oppressive heat of the noontime sun, and the Chola forces saw themselves converging around the ramparts of the fort. Aniruddhan's prediction had been proven to be drastically wrong, for he had anticipated stiffer resistance from the army. Even the miniscule minority of Aryapriya's loyalists could not do much. The civilians' weapons, harkening back to a martial past, had been confiscated by the government. The citizen committees of a few neighbourhoods attempted to resist, only to be slaughtered, their blood splattering upon the streets and upon the walls of houses.

With the noontime sun prevailing rather forcefully as a witness, the Chola marched to the zenith of their successes as the army surrounded the fort on all sides—Rajendra had led the army from the north, Aniruddhan from the west and Vandiyathevan from the south. The troops stormed the star-shaped fort.

At the centre of the star lay the Chola army's target— Governor Aryapriya's palace. The Chola army fought ferociously, defeating the Sepang army with utmost ease. They stormed into the governor's palace. As Aniruddhan had predicted, the palace was heavily guarded; elite guards, highly trained and fanatically loyal to Aryapriya, had been barricaded in the fort, hoping to draw the Cholas in.

The hillock was occupied exclusively by the fort. There were numerous secret underground passages linking the fort and palace to the rest of the country. This was where Aryapriya had fled to, intending to come out of the exit at the stables at the rear of the fort and travel on horseback to his brother Abhinava's court further inland. He took with him as hostages his female Tamil employees and a retinue of still-faithful Sepang guards. Although the fort was well-planned, the passages below were decrepit from disuse. This worked to the advantage of the Cholas.

Having annexed the hinterland and captured the fort, the Cholas started infiltrating the third layer—the underground passages. Aniruddhan, who had deployed troops to guard the towers as they advanced, noticed a tiny wooden staircase close to the entrance. He, accompanied by Vandiyathevan, Rajendra and a small coterie of troops, climbed down the creaky stairs that led into a small room and followed along the single unlit passage, leading to a small clearing.

Vandiyathevan's normally impassive face was betrayed by surprise, relief and joy simultaneously.

Aryapriya had been discovered.

While Aryapriya observed Vandiyathevan's and Rajendra's entry, he failed to observe Aniruddhan's presence. He quickly drew a sword from his pantaloons and declared, 'I will release these Tamil wretches only if you leave immediately!'

His eerily low-pitched voice momentarily unnerved the normally unflappable Vandiyathevan, but Aniruddhan was quick to react. He swiftly and discreetly slipped into a dark alcove in the dingy chamber. He readied his bow and drew a steel arrow dipped in cobra venom from his dark brown quiver. He recalled his education in Marthandan's gurukulam. The steel arrow, if shot at the point where the collarbone and the spine intersect, would lead to instant death. The poison was just a precaution.

Aryapriya was dead.

The terror of the Tamils was dead.

Empire of the Cholas ॐ 71

10

As the warm afternoon began to wane, a procession emerged from a narrow gap between the heavy steel doors. From those curtains of what looked like liquid silver falling unto the earth scarred by the militaristic fixtures of an oppressive regime, emerged a line of soldiers, sombrely marching down the incline. They seemed to form a parasol of sorts with their shields and their spears, their eyes firmly averted towards the dusty ground or the scrub that surrounded the ramparts.

Behind this parasol of steel stood the Tamil women of Kadaram, scantily clad in whatever clothes the soldiers could find in the palace, for the palace had been thoroughly evacuated of both the architects of their miseries, as well as the robes they wore. The Cholas, for their own part, had vastly underestimated the number of women who were held prisoners in the fort; their blankets and robes could barely clothe the women.

And hence, a strange parade filtered through the streets of Kadarapattinam.

As the scantily clad procession headed into the city, with Rajendra, Aniruddhan and Vandiyathevan at the helm, the hoi polloi of the city congregated to attempt to catch a glimpse of the women. The women had a reputation, apparently, of being great, exotic beauties. The city had hitherto only heard rumours of their existence, but for the first time, it was their chance to gaze upon their beautiful faces.

Seeing the spectacle at hand, Rajendra suddenly stopped the procession. Aniruddhan looked confused and turned to Rajendra. What he saw in Rajendra's eyes was a fire—a rage. Knowing his dear friend, Aniruddhan attempted to restrain him from doing something rash; but can a leaping tiger ever be tamed?

Rajendra swiftly scaled up to the vacant deck of a house. From atop, he could see the roof of steel formed by the shields slithering across the city like a simpering snake. Rajendra looked down at Aniruddhan, resigned to expecting the unexpected, and a confused Vandiyathevan. And then, Rajendra looked upon the curious citizens of Kadarapattinam, straining to see what lay behind the iron and steel curtain, a peek here, a snatch there.

Rajendra had enough.

'You people have no shame?' His voice boomed, halting the advance of the troops. The rhythmic marching of the troops had suddenly ceased, setting Rajendra's fury centre stage.

'They are your sisters. They are your daughters. They are your mothers. They are your wives. And yet, you gawk at them like animals? What, have you men never seen a woman before? Is this your first encounter with the female form?'

Silence hung pregnantly over the street. Vandiyathevan's eyes expanded like drops of oil on a steel plate. He looked urgently at Rajendra, his annoyance burrowing into the prince's skull.

'What I say may be unbecoming of my station as the Prince, or as a representative of the Chola Empire, but I have a moral impetus here as a human being to castigate your animalistic manners. How long or how far we have marched through this metropolis, only god knows. But both Emperuman and I know how many of the people of this metropolis have offered clothes—zero! Not a single man, woman or child!'

Some of the citizens on the street hung their heads in shame.

'We may have shrugged off an oppressive political regime, but we must also shrug off the regime of our collective apathy towards other humans. These are vulnerable women, who have been through untold trauma and suffering. As have you. They are not objects of fascination. They are not your fantasy. And if you see them as not one of yours, your sisters and wives and your daughters, then you should hang your head in shame. For as long as the Vedas reign, for as long as the *parijata* flower remains fresh, feel the shame.'

Rajendra climbed down and looked at Vandiyathevan, who glared at him. Rajendra rolled his eyes.

Meanwhile, the residents retreated into their houses and came out with robes of silk. Sequestered away from the prying eyes of tax inspectors, these silks came out, wrapped in delicate leaves, to prevent moths from making a meal out of them, to adorn the bodies of their sisters, their mothers, their wives, their daughters.

The procession continued, except with the women shivering no more, their bodies covered in the finest robes of Kadarapattinam's crème de la crème.

The ship's journey back home should have been jubilatory, yet it was sombre. As the ship pulled away from the shore, and Rajendra returned to his chamber on board, Vandiyathevan locked eyes with him. Rajendra tried to close the door to the chamber, but it was too slow for his uncle to say, 'Ilavarasey! Will you condescend to grant an audience with me?'

Phrased as a request from a subject, the prince knew that not acceding to his uncle's request would lead to hell at home. Sighing internally, Rajendra put up a brave face and invited his uncle to the chambers.

Vandiyathevan sat down, placing one leg upon another. He motioned for Rajendra to ensure that no one was at the door, and asked him to close the door. As Vandiyathevan sat, the ilavarasan stood, his arms folded.

Vandiyathevan smiled. 'Ilavarasey! I merely have one question, and I humbly submit that you answer.'

Rajendra shuffled, knowing what the question was.

'What was going on in your mind when you delivered your delightful little jeremiad about fraternity? Do you realize how risky what you just did was and how it could have angered the elites of Kadarapattinam? What it says about our land?'

The vocal Rajendra fell silent, as his uncle burrowed into the depths of his soul.

Rajendra mumbled, 'The dungeons...those women...they couldn't even speak properly...and they looked...skeletons.' He spat out each word with what seemed like a great force from within, but to Vandiyathevan, Rajendra was barely audible.

Vandiyathevan softened.

'*Kuzhandai*! It is our Kshatriya dharma towards the downtrodden. And by so heroically leading the effort to rid the world of that rakshasa who tormented these women, you have fulfilled your dharma. Haven't you listened to our Raja Guru, my dear nephew? He quotes from the shastras that we humans will not be free of all this pain and suffering till our release from *samsara*. Till then, it is our duty as humans to perform our duty, our dharma, without any expectation of any reward or change. The world around us is full of Aryapriyas, who oppress our people, despite our Chakravarthy's stature and efforts. As the warriors of Chola Nadu, we must use *all* four tools of diplomacy, *sama, dhana, bhedha and danda*—conciliation, gifts, reasoning and aggression—to defend our people. All you can rely on is this dharma, *pillai*. Let that be your lodestone.'

As Vandiyathevan departed from his quarters, and Rajendra began resting in his, uncle and nephew, royal and noble, were both afflicted with a shared malaise, insomnia. As they closed their eyes, rocked like babies in the cradle that was the ship, they could not see the ambiguous, shapeless grey that enticed them towards a dreamless, vacant sleep; they only could see strange visions.

For Rajendra, it was the sight of the skeletons, the ghosts of Kadaram, the unseeing eyes of the people, the horrors of war.

But for Vandiyathevan, it was a confusing image—a man on the throne of the Cholas, but was it Rajendra? Or the Chakravarthy himself? He couldn't tell.

The magnificent vessels of the Chola fleet were visible from the terraces and temple *gopuram*s of the coastal town of Arikamedu, which was still developing into a full-fledged port. Lavish preparations for welcoming the victorious forces had been made. Caparisoned elephants, the finest ensemble of Chola Nadu's court musicians, the royal priest and his contingent, key courtiers accompanied by their wives and led by the sapient prime minister, Aniruddha Brahmarayar, and the proud citizens of Tamizhagam were awaiting the return of the naval fleet. Also present were Subbiah, Angayarkanni and Kayalvizhi.

The stately vessels reached the harbour. The army which had conquered Kadaram returned to a tumultuous welcome. The welcoming sound of conches, *nagaswaram* and *thavil,* along with the hymns chanted by the priests to bless the victorious forces and to ward off the evil eye, resonated in all four directions. The priests welcomed the forces with a *purnakumbham.*

When Vandiyathevan, Rajendra and Aniruddhan disembarked the ship, Angayarkanni and Kayalvizhi performed the *drishti kazhithidal* ceremony to ward off the evil eye. It was then that the eyes of Rajendra and Kayalvizhi met. The fires of the *homam* had ascended upwards, plumes of dark smoke reaching the sunny blue skies, a stairway for the gods to descend to the world of the mortals and witness the triumph of Chola Nadu. It was through this smoke that Kayalvizhi saw Rajendra Chola.

He stood amongst the royals, bedecked in the silks of royalty and wearing his battle scars like prized ornaments. And she stood amongst the courtiers, clad in resplendent silks, wearing exquisite pearl jewellery from Pandya Nadu—gifts from her uncle.

Kayalvizhi looked at the rest of the royal family, bedecked in their silks and ornaments, soberly concentrating on the hymns the priests were chanting, seemingly obscured by the smoke from the homam.

But she only saw Rajendra.

And likewise, Rajendra could see no one through the veil-like smoke—except Kayalvizhi.

He looked at the rest of the courtiers, sporting various garments, depending on their importance and their affluence. He saw their varying levels of interest in the long-drawn hymns of the priests.

And then, their eyes met, and nothing was the same again.

His dark eyes burrowed into her feline eyes, and her feline eyes probed his dark eyes. They didn't blink. They didn't look away. They didn't even move, even as the searing, blinding dark smoke penetrated their eyes directly, as they were the closest to the fire.

They just gazed into the windows of their souls.

The ceremony, the hymns, the chants, the people, the clothes, the temple, the society they lived in, their past, their present, their future—nothing mattered, except their love for each other.

Kundavai was watching through the smoke too, standing beside Vandiyathevan. She observed the two youths of Chola Nadu from very different backgrounds falling in love. And immediately, her past flitted before her eyes, like a montage of scenes from an exotic puppet-show. She remembered her falling in love with Vandiyathevan, which couldn't keep her from smiling.

At the end of the ceremony, Aniruddha Brahmarayar made a stirring speech hailing the valour of the soldiers in their efforts to conquer Kadaram and liberate the oppressed Tamils. The women of Chola Nadu showered flowers on the soldiers, who then boarded open carts festooned with flowers. The soldiers were taken in a procession around Arikamedu. Crowds thronged the streets of Arikamedu and cheered the army. A special prayer ceremony and a lavish feast were organized at the Shiva temple for the soldiers, who then retired to a specially set-up army camp to recuperate.

The army was to return to Thanjavur in a week, where the Chakravarthy and senathipathi of the Chola Empire, Raja Raja Chola, would initiate each of the victorious soldiers into the Order of the Tiger—the highest military order conferred on the infantry.

Rajendra, Aniruddhan and Vandiyathevan were eager to return to Thanjavur. It had been months on end of incessant hard work, braving an uncompromising sea, battling menacing pirates, conquering Kadaram, making arrangements for the freed Tamils to return home, and finally sailing back home amidst concerns about dwindling supply of victuals and an inclement weather. The victorious army would take four days to traverse the emerald green countryside to reach the capital, Thanjai.

The people of Chola Nadu had thronged the route the army took to the capital city, cheering the victorious warriors, extending hospitality, and mostly importantly, asking them to narrate how they vanquished the Sepangese army.

Chola Nadu's villagers lay out elaborate feasts of lunch and dinner for the passing army, set up camps for the army to retire at night, and also invited them to the major temples that lay en route to Thanjai where special poojas were performed for their well-being. The denizens also set up *neer pandal*s and *mor pandal*s for the passing army.

The royalty, nobles and their families alternated between riding horses, walking, and being ferried in palanquins while travelling from Arikamedu and Thanjavur. It just so happened that Rajendra and Kayalvizhi opted for the same mode of transport, thereby creating several opportunities for conversation, mirth and leg pulling without attracting attention for apparent breaches of protocol...or so they thought.

Men and women of the royal contingent sat in two separate rows facing each other as meals were served on banana leaves. During the first dinner served after the army's return, Kundavai Pirattiyar invited Angayarkanni and Kayalvizhi to sit beside her and coincidentally, opposite Rajendra. This seating arrangement became a norm for the rest of the journey, a development that did not fail to catch the attention of Aniruddha Brahmarayar, Vandiyathevan and Aniruddhan. One of the trio was observant, another amused and the third, concerned.

The victorious troika finally entered the Chola capital of Thanjavur.

Even as Vandiyathevan, Rajendra and Aniruddhan were riding across the moats of the Thanjavur Fort, Raja Raja Chola was in his palace talking to Vellaiappan. They shared an intellectual camaraderie and a sense of love for the denizens of the land of Ponni, the Golden River. The battle-scarred, ageing Chakravarthy looked regal. Vellaiappan, on the other hand, was in poor health. A few months earlier, he had tripped and fallen down the staircase of his Nagapattinam residence and had not yet fully recovered. He still limped perceptibly and his shoulders stooped.

Vellaiappan stated, 'Arasey! Senathipathi Vandiyathevan, Ilavarasan Rajendra and Aniruddhan must be returning to Thanjavur any time now. This is a momentous overseas victory surpassed only by your conquest of Eelam decades ago. The Tiger flag flutters majestically not only across Dakshina Bharata but also at the forts of Eelam and Kadaram. You must be a proud man today.'

Raja Raja Chola replied, 'Yes, Vellaiappa, I am proud of and happy about our victory. But my conscience pricks me. The human cost of victory has been immense. We recruited a large army for this expedition. By the grace of the three-eyed Lord, our side has not suffered many casualties. But how do we feed this army and employ it suitably going forward?

Don't you know that an idle army does not bode well for a country's harmony? My daughter, Kundavai, is willing to contribute the produce of her lands towards the upkeep of the army. But that is not enough. I am at a loss, wondering how to keep the army occupied.'

'King of Kings, the victories are well-deserved. Upholding justice is no mean task, but the Chola Empire will rise to the occasion under your able guidance. When the future is not clear, one ought to look at the past for guidance. Arasey, your own ancestor Parantakar laid a golden Chitambalam on the Chidambaram temple about a hundred years ago to commemorate his victory,' reminded Vellaiappan, and paused.

'What do you suggest I do, Vellaiappa?' enquired the now attentive Chakravarthy.

'Chakravarthy, build a temple whose dimensions will take at least a day to measure, months to plan, years to construct, which will stand regally for millennia proclaiming the might of your empire. Build a temple which will showcase the rich artistic and cultural heritage of the Chola Dynasty and its subjects. Build a temple to honour the Gods who have blessed you and protected you during times of trials and tribulations. Build a temple to assuage your troubled conscience, to employ the vast army of this nation and to motivate your citizens.'

The Chakravarthy sat silently, lost in an ocean of thoughts. For a moment, he pondered the audacity of Vellaiappan, the audacity of a minister to engage the emperor of one of the most powerful realms in what had effectively been an impassioned lecture. And then, the Chakravarthy remembered that it was this that was his favourite quality in Vellaiappan—the way he questioned authority and tread on its toes so adroitly when few others would dare.

He then spoke like one possessed, 'Vellaiappa! Your idea has indeed reminded me of my youthful aspirations! As a young man in Eelam, I could not help but marvel at the towering viharams touching the heavens across the land, commemorating their lord, and thought, "If Eelam, a tiny isle, can honour their gods in such a magnificent manner, why can't we do the same in Chola Nadu, which is blessed by Him with such natural bounty?" Alas, that ambition of mine had been subsumed by the responsibilities of kingship, lost in the murky, swirling seas of time. But now, I feel like I have been awoken from a long slumber. I am forever indebted to you for that, Vellaiappa—forever indebted.'

And then, the Chakravarthy summoned his ushers and announced regally, 'Summon Kunjara Mallan Peruntachchar, the courtiers, the chiefs of kottams, the thalapathis and the dhanadhikari. By the grace of Emperuman, we will build a temple—the largest, the tallest and the most magnificent in the three worlds—which will grace Thanjai for eternity.'

11

Ilavarasan Rajendra, soon after returning from Kadaram, made it a point to visit Vellaiappan's stately manor, with its multiple courtyards illuminated at night with oil-fed silver lamps dangling sensually from the earthen tiles that adorned the roof, sourced especially from Athangudi in the Pandya country. He invariably visited the manor a few muhurthams before noon and had his lunch there. The crown prince of the Chola realm visited Vellaiappan's residence to assess the Kadaram expedition without the distractions in the palace and to train and strengthen the already formidable Chola army. Angayarkanni urged the crown prince to stay back for lunch, to which he acquiesced, not unwillingly. He rather relished the informal environment at Vellaiappan's home. It just so happened that Kayalvizhi joined him and Aniruddhan at lunch almost every day.

During one such visit, Aniruddhan had to run a few errands for Vellaiappan. Thus, Rajendra and Kayalvizhi had the rare opportunity to share a meal and converse, with just the kitchen staff in Vellaiappan's household around, serving them food.

'Did you hear, Ilavarasey?' asked Kayalvizhi, between mouthfuls of rice and fragrant meen kozhambu made from the day's catch.

'Hear what?' retorted Rajendra, his ears perking up.

'I heard my father inform my mother that the

Chakravarthy is constructing a temple like none seen before; one whose scale and grandeur future emperors will struggle to match, let alone surpass. Ilavarasey! My father said that he had reminded the Chakravarthy of his youthful ambitions of building a monument that would outshine the imposing viharams of Sinhala,' remarked Kayalvizhi. 'Would you be aware of such plans perchance?'

Rajendra chuckled and declared, 'Of course, I am aware of the Chakravarthy's intentions, dear Kayal. I am also aware of something your father is not yet aware of. The Chakravarthy is going to convene a team, Kovil Kattum Kuzhu, which will include your father, brother and, of course, the crown prince of Chola Nadu.'

Kayalvizhi retorted, 'Humility is evidently not the virtue of the ilavarasan of Chola Nadu.'

Rajendra shot back, 'Neither is deference a virtue of the daughter of Chola Nadu's minister of agriculture.'

Kayalvizhi rolled her eyes and countered, 'Why do you then visit the daughter of Chola Nadu's minister of agriculture every day? There must be innumerable maidens at the *anthapuram*, bowing to you. Why don't you visit them?'

To this Rajendra responded in a placatory tone, 'The heart craves for that which it does not have, Kayalvizhi. Besides, I heard you mention to your mother that you wished to visit Subbiah *thatha*'s cousin Sivakozhundu thatha's jewellery store in Thanjavur's *market*. I also heard you say how you yearned for the peanuts fried in ghee till they looked and smelt as rich as nuggets of gold, and the boat rides in the pond close to his house that Sivakozhundu thatha treated you to when you were a kid. The least the ilavarasan of Chola Nadu can do is to satisfy this desire of yours.'

Kayalvizhi raised her eyebrows and enquired, 'Has there

been a change in palace protocol that permits you and maidens in the anthapuram to venture out sans chaperones? If not, do you think that the minister of agriculture's daughter, by virtue of being a commoner, will consent to step out with you alone?'

A rather defensive Rajendra stammered, 'I have never ever invited the anthapuram maidens for an outing. Neither did I imply that we flout protocol and step out alone. I wanted to seek your consent before soliciting Ilavarasi Kundavai's help.'

Kayalvizhi smilingly stated, 'As Ilavarasi Kundavai's faithful companion, I will accompany her wherever she commands me to. The ilavarasan of Chola Nadu is bound only by the orders of the Chakravarthy, who I am sure will not demur if his offsprings wish to go on an outing.'

An elated Rajendra took leave of Kayalvizhi and Angayarkanni and seemingly apparated to the palace. He did not recollect mounting his horse or riding back. A formless, joyous force transported him across Thanjavur, enveloping him in a bubble that made the trees and the road and the traffic around him fade into a barely cognizable blur. Rajendra cheerfully instructed one of the palace guards to take his favourite horse to the stables, taking the attendant by surprise, and went to Ilavarasi Kundavai's chambers in the anthapuram.

Kundavai embraced him and quipped, 'Anna! I thought I had to visit Minister Vellaiappan's house to talk to you. I'm so glad you found time to visit me. How have you been?'

Rajendra sheepishly explained, 'I have been well, Kundavai. A war does not end with fighting. We need to understand what we did right and wrong. The army needs to be applauded for its successes and trained so that mistakes are not repeated. It is not possible to discuss these things with Aniruddhan in the palace without interruptions. So, I visit him at his home.'

Kundavai retorted, 'How will having lunch with Kayal every day strengthen our army, Anna?'

Rajendra was momentarily rendered speechless. But he managed to extricate himself from the corner by countering, 'You know so much about my whereabouts! Impressive, Kundavai, especially when everyone in the anthapuram and beyond are buzzing with the news that Ilavarasi Kundavai is personally supervising the living arrangements of our guests from Vengi.'

All Kundavai could manage was a squeaking 'Anna!', her cheeks ruddying as she became bashful.

Fortunately for her, someone knocked at the door. Kundavai quickly opened the door and allowed her lady-in-waiting to step in. The lady-in-waiting said, 'Ilavarasey, the Chakravarthy has asked you to join him, Aniruddha Brahmarayar and the princes from Vengi at the palace temple for the evening prayers and subsequently for deliberations at the terrace adjoining his quarters.' Having said that, she retreated.

As Kundavai closed the door, the levity that prevailed thus far also exited.

Rajendra enquired, 'Kundavai, I have been meaning to ask you. I was rather surprised that the princes from Vengi came here unannounced and Appa did not immediately summon me. I asked Brahmarayar about this; he promised to apprise me once he became fully aware of the situation. That was the last I heard from our wise prime minister. The Chakravarthy's desire to keep the Vengi princes' visit low-key is evident from his not announcing a state banquet in their honour thus far, and holding deliberations at his living quarters and not at the royal court's chambers. What is going on? Are the Vengi princes our guests or refugees?'

Kundavai replied, 'Anna, sometimes I wonder if the bonds of trust and affection that bind Appa and Brahmarayar are stronger than our familial ties. While I understand their relationship predates our birth, I cannot say that I'm not envious. Anyway, to answer your question, the Vengi princes did come here unannounced and uninvited. Their father—Maharaja Danarnava—was slain in a battle. On his deathbed, the dying king commanded his sons—Shaktivarman and Vimaladityan—to retreat to Thanjai and seek our Chakravarthy's counsel. Maharaja Danarnava had also ordered the brothers not to continue with hostilities without consulting Appa. So, the two princes hurriedly conducted their father's last rites in a forest and rode non-stop to Thanjavur, accompanied by a small contingent of loyal cavalrymen. The Chakravarthy did not think it necessary to inform us, his adult children, of this development. *Amma* and Anirudha Brahmarayar summoned me and asked me to oversee the guests' living arrangements. They asked me to enlist as few ladies-in-waiting and ushers as possible and said that this task was to groom me to assume the responsibilities of a Maharani at a future date. Both of us now know it's not the entire truth.'

Rajendra listened attentively to Kundavai and could not help remark, 'So, your enthusiasm for overseeing Shaktivarman's and Vimaladityan's living arrangements stems just from your desire to comply with the Maharani's and Brahmarayar's instructions?'

Kundavai remonstrated, 'Anna! Despite having to flee, the dignity in their bearing and their resolve to retrieve their kingdom is worthy of admiration. They are not defensive about their defeat; they view this as a temporary setback they will ultimately overcome. Unlike certain pompous feudatories we meet at state banquets, these princes are so rooted. They merely stated what transpired at the battlefield, without vilifying their adversaries or exaggerating their father's and their exploits. Ilavarasan Shaktivarman, who has been anointed to succeed Maharaja Danarnavan, has been housed in a guarded chamber for security reasons. His younger sibling, Ilavarasan Vimaladityan, has been accommodated in the guest wing of the palace, so that he can engage with the small Vengi contingent in Thanjai and keep his ears to the ground. Though he discharges his duty seemingly normally, the sorrow of losing his father in the battle and having to flee is palpable. I only have to initiate a conversation with Ilavarasan Vimaladityan, and one of amma's ladies-in-waiting miraculously materializes with an errand from her.'

A bemused Rajendra suggested, 'I would like to meet this Vimaladityan one-to-one and understand how the renowned Vengi force was vanquished. I will invite him to spend a day with me wandering the streets of Thanjai incognito. You too need a break from all this palace intrigue. Why don't you take a few of your friends to the riverside palace and summon astrologers, soothsayers, jewellers, silk merchants and purveyors of any other product you fancy?'

Kundavai shot back, 'Needless to mention, your incognito expedition in Thanjai will coincide with our visit to the riverside palace; Kayal will accompany me and our paths will cross.'

Kundavai squealed in annoyance and delight when Rajendra tugged at her tresses as he left her chamber.

Ilavarasi Kundavai was getting dressed to head to the riverside palace with her friends, when Kundavai Pirattiyar walked into her chamber.

'Kuzhandai, I understand you are visiting the riverside palace with your friends,' enquired the Chakravarthy's sister.

'Indeed, *Athai*. I have been bound to the palace, overseeing the living arrangements of the princes from Vengi. Rajendra suggested I step out for a while.'

'Your uncle informs me that Rajendra and Ilavarasan Vimaladityan too are going to spend the day in Thanjai, incognito.'

'Is that so, Athai?'

'You were unaware of this, kuzhandai?' asked Kundavai Pirattiyar, as she fastened a necklace on to the neck of the Ilavarasi, who was sitting in front of a mirror. Their eyes met for a moment as they looked at each other through the mirror.

The Ilavarasi remained silent.

Kundavai Pirattiyar continued, 'In our youth, we believe that the elders in our family unnecessarily panic and are overprotective. When in love, we think no one is aware of our feelings.'

'Athai, I'm in love with no one.'

'True, Rajendra is as oblivious to Kayalvizhi's existence as you are to Vimaladityan's,' remarked Kundavai Pirattiyar.

As the Ilavarasi began to say something, Kundavai Pirattiyar continued, 'Kuzhandai, why are you so embarrassed about falling in love? We cannot control with whom we fall in love. The challenges facing a princess falling in love with an exiled prince far exceed those of a princess falling in love with a commoner. Be conscious of your stature as the Ilavarasi of Chola Nadu and the royal family's responsibility to safeguard Vimaladityan; he is second in line to the Vengi throne.' Kundavai Pirattiyar then removed a scabbard with a small dagger from amidst the pleats of her saree, tucked it into the Ilavarasi's saree and walked out.

చ

Ilavarasi Kundavai, Kayalvizhi and four other friends, their hairs ringed by strings of jasmines and dressed in colourful silk sarees and exquisite pearls and corals, sat in three palanquins that were ferried towards the riverside palace. Kundavai and Kayalvizhi shared a palanquin. Two horsemen rode ahead of, and two behind, the three palanquins. Rajendra and Vimaladityan, disguised as cavalrymen, had left the palace on horseback a *muhurtham* ago.

A hearty brunch awaited the women when they reached the riverside palace. Shortly after the sumptous brunch, the women headed to the large koodam with mirrors fixed to the walls, where silk merchants and jewellers awaited them. Thick, multi-coloured *jamakalam*s were spread on the floors, on which the Ilavarasi and her companions sat. A few ladies-in-waiting waved hand-held fans in the background, while others served water, neer mor, *elaneer* and *panagam* out of intricately ornamented silver jugs.

The merchants displayed their wares that Ilavarasi Kundavai and her companions viewed, caressed and tried with much gusto. They set aside the silks and jewellery they wished to buy. One of the visiting merchants inscribed on a palm leaf the list of wares the Ilavarasi and her coterie had purchased and submitted it to Kundavai, who read it and handed it over to her lady-in-waiting, instructing her to give it to the palace retainer when they returned. Kundavai then handed over a ring bearing the royal insignia to the merchant, so that he could visit the palace and collect the payment.

Towards the end of the shopping spree, Kundavai and Kayalvizhi were distracted. They frequently looked towards the entrance as though they were expecting someone.

As the silk sellers and jewellers were leaving, two men arrived on horseback. They produced the royal insignia to the guards, who ushered them to the Ilavarasi's presence. One of the men said, 'Ilavarasi, an elderly jeweller, Sivakozhundu Pathar, has preserved rare and unique designs inscribed by his ancestors on palm leaves. These manuscripts are very old and may disintegrate during transit. He beseeches you and your friends to pay his humble abode a visit and choose the designs. He is keen to craft jewellery for you during his lifetime.'

Much confusion prevailed among Ilavarasi Kundavai's companions as the princess of the realm seldom visited a jeweller. Kayalvizhi, at this juncture, interjected. 'Ilavarasi Kundavai is not keen to inspect jewellery designs or jewellery now. She wants to go on a boat ride.'

To which, the second man, whose voice sounded familiar to all assembled, pronounced, 'Even Mother Nature is eager to fulfil the Chola Nadu's beloved Ilavarasi Kundavai's wishes. There is a pond behind Sivakozhundu Pathar's house. Boatmen are also available there to ply boats.'

Ilavarasi Kundavai replied, 'In that case, I am keen to see Sivakozhundu Pathar's offerings and then go on a boat ride.' Her companions had unravelled the visitors' identities; they suppressed their giggles.

Rajendra and Vimaladityan led the women out of the palace. While the two men mounted their steeds, the women sat in their palanquins. The two princes rode towards Sivakozhundu Pathar's house followed by Ilavarasi Kundavai's contingent.

12

Sivakozhundu Pathar paced in and out of the mansion that encompassed his home, jewellery store and safe. His wife Tirupurasundari Ammai excitedly commanded her staff to meticulously peel the skin off roasted peanuts, roast cobs of corn and arrange silver plates, bowls and tumblers attractively in the koodam. A dozen of Sivakozhundu Pathar's apprentices appeared to be at work in the *mandapam* adjoining the koodam, but in reality were observing the entrance to the mansion with bated breath. The *kolam* outside the gate and at the mansion's entrance was more elaborate than usual, the slender white tendrils of the rice flour glimmering enticingly in the late afternoon sun. The *pathar* had posted a few men at the gate to usher in the visitors.

An alley from the rear entrance of the mansion led to the pond. Since morning, the domestic helpers in the jeweller's house had scrupulously cleaned the alley, removing twigs, stones and thorns, and levelling it with sand from around the pond and the banks of the Kaveri.

Why was the jeweller's household abuzz with excitement and a certain nervous tension on a regular working day when neither a festival nor a family celebration was underway?

That morning, two young men of regal bearing had paid the pathar a visit. Sivakozhundu Pathar, who could smell affluence that lay aeons away, was not deceived by the warriors' robes the young men had donned. He requested them to be seated and asked one of his apprentices to fetch water and elaneer. When the pathar asked the young men how he might be of assistance, they made a strange request.

The young men said that they belonged to the Chola cavalry and that Ilavarasi Kundavai and her companions were desirous of viewing the pathar's jewellery at his store and then going on a boat ride in the pond behind the mansion. The pathar was perplexed. Tanks and ponds that were larger and far more scenic than the one behind his mansion abounded the palace complex. He offered to visit the palace with his jewellery and display them to Ilavarasi Kundavai and her companions. The young men insisted that he should host Ilavarasi Kundavai and her companions. They said that the palace would be sending the boats and the boatmen and that the household's routine would not be disrupted. This reassurance only served to make the pathar more anxious.

It was then that one of the pathar's apprentices, under the guise of serving elaneer, whispered into his master's ear. On realizing that Ilavarasan Rajendra was one of his visitors, Sivakozhundu Pathar immediately agreed to his request. The crown prince warned the pathar that news of the Ilavarasi's visit should be kept a secret, that neighbours ought not to be informed, and nagaswaram and thavil vidwans ought not to be engaged to welcome the royal contingent. The two princes also instructed the pathar that the house ought not to be decorated and should look like it currently did. The dumbstruck pathar nodded in agreement and saw his visitors off.

Sivakozhundu Pathar's young apprentices, who were agog with excitement, were unable to restrain themselves after the princes left. The apprentices informed the pathar that the retainers in the palace and Vellaiappan's household had informed them that Ilavarasar Rajendra and Ilavarasi Kundavai were in love with Kayalvizhi and Ilavarasar Vimaladityan, respectively. The apprentices believed that the pathar was indeed fortunate that the royals had chosen his abode as the site of their rendezvous and that the sky was the limit for his jewellery business henceforth.

For a change, the pathar was more concerned about his head exploding than his business expanding. He was justly scared of incurring the Chakravarthy's wrath. His practical wife, Thirupurasundari Ammai, reasoned that the pathar had really no say in the matter and that the household should prepare for Ilavarasi Kundavai's visit. They could decide whether or not to tip Subbiah, Aniruddha Brahmarayar or Kundavai Pirattiyar off after the Ilavarasi's visit.

The gates of Sivakozhundu Pathar's mansion swiftly opened as Ilavarasi Kundavai's contingent led by Rajendra and Vimaladityan entered the street. Once all the palanquins and horses entered the compound, Rajendra gestured to the pathar's men at the gate, who closed the gates immediately. Ilavarasi Kundavai, Kayalvizhi and her companions alighted from the palanquins and walked towards the mansion.

Thirupurasundari Ammai, flanked by the womenfolk in the pathar's household, performed an *arathi* and welcomed the royal visitors. Once everyone was seated in the koodam, the apprentices displayed the jewellery, while the pathar described the design aspects of each piece. Roasted peanuts, corn and raw mangoes were served to the guests along with elaneer, neer mor and panagam. It was then that Thirupurasundari Ammai seated herself next to Kayalvizhi, embraced her and asked, 'Did you remember the existence of this old couple just now, Kayal?'

An embarrassed Kayalvizhi replied demurely, 'Not at all, *paati*. I have been meaning to visit you. Between relocating from Nagapattinam to Thanjai, and my music classes and duties as Ilavarasi Kundavai's companion, I was unable to visit you. I missed you two sorely. In fact, it was I who suggested we visit you today. I promise to visit you more frequently henceforth.' Thirupurasundari Ammai did not reply.

The royal contingent viewed the jewellery for about a muhurtham, purchased a few pieces and then expressed their desire to go on a boat ride. They were led to the pond through the rear entrance, to find three boats waiting for them. The pathar, his wife and the Ilavarasi's companions observed that while Rajendra and Kayalvizhi headed to one boat, Kundavai and Vimaladityan headed to another. Ilavarasi Kundavai's four companions had no choice but to board the third boat. It was then that one of the companions, Mangai, instructed the boatman to row in the direction the boat carrying Ilavarasi Kundavai and Vimaladityan had headed. He wordlessly rowed in the opposite direction. An annoyed Mangai asked the boatman why he did not have the courtesy to inform her that he was instructed to row in a particular direction. The boatman continued rowing without reacting and responding. It was then that the ladies realized that all three boatmen were hard of hearing and mute and were instructed to row in designated directions beforehand.

Rajendra and Kayalvizhi alternated between bantering casually and falling into companionable silence, while admiring the imminent sunset, the sounds of birds chirping, and the ripples caused by the gentle breeze gliding across the pond. Conversation between Kundavai and Vimaladityan was, at least initially, decorous.

'Ilavarasi! I am indeed indebted to the Chakravarthy and his family for not just giving Anna and me refuge but also treating us as one of your own. This means a lot to us, especially after losing our father and the misfortune that befell our kingdom recently.'

'Ilavarasey! The rulers and denizens of Tamizhagam are not fair-weather friends. We stand with our allies through thick and thin. Centuries ago, the Sinhala prince, Ilavarasan Maravarman, sought refuge at Kanchi during Mahendra Varma Pallavar's reign after he was ousted from his empire. Mahendra Varma Pallavar not only hosted Maravarman for years but also provided him with an army that vanquished the Sinhala prince's adversaries and reinstated him on the throne. Hospitality and fair play courses through our veins.'

'I agree with that. Ilavarasan Rajendra was under no obligation to show me around Thanjai today. Yet, he did so. In accompanying him incognito and taking in the sights and sounds of Thanjai, I experienced freedom and lightness of spirit that I have not felt for long. Similarly, while you were tasked with organizing my brother's and my living arrangements, you did not have to meet me every day and enquire about my well-being. Your visits provided me much solace, especially since I am unable to freely communicate with my brother despite living under the same roof. You, who are destined to be a chakravarthini of a vast empire in a few years, do not have to go through so much trouble for my sake.'

'Ilavarasey, this is not the first time you are mentioning that my behaviour is unbecoming of a future chakravarthini. Do you find my attentions repugnant? I will refrain from speaking to you henceforth, if that is the case. You may be rest assured that your unwillingness to befriend me will in no way affect my father's decision to support you and your brother.'

'Repugnant? You, Ilavarasi? That was the last thought in my mind! Since you have spoken so plainly, I beseech you to allow me to do so, even if it may be inappropriate. I was drawn to you even before I knew you were Chakravarthy Raja Raja Chola's beloved daughter. You may not recollect this. When the Vengi contingent, my brother and I reached Thanjai, we were led to the palace stables to hand over our horses. That was when you and Kayalvizhi also rode into the stables. You dismounted from your horse, led it to a vat to quench its thirst, and then started conversing with the stable hands. You were enquiring about their well-being. I was struck by your caring nature and beauty. It was only when your mother and Brahmarayar introduced us, I became aware of your identity. The Vengi kingdom is akin to this pond in comparison to the ocean-like Chola kingdom. It is my brother, Shaktivarman, who will ascend the throne when we wrest our kingdom from our adversaries. I have been groomed to be the senathipathi of the Vengi army, a calling that suits my character and aspirations. Ever since I became aware of your identity, I keep reminding myself, rather unhappily, that I ought not to forge relationships above my station.'

Kundavai's heart skipped a beat. She had imbibed her athai's virtue of treating commoners with respect and affection. However, her running into Vimaladityan in the stables on the day of his arrival at Thanjai was not entirely coincidental. As she, Kayalvizhi and her companions were returning to the palace after a ride in the nearby woods, she had observed the Vengi contingent riding towards the palace. Leading the contingent were Shaktivarman and Vimaladityan. The fleeing contingent did not carry its standard; she had been unable to ascertain their identity. While all the other riders looked despondent and weary, resolve shone through one of the warriors leading the force—Vimaladityan. Curious to ascertain his identity, she had gestured to Kayalvizhi. The two women had followed the cavalry to the stables. She had not been able to bring herself to initiate a conversation with a stranger. But she had overheard the stable hands mentioning that the contingent had fled from Vengi. Later during the day, her joy knew no bounds when her mother and Aniruddha Brahmarayar introduced her to the Vengi princes and tasked her with their living arrangements.

Ilavarasi Kundavai smilingly replied, 'I seem to share several similarities with my athai. She too fell in love with and married a brave warrior, Vallavaraya Vandiyathevar, who is now the senathipathi of the Chola army. Some princesses are drawn to power, others to strength of character and valour. My athai and I belong to the latter category.'

'I must be the most fortunate man in this world, Ilavarasi. While your willingness to marry the senathipathi of a much smaller kingdom is heartening, your parents will be disappointed.'

Kundavai burst out in fits of giggles. She assuaged Vimaladityan's concerns saying, 'Ilavarasey, it was my father who reasoned with my grandfather, the great Sundara Chola, when my athai and Vandiyathevar were desirous of marrying. As you can see, Rajendra is smitten with Kayalvizhi. My family is not unaware of their meeting today. Members of the Chola dynasty value character over titles and wealth.'

Vimaladityan replied, 'I'm indeed blessed. But I do have

one request. My brother's and my priority is to build our forces and recover our kingdom. The Chola forces have also just returned from Kadaram and are embarking on building a colossal temple of peerless splendour. I cannot broach the subject of our marriage with your father until I have established my credentials. I must make myself worthy of seeking your hand in marriage. Both of us should wait for the right time to broach the subject of marriage.'

'I could not agree with you more, Ilavarasey. We, Chola women, aim to strengthen our menfolk. I assure you that we will seek our elders' approval for our marriage only when you are confident of winning back your kingdom and the temple construction is progressing smoothly. Till then, please do not hesitate to ask for my assistance. I am a descendant of an illustrious lineage of valorous women of Bharata Kandam, such as Kaikeyi, Sathyabama and my athai, Kundavai Pirattiyar.'

An intimate calm descended on the boat occupied by Ilavarasi Kundavai and Vimaladityan, following this heartfelt exchange, after which the boatman pointed to the setting sun. Kundavai gestured to him to row towards Sivakozhundu Pathar's mansion. Kundavai and Vimaladityan reached the banks to find Rajendra, Kayalvizhi and the Ilavarasi's companions waiting for them. The group walked back in silence to the pathar's mansion. They were met by an uninvited guest—Aniruddhan.

The fearless Kayalvizhi was unable to look at her brother in the eye. Neither was Rajendra. Kundavai however had the presence of mind to salvage the situation saying, 'Aniruddha! How nice to see you. Athai had warned us to keep Ilavarasar Vimaladitya's incognito trip low-key. So, Anna did not invite you, albeit reluctantly. Kindly accompany us to the palace and stay for the night. It's *pournami*, the moon will be blazing in its full glory, illuminating us all in its effulgence. Dinner will be served on the palace terrace, followed by music and dance performances. Kayalvizhi and you must join us for the festivities and return to your home tomorrow.'

'Your wish is my command, Ilavarasi,' remarked a deadpan Aniruddhan.

The royal contingent thanked and took leave of Sivakozhundu Pathar and Thirupurasundari Ammai and headed back to the palace.

As the palanquins made their way to the palace, Kundavai excitedly squeezed Kayalvizhi's hands and stated, 'Kayal, I have much to share with you.'

Kayalvizhi replied, 'I let down my brother, Ilavarasi!'

Kundavai consoled her saying, 'Don't be sad! We will make amends.' The two friends embraced each other.

13

Kunjara Mallan Peruntachchar was a gifted architect who lived in an expansive mansion at the heart of Thanjavur. He was a skilled practitioner of Agama Shastra and had penned a commentary on the subject. He had built several temples across Chola Nadu, and it was almost impossible to be a citizen of Chola Nadu and not to have visited a temple built by him.

Kunjara Mallan was a tall, lean man, with large, bulbous eyes and a stubby nose. Dimples appeared on his oval face when he smiled, softening his otherwise rugged countenance. He was happily married with three sons, all of whom were his understudies.

The Chakravarthy and Kunjara Mallan had a close rapport, bound by their interest in sculptures and their love for Tamizhagam.

When the Chakravarthy conveyed his long-time dream—his vision of a temple whose scale and grandeur outshone those of others in Eelam, the erudite peruntachchar didn't bat an eye. He simply asked what unique features the Chakravarthy would like to incorporate in the temple.

The Chakravarthy was momentarily taken aback by the peruntachchar's tranquillity. Regaining his composure, he elucidated, 'Ayya, I ask this of you. Build a temple that is unequalled in grandeur, size and intricacies in all the three worlds. I request you to build a temple that will instill pride and confidence in the Chola people. I want to build a temple that will stand for eternity, showcasing the rich culture, heritage and art of our race, the diligence of the citizens of Chola Nadu, and the vision and splendour of my dynasty. Use your rich imagination and creativity to build a temple that has no parallel to date and will have none in future.'

The peruntachchar was silent for a moment. He then affirmed, in his rich, deep baritone, 'Arasey! By the grace of Emperuman and with your support, I will be able to construct such a temple.'

The Chakravarthy, a man who usually did not show much emotion, was elated. Smiling, he announced, 'I will immediately convene a *Kuzhu* under your stewardship to construct the temple and will also allocate the necessary funds.'

He looked back and breathed a sigh of relief. No enemy soldier was on his tail as he rode his horse across the thick foliage in the direction of the capital of Sepang. He was lucky; unlike the corpulent Aryapriya, he was slim and was a skilled horse rider. He was a courtier of the erstwhile governor of Sepang. He was fleeing Kadaram, which was now under the control of Tamils. The border between Kadaram and other provinces in Sepang wasn't clearly demarcated. He didn't know when he would be able to ride at a normal pace. Bandits and thieves who preyed on merchants transporting goods to and from the port infested the road from Kadaram to Sepang.

It was night time when he believed that he had reached the safer area near Sepang. Seeing a merchant caravan, he immediately rode towards it and asked if he could join it on its journey to Sepang. He possessed a few spears and a bow with a quiver full of arrows.

His request wasn't turned down by the merchant contingent, who understandably feared bandits.

He was on his way to Sepang.

When the Chakravarthy announced his plans to build the greatest of temples in Bharata Kandam, his courtiers posed several hurdles.

The dhanadhikari, a man who was characterized by prudence and financial suavity, worriedly enquired, 'Chakravarthy, this is an idea which, in my opinion, will not only employ our army but also make our citizens justly proud of Chola Nadu. But the cost will be considerable. Paying for the stone and raw materials and employing artisans and labourers will deplete our treasury. Temple construction isn't cheap and a temple of this scale will take decades to construct. Arasey, the Kadaram expedition was a significant drain on our treasury. We have just enough money in our coffers to survive. If the rains were to fail for a few years during the period of the temple construction, how will we support the nation?'

Prime Minister Aniruddha Brahmarayar replied, 'The respected dhanadhikari has admirably discharged his duty by emphasizing the risks the temple construction is fraught with. He has however failed to account for the wealth the Kadaram expedition yielded. Also, the temple construction will cause our merchant community's profits to increase and a rise in the incomes of those working on the temple site. Our taxes will also increase. May I request our dhanadhikari to advise us how much may be spent on temple construction every year after keeping aside enough money to meet contingencies like floods and droughts?'

Next spoke Chezhian, the quick-minded chief of the Kudandhai Kottam: 'Arasey! I hear the temple will be built of stones.'

The Chakravarthy nodded.

Chezhian continued, 'There are no hills in the vicinity. The only way we can get stone for your temple is by quarrying it from distant places, and even then, stone must be transported over a great distance! How is that possible, Arasey?'

Aniruddha Brahmarayar assuaged Chezhian's concerns saying, 'Respected Chezhian, we have many quarries in Senji and Pachaimalai, most of them owned by the Chakravarthy and his dynasty. We can arrange to bring stones from there. Remember, our land is blessed with bountiful natural resources. All we require is the wisdom to use it.'

Vandiyathevan, the senior-most military official in the court, proudly declared, 'Our neighbours must have heard of the ferocity of the Chola soldiers in the Kadaram campaign by now. They fear our military might. Hence, it is highly unlikely that anyone is going to attack us. So, we will deploy enough forces to safeguard our borders and the rest may be deployed to construct the temple.' The Chakravarthy nodded in agreement.

Next spoke Kundavai Pirattiyar, the beloved and learned elder sister of the Chakravarthy, who exercised great influence over him. She said, 'Thambi, by the grace of Lord Shiva, I will pay the wages of the artisans employed to construct the temple.'

Kundavai's magnanimity made the king happy. Other courtiers soon joined in, donating significant sums of money for the temple's construction. The Chakravarthy was relieved that money had started flowing in to fund the temple construction.

Kundavai, Vandiyathevan, Brahmarayar and the dhanadhikari exchanged almost imperceptible smiles. Their behind-the-scenes collaboration had garnered support for the Chakravarthy's dream project and helped bring about the discipline they wished to impose for the good of the nation.

※

Sepang's picturesque capital was located on a small hill overlooking a river. Splashes of vivid green jungle were visible even in the urban downtown. It wasn't a planned city; instead, it had grown organically, from a hunter settlement to a small city. The 'city' was not populous—most of its people lived on the three streets in the hillside. Its strategic location as the midpoint on the road from Kadaram to the eastern coast was its strength. The centrepiece of the city was its market, a cacophony of live chickens, cows and other poultry. The merchant contingent had dropped off the sole surviving courtier at the central market, and they made their merry way eastwards. He felt healthy and nourished as the fellow merchants had taken good care of him during the journey. Hence, he rode his fine horse quickly and energetically, albeit worriedly, to the King's palace.

Abhinava was practising his zither when the guards admitted the courtier. He stopped playing, placed the instrument on a silk cushion, and looked up at the courtier who bowed to him.

'Greetings, courtier. How are the affairs in the province of Kedah? Is my brother well? Are taxes and levies being collected regularly?' squeaked Abhinava.

'Your Highness, I don't know how to say this...,' the

courtier's sonorous voice trailed off.

'Don't fear, dear courtier. Tell me, how are the affairs at Kedah?'

'King, we've lost Kedah to the Tamils,' quivered the courtier fearfully.

'And Aryapriya?' asked the king gravely.

'Dead. Killed by the poisoned arrow of a Tamil warrior,' squeaked the courtier.

'You may leave now,' ordered the king to the courtier, who did as he was told.

'Guard! Summon the chief of spies!' growled a furious Abhinava.

The guard bowed, and scuttled away.

The wheels of revenge had started turning.

14

The pond behind Sivakozhundu pathar's mansion had led an uneventful existence. In the old days, it was used to water the fields of the farmers who tilled their lands around it. When the Cholas moved their capital city from Uraiyur to the now bustling Thanjavur, the pond was located at the edge of the city, just where the bazaar ended. Mango and banyan trees surrounded the pond, hiding it from public view. Few people, who knew of the pond's existence, went for coracle rides after a day of shopping in the bazaar, but the pond had mainly led a placid, uneventful existence.

Until, of course, the crown prince of the Chola Empire, Rajendra, and Kayalvizhi began using the pond for their rendezvous, away from prying eyes. After the court moved to Thanjavur en masse to focus on the temple construction, the duo frequently visited the pond, always in the evening, away from the eyes of the public at large. They'd watch the sun set, share court gossip or discuss the latest developments in the temple construction, but seldom beyond. They enjoyed each other's company, but with time they began to start feeling something more. Was it a mere desire to not miss their weekly meetings? It was not. Was it an inane craving for the honeyed voice of each other to trickle into their ears, like a slow drip of cold water from a leaky wooden ceiling in the hut of a peasant? No, it was not that either. Was it mere appreciation of the beauty of each other, that when asked about the ideal physical qualities in their mates, their description would be of each other? Again, no, it was not that either. Yet, try as they might, neither Rajendra nor Kayalvizhi knew what precisely it was.

The silent, antediluvian pond, having seen a city rise from the ground and the vagaries of its inhabitants who frequented it, would have known what it was. Yet, alas, ponds are not sentient. Its silent observations of the blossoming relationship between Kayalvizhi and Rajendra, the most momentous event in its life, would be unarticulated. Any communication of emotion would have to be by those involved, not by the ponds and the trees which witnessed their emotions flower like a pearl-white lotus in a pond.

Early one morning, as Kayalvizhi finished giving lessons on the *yazh* to one of her students, Angayarkanni approached her and said, 'Kayal, I have procured a special oil from the markets recently. The shopkeeper said that if applied to the scalp, the person's stress will be relieved and there will be a lush growth of dark hair. Come here, let me apply it on your head.'

Kayalvizhi smiled, and changed into an older saree. She followed her mother into the bathing area of their mansion and sat on a wooden stool. Angayarkanni sat herself on another teak-wood stool and opened the oil vial. As Angayarkanni proceeded to massage her daughter's already lush hair, she cautiously said, 'Kayal, I have observed that you and the ilavarasan have been spending a lot of time together.'

Kayalvizhi turned back at her mother; her eyes dilated with embarrassment as she said, 'Amma! He is just a friend! Nothing else! Why would you even assume anything? You know that my first love is music! Plus, we have known each other since we were children. Why can't we talk? Is that such a crime?'

Angayarkanni smiled inwardly, as she was reminded of her love for Vellaiappan. She said, 'I didn't say anything, you did!'

'I know what you are about to say next!'

'Really? That sure is news to me!' said Angayarkanni sarcastically, her brows rising to form delicate arches above her eyes while she continued to rhythmically massage her daughter's hair.

Kayalvizhi stayed silent.

'Kuzhandai, my dearest daughter Kayalvizhi, it is but natural for all girls to fall in love at this age '

'I am not "all girls"! And I am not in love!'

'My mistake, you're not in love. But just remember, Appa and I know the feeling of falling in love despite all the odds being stacked against you. Subbiah thatha nearly drove Appa into the streets after he discovered that we were in love. Though Appa and I will support your choice of life partner, arranging your marriage with the ilavarasan is beyond our ken. The royalty has several other considerations besides mutual affection while choosing a spouse. You may point out that Kundavai Pirattiyar married below her station. Just remember, she is a woman who was unlikely to succeed to the throne. Since she was determined to continue living in Chola Nadu, the royal family had no choice but to acquiesce to her marriage with Vandiyathevar.

'I also hear stories of Ilavarasi Kundavai and the exiled Vengi prince, Vimaladityan, being in love. The Chakravarthy has reasons for turning a blind eye to, or even tacitly encouraging, this dalliance. Once again, Ilavarasi Kundavai is unlikely to ascend the throne. By assisting the exiled princes in retrieving their kingdom, the Chakravarthy is essentially creating a protectorate and loyalists who will support Ilavarasar Rajendra becoming the undisputed Chakravarthy of Dakshina Bharata.

'You are the apple of our eyes and you lord over this household. Even if the Chakravarthy consents to your marriage with Ilavarasan Rajendra, he will marry women from other royal families. If you two were to be married, your sons will never ascend the Chola throne. You will never be the Chakravarthini. Do you have it in you to play a subservient role in the royal household?'

'Amma, we are not in love!'

'Okay, okay! Got it. Do you want some panagam? I had Muthamma make some. It is a hot day...'

Rajendra visited Aniruddhan the next day at Vellaiappan's house. Angayarkanni greeted Rajendra with warmth and respect. As she walked to the kitchen to instruct the cooks to serve lunch, she glanced at Kayalvizhi from the corner of her eye. Kayalvizhi looked away. Soon after lunch, Vellaiappan summoned Aniruddhan to the palace to assist him with some matters relating to the agricultural ministry. Kayalvizhi and Rajendra once again had an opportunity to converse at the former's home without a chaperone. Inevitably, the conversation drifted to the topic of parents.

'Ilavarasey, you will never believe what my mother told me yesterday!' said Kayalvizhi, her voice barely concealing her irritation.

'What? Did she ask you to find a bride for me?' teased Rajendra as he feigned horror.

Kayalvizhi rolled her eyes and shot back, 'Ilavarasey,

commoners, especially women of mixed race, are not enlisted to find a bride for the nation's beloved crown prince.'

Rajendra guffawed and replied, 'How unfortunate!'

'But anyway. Where was I? Oh yes. My dear amma thinks both of us are in love. She said Kundavai Pirattiyar and Ilavarasi Kundavai may marry as they wish as they do not have a claim to the throne. However, even if the Chakravarthy were to consent to our marriage, I will occupy a subservient position in the royal household.'

Rajendra icily asked, 'What did you say, Kayal?'

'I informed my mother that I was not in love with you.'

'Are you not, Kayal? Then why have you been trying to spend time with me by hook or by crook? Why did you come on boat rides with me unchaperoned? Is this the way you behave with all of Aniruddhan's friends?'

'Mind your words, Ilavarasey. You are casting aspersions on my character. Was I the one trying to spend time with you? Why should the Ilavarasar visit my house everyday under the pretext of meeting my brother and speak to me more than he does to my brother?'

'I never denied being in love with you, Kayalvizhi, whereas you denied being in love with me to your mother. So, to whom are you stating the truth? To me or to your mother? Also, when your mother said that you will occupy a subservient position after marrying me, why did you not deem it necessary to defend me?'

'My mother did not say anything wrong, Ilavarasey! If we were to be married, will I be anointed as a chakravarthini?'

'Are you in love with me or the throne, Kayalvizhi?'

'Will you promise me that you will marry no other woman besides me?'

'I can promise you, Kayal. But I will not be able to keep

my word. We both know that I will have to marry other women to cement political alliances. How does that in any way diminish the love and friendship we share?'

'Wasn't Lord Rama a Chakravarthy? He married only Sita. Don't use statesmanship to justify your roving eye, Ilavarasey!'

Rajendra stormed out of the house. A distraught Kayalvizhi fled the room to seek refuge in her mother's lap. She ran into a horrified Angayarkanni, who was standing immobilized in the adjacent chamber.

15

One evening, as Ilavarasi Kundavai and her brother, Ilavarasan Rajendra, sat on the banks of the Kaveri, gossiping as the fish nibbled on the skin of their toes, staring into the setting sun, she asked with a start, 'Anna! I almost forgot to tell you! Kayal is visiting me at the palace tomorrow to show me some new jewellery her grandfather bought from Korkai. Would you like to join us at the anthapuram then?'

'Me? At the anthapuram, Kundavai?! I hope this comment was made in jest! I am a blue-blooded warrior, the Crown Price of Chola Nadu and heir apparent to the peerless Raja Raja Chola! Do you seriously think giving you company while you and your companions engage in frivolous pastimes like scrutinizing each other's jewellery is worthy of the ilavarasan of Chola Nadu?' retorted Rajendra, his body moving away from his sister in a sharp motion of affront.

'The ilavarasan of Chola Nadu, till a few weeks ago, had no compunctions about accompanying me and my friends to our shopping expeditions in Thanjavur. If my memory serves me right, he even spirited away one of my friends, whose name is Kayalvizhi, for a boat ride in a secluded pond. It is this Kayalvizhi who is visiting me tomorrow, ostensibly to show me the jewellery her grandfather bought for her. Why this uncharacteristic unwillingness to meet Kayalvizhi? Have you suddenly become aware of your stature as the ilavarasan of Chola Nadu or has someone else caught your eye?' asked Kundavai, only half-jokingly.

Rajendra glared at Kundavai; her last remark had touched a raw nerve. Kundavai's mind dwelt on Rajendra's strange behaviour. When Rajendra and Kayalvizhi spoke, Rajendra's eyes gleamed like the light of a solitary oil lamp lit in a temple, spreading molten gold around the cavernous space and making it so much warmer. Kayalvizhi too relaxed, tucking the strands of her hair behind her ears like she was a smitten teenager—the same Kayalvizhi who could ride a steed as well as the finest horseman of Chola Nadu, who seldom spoke of herself. And now? Rajendra, a kid she had known to be honest all her life, was equivocating! Something was evidently not right. Kundavai took it upon herself as her mission to find out what transpired between her best friend and her dearest brother.

Kayalvizhi came to the palace the next day, and Kundavai was all too eager to receive her. As they discussed the intricacies of the craftsmanship of the pearl beads, Kundavai tried to string in questions about Rajendra. Yet, Kayalvizhi's response was so evasive that Rajendra's seemed unambiguous by comparison. Kundavai was stupefied—two of the people who seemed the most transparent to her had suddenly become as opaque as a piece of ebony wood. Evidently, something had transpired between the two of them, thought Kundavai—something that had changed how they saw each other forever. What could it be? Kundavai explored the possibilities—a misunderstanding between the two lovers, jealousy, or probably a development that the much-in-love Ilavarasi Kundavai found too unpleasant to even contemplate. She could only conjecture; Ilavarasi Kundavai was as unsuccessful in unearthing the truth as a pearl diver off the shores of Mamallapuram.

At that moment, a thought struck Kundavai's mind—if she wants to retrieve pearls from the sea, she needed to dispatch a pearl hunter to Korkai and not Mamallapuram! Kayalvizhi and Rajendra needed a discreet location to meet and talk to each other. But they did not want to see each other! How could she engineer a meeting between Kayalvizhi and Rajendra? A plan began forming in Kundavai's mind, and she began making the preparations.

Ilavarasi Kundavai, launching a flurry of preparations to contrive a rendezvous between Kayalvizhi and Rajendra, did not escape Kundavai Pirattiyar's watchful eye.

※

'Where is everyone else?' asked Kayalvizhi to Kundavai. The duo was at the royal marinas of Nagapattinam, waiting for the rest of the coterie of friends to turn up. A recently retired naval ship in the Imperial Chola Navy had been converted into a pleasure boat for the royal family, and Kundavai had meant to invite her entire group of friends, including Kayalvizhi, to go on a one-day expedition at sea. At least she wanted to, but rather unfortunately, she forgot to invite the rest of the group, save Kayalvizhi.

'Ayyo! Didn't I tell you? Their palanquins turned back to Thanjavur at Needamangalam! Soundari fell sick, apparently. In the morning, she was fine. By the afternoon, she was in the throes of a fever. Utterly delirious, apparently! Thought all her friends were her long-gone great-grandparents. So they turned back and went to Thanjai. But worry not, Kayal, I've ensured that the best vaidhyars will attend to Soundari. Let's just enjoy this excursion,' said Kundavai.

Kayalvizhi silently raised her eyebrows, her expression

inscrutable, and boarded the ship. A lady-in-waiting led her to her quarters, and another kept the ornate wooden chest she carried her clothes in, taking it to her room. Kayalvizhi watched the ship sail out of the docks, further and further away from Nagapattinam. From her windows, she could see the scores of fisherfolk in the sea returning to the coast, their wooden hulls rocking gently in the breeze. Feeling hungry, Kayalvizhi wandered out of her room, and into the central deck of the ship. There, she saw Kundavai sitting on a bench near the hull of the ship, talking animatedly to a man. As she approached and touched the shoulder of Kundavai, the man turned back too, to reveal it was Rajendra!

'Ilavarasi! Is this why you brought me on this excursion? So I would have to talk to ilavarasan again? The last time we met, I told you that I did not want to talk about him. I am hurt that you should disregard my feelings!'

Rajendra was stupefied, his eyes glazed in that same vacant expression that came on his face during the last conversation. His heart began to sink glacially into an icy pit which had replaced his stomach, and his senses were dulled, unresponsive like a man unconscious. Thus, he did not hear his sister try to reason with Kayalvizhi to remain calm, and to just talk to Rajendra, her friend. His eyes remained unseeing to Kayalvizhi storming into her quarters, a concerned Kundavai in hot pursuit. His body unfeeling to the movements of his legs into his quarters, lying down, eyes shut as the middle-day sun blazed onto his face.

All he could see, hear, feel—was the sound of a yazh, being strummed by Kayalvizhi, somewhere in the distance.

Near sunset, Rajendra arose, not feeling himself. He knew he had to say something, do something, about Kayalvizhi. And thus he walked out, to see Kayalvizhi leaning against the stern of the ship against the setting sun, humming a tune. As he walked towards her, his heart racing, Kayalvizhi turned around, her face impassive. But Kayalvizhi did not flee this time.

Rajendra's heart ceased racing, and his legs began running.

Kundavai watched as her dearest friend and her beloved brother locked themselves in an ardent embrace against the setting sun off the shores of Nagapattinam. She didn't need to hear the words, for all she could see illuminating the edge of the ship was pure, unadulterated love. Kundavai walked away observing Rajendra and Kayalvizhi lock lips, thinking of her and the valorous Vimaladityan.

16

One bracingly cold day just after the harvest festival of Pongal, as the sun rose over the city of Thiruvarur, a retinue of chariots and palanquins made their way down the dusty streets leading to the Thyagaraja Swamy temple. Neither the low-hanging mist—a heady mixture of the crop stubble burnt in the recently-concluded *Bhogi* festival and the mist that accumulated every morning in the early part of the month Thai—nor the gentle early morning drizzle of rain as sharp as cold steel spears, seemed to deter the contingent as they made their way to the heart of the city. Parking in the specially erected royal pandal, on the vast empty field that sat opposite the temple, used by the townsfolk as a public space for concerts and religious discourses, the passengers in the chariots disembarked to reveal some of the most powerful and important people in the Chola Empire.

The flower sellers and the touts, setting up their shops along the magnificent stone walls of the temple, espied through the early morning mist a veritable galaxy of *deva*s and *devi*s disembark. Out came the Chakravarthy himself, decked in the finest blue silk robe, under an umbrella bearing his personal insignia. Another umbrella bearing the insignia of the Chakravarthy's sister, Kundavai Pirattiyar, emerged, barely concealing the elaborate set of jasmines and hibiscuses she wore in her head supported by an ornamental jade headpiece. Other umbrellas emerged, bearing the insignias of Kunjara

Mallan Peruntachchar, Vellaiappan, the wizened Aniruddha Brahmarayar, Dandanayakan and Ilavarasan Rajendra. Only Aniruddhan, being the son of a minister, was guarded by an umbrella not bearing the insignia of any kottam or *kulam*, but instead one bearing the insignia of the Imperial Army. An air of pomp pervaded the field, as far as the touts could tell—a fact supported by the presence of a yazh player who wore a pure white robe and a look of contentment, and by multiple priests.

The touts and flower-sellers looked on curiously, squinting their eyes as they saw a spire of smoke rise from the heart of the field, straining their ears for the faint sounds of the yazh and a singer—a song on Vinayaka, it seemed, something about granting propitious beginnings. And just like that, the coterie had dispersed into the chariots, their pageboys carrying woven bamboo baskets brimming with frangipani and fruits—*prasadam* from the prayer, evidently. The chariots then made their way across the road, and the touts and flower-sellers could catch a glimpse of these devas and devis as they seemingly glided into the temple, their feet barely seeming to touch the ground as the silk seemed to sashay for them while the wearers looked on serenely, into the magnificent Maha Mandapam, the biggest mandapam, bedecked with paintings of incidents from the Thiruvisaippa, a composition of a Chola dynast.

Little did the onlookers realize the import of what they'd seen—the formation of a Kovil Kattum Kuzhu.

Raja Raja Chola was aware that the successful construction of a temple of such scale and grandeur was a community initiative. So he formed a Kovil Kattum Kuzhu. The Chakravarthy decided that he and the architect, Kunjara Mallan Peruntachchar, would jointly helm this Kuzhu. In addition to his resourceful and loyal ministers Vellaiappan and Aniruddha Brahmarayar, he enlisted the services of his dear brother-in-law Vandiyathevan, the army general Dandanayakan, Rajendra, and Aniruddhan. No project that the Chakravarthy embarked on was complete without his esteemed elder sister and Vandiyathevan's dear wife, Kundavai Pirattiyar.

The members sat themselves on raised platforms made from fragrant sandalwood, the finest brought from the western reaches of the Chola Empire. The Chakravarthy was seated in the highest of the platforms, with two tall attendants fanning him on either side. From the vantage point the Chakravarthy enjoyed, a sea of heads descended towards the ground. To the left, the Chakravarthy saw his beloved sister, Kundavai Pirattiyar, and to his right, a seat was reserved for Vanathi, the Chakravarthy's most beloved consort. At the next level, fanning outwards, was the wizened prime minister of the Chola Empire, Aniruddha Brahmarayar, the rich brown of his head reflecting the iridescent sunlight of the early morning light filtering into the hall. Opposite Brahmarayar sat Vellaiappan, leaning forward eagerly. At the next level, Kunjara Malla Peruntachchar sat anxiously, flanked by two of his assistants carrying heavy bales of olive-green palm leaves glowing like blocks of emerald, his expression pensive. The lowest rungs were occupied by Aniruddhan and Rajendra, the platform low enough for their silk robes to brush against the fine layer of sand that had accumulated on the floor, brought in by the wind from the wide field opposite.

As the Chakravarthy cleared his throat, the courtiers became very silent. 'Friends, we are gathered here, as you well know, to celebrate the genesis of a new era of our glorious empire. Today, we celebrate the birth of a temple so large, so magnificent, so important that it shall dwarf all attempts to rival or surpass it in the past, present or the future. We celebrate the birth of a temple that shall unite our nation, an ascendant star in the firmament of the great peoples of the world, and secure its unity, its harmony and its cohesion. We celebrate the birth of a temple that shall be remembered for aeons and aeons, that shall draw the world to it. Even though the temple does not exist in a physical form, in our minds, we have already built it as an edifice representing the might of our empire. We, the Kovil Kattum Kuzhu—the consortium of temple builders—are here today to realize the temple in the physical form, so the world may see with its eyes what we do with our mind's eyes.'

Just as the import of the Chakravarthy's words were sinking into the gathering, the Chakravarthy's sister spoke up, 'How well-articulated, arasey! Moreover, in order to further consolidate the importance of the temple, I believe we should build it in Thanjavur.'

Silence prevailed for a while, as the shock of Kundavai's statement percolated among the audience. Ilavarasan Rajendra, from the end of the hall, began speaking up, 'My beloved Athai! In your wisdom...'

The ageing Aniruddha Brahmarayar strained, leaning forward trying to hear Rajendra. Noticing that, Vellaiappan raised his palm in the ilavarasan's direction. Getting the hint, the ilavarasan began again.

'My beloved Athai! While I attempt to cast no aspersions on your infinite wisdom, your wit and your observations, I do find myself questioning you at this moment—not out of imprudence or arrogance but out of genuine curiosity. We have many large, important cities in our land. There's our very own Aarur. There's Kudandhai, nestled on the banks of the Golden-Hued One. There are our holdings in erstwhile Pallava country—Mayilai and Kanchi. Our old capital, Pazhayarai, is also firmly in our control. We have just gained control of the Chera Kingdom. But why Thanjavur?'

Kundavai's lips curled upwards. 'Rajendra, that was a beautifully articulated question. I suggest Thanjavur for practical and symbolic reasons. Several foreign emissaries, scholars, artists and travellers flock to the all-powerful Chola capital. It would be easier to solicit their counsel during the construction phase and showcase our glory to the world more immediately once the temple is constructed. Imagine, an edifice that makes our capital one of the great ones of Bharata Varsha—which elevates it to the stature of Kashi, or Kanchi, or Ujjayin.'

Kundavai continued. 'As this erudite *sabhai* is aware, it is not as though Thanjavur is bereft of importance, or history, or pedigree. Thanjavur is a symbol of victory and an ancient seat of power. Our shastras tell us that it was in our very own Thanjai that Mahavishnu decimated the demon Thanjan, after whom the city is named. Our very own ancestor, the great and esteemed Vijayalaya, made it his capital city. Being on the banks of the Golden River, it possesses immense importance for the control of the empire, for he who controls the Golden River controls the gold that abounds on its banks. Yes, Ilavarasey, I concede that there are greater cities that populate the rich lands that Emperuman has entrusted unto us. But, imagine how posterity would remember us if we develop what has hitherto been an administrative and diplomatic centre into a city of great importance, attracting people from around the world to its markets, its temples, its auditoria!'

The entire gathering nodded silently in assent.

The Chakravarthy turned to his right and asked the venerable peruntachchar, 'Respected Peruntachchar! I see you've brought elaborate manuscripts pertaining to the temple and how you see it taking shape, based on our many conversations over the years. Share them before your peers!'

The peruntachchar stepped forward. A man of noble bearing, he rose from his seat, rearranged the angavastram across his shoulder, and sat on the elevated platform in the middle of the hall. Two of his disciples laid out the manuscripts, as the peruntachchar instructed them in calm, hushed terms. The disciples retreated a little way back, and the peruntachchar began to speak.

'Esteemed Chakravarthy, the wise and munificent Kundavai Pirattiyar and respected courtiers, grandeur and elegance are to be the main features of this expansive temple. I propose that the temple be located on a plot of land whose length is twice its width and that it spans an area of more than 3,000 *kuzhi*s. It should be surrounded by a wide moat and high walls. This will create the right ambience and protect the temple during times of conflict. Further, moats stabilize the large structures they encircle and help maintain a stable level of groundwater; they act as a reservoir that prevents groundwater from falling too low or rising too high. The temple will have four entrances in the four cardinal directions to make it accessible to visitors from all the directions. These plans will demonstrate the same.'

Immediately, the students of the peruntachchar distributed the manuscripts to each member of the Kuzhu. Approaching Kundavai and the Chakravarthy, the student passed on the unrolled manuscripts into the hands of sentries, who held it up for the royal personages.

The peruntachchar adjusted his angavastram, patting down the smooth cotton with his worn hands, and continued, 'The grandest of all entrances to this temple is to be in the east—the direction in which Surya Bhagavan ascends the skies every morning, to represent our glorious Chakravarthy's ascent to power. Two smaller temples, one dedicated to Ganapathy and the other to Murugan, the worthy sons of the blue-throated Shiva, will be constructed at this entrance so that devotees may pray for the obliteration of all obstacles and for their well-being as they enter the temple premises.

'A lofty *gopuram* will adorn the eastern entrance to commemorate the might of the Chola dynasty. Once devotees cross the shrines of Ganapathy and Murugan, they will enter the still expansive inner courtyard.'

In the pause, Vellaiappan interrupted the peruntachchar, 'How long do you anticipate the inner courtyard to be?'

'I have not yet calculated its exact dimensions, but I visualize its length to be twice its width.'

Vellaiappan nodded in assent.

'The temple complex will have four wings to exhibit the

architectural, artistic and altruistic heritage of our storied land. The essential constituents of a large temple—the ceremonial chambers, temple kitchen, store rooms and the feeding halls—will be constructed in the eastern and southern wings of the temple. The northern and western wings of the temple will house frescoes of the 64 forms of Shiva and sculpted lingams from across Bharata Kandam.

'The main temple itself will be located at the western end of the courtyard, preceded by a hall filled with frescoes and lingams. The lingam at the temple's sanctum will be the tallest, widest and most perfect in all the three worlds. All the integral components of a temple: the *garbagriha*, the pillared corridor around the temple, the Maha Mandapam, the hall for the temple paraphernalia, the shrine of the Chola dynasty's deity Thyagaraja and the music hall will be present in the temple complex. The vimanam of the main temple from the basement to the top will be thirty-five-and-one-quarter-paagams high—the highest vimanam in the world—and will consist of thirteen tiers.'

At this point, Aniruddhan interjected. As the entire hall turned towards him, he asked, in a loud, clear voice, 'Such a large compound necessitates multiple large entryways, so that people may disperse in a safe and orderly fashion. What are your plans in this regard, Ayya?'

Peruntachchar smiled and adjusted his angavastram ever so slightly. 'Safety is an important concern, Aniruddha. That is why I have intended for the temple to have two main portals, with the names Keralantakan and Rajarajan, named in honour of the Chakravarthy who has opened the floodgates to a new era of our glorious land. These entrances will be embellished with large Dwarapalakas to guard the entries of the temple. To enhance the significance of the temple, they will be carved out of one stone, which, as you know, is a rare and unusual challenge. This will enhance our temple's grandeur and convey the might of our empire.'

Silence prevailed in the hall. 'I would like to thank the Chakravarthy for placing enough trust unto my fragile, undeserving shoulders to spearhead such a massive project. The strengths of my presentation are borne of my fathers and forefathers who, as my gurus, taught me all I know, and the errata are borne upon me. Of course, these are very preliminary plans; a lot of the finer details will evolve over time, and with the help of your sagacious guidance emerge from your infinite wisdom. However, if any members of this esteemed gathering have any questions, I shall do my best to answer them.'

As Kunjara Malla Peruntachchar concluded his speech, the Kuzhu, overawed by his eloquence, his intelligence and his humility, broke into applause. In the distance, the magnificent brass bell of the temple could be heard loud and clear, drowning out everything else. The Chakravarthy descended from his seat, walked down and approached the peruntachchar. As the peruntachchar hunched forward, bending towards his feet, the Chakravarthy gently clasped him by his shoulders and held him close in a warm embrace. Mounting the central platform, the Chakravarthy announced, 'With the consultations of the royal astrologers, the *bhoomi pujai* ceremony will be scheduled.'

17

Like moths dancing in front of an incandescent flame, the court was once again drawn to each other, united by a common cause and the intensity of their devotion to it. One of the pleasure domes of the Chakravarthy in the royal palace compound in Thanjavur was repurposed into a communal meeting space dedicated to the construction of the temple. The house flanked a gentle turn in the Kaveri, which enveloped it on two sides, and was surrounded by frangipani trees whose blossoms carpeted the dusty yellow earth in a layer of wistful, optimistic pink. The wide, colonnaded verandah of the pleasure house which wrapped around it was seldom empty. Neither were the spacious interiors, with their dramatically high teak ceilings decorated with vivid scenes from day-to-day life. The siesta room, facing one end of the Kaveri, was converted into an extensive library under the supervision of Vellaiappan and Aniruddha Brahmarayar, with multiple rare handwritten manuscripts copied by hand from the Choodamani Viharam in Nagapattinam. The main meeting chamber, a circular room around which all members of the Kuzhu had assembled, had natural light filtering in at all times of the day. Leading out of the room was a set of low stone steps, which led directly into the Kaveri itself.

On some evenings, it was just the venerable peruntachchar and the Chakravarthy, sitting down and discussing the specificities of quarries from which the stone may be sourced.

Another late night, it was the venerable Kundavai Pirattiyar, taking her post-dinner constitutional along the banks of the Kaveri in the company of the Ilavarasan Rajendra, illuminated by the waxing moon and their conversation about workers' accommodation. Some days, after a sumptuous lunch was served in the central courtyard of the house, Aniruddha Brahmarayar lounged in the cushioned ante-chamber set towards the front of the house, watching the bamboo swaying in the wind, deep in contemplation about the state of the temple.

On the days that the entirety of the Kovil Kattum Kuzhu did convene in full strength to discuss the state of the temple's construction, it seemed as though all the *graha*s had descended onto the planet Earth. One such early meeting, set in a balmy afternoon in the month of Aippasi, proved to be particularly fruitful. The late-afternoon rains had just drawn to a close, and the grounds of the pleasure dome were fragrant with the smell of petrichor and the sweet, frail berries which had fallen in the course of a languorous shower. The earth was damp enough to leave the brief imprint of the wheels of the variety of chariots which drew into the colonnaded entrance of the pleasure dome—the wide brass ones of the Chakravarthy and his family, the narrow ones of the various courtiers. These patterns seemed to form an intricate kolam, a pattern of a lotus looping in and out of itself, almost to propitiate the meeting that was to unfold within the chambers of the Kovil Kattum Kuzhu.

As the group assembled, settling into the semi-circular room, an attendant placed a specially prepared serving of panagam in a gold-rimmed silver cup, emblazoned with the national emblem of the Chola realm. Each member solemnly consumed the offering, hoping that the fruits of their endeavours would be just as sweet as the jaggery drink. As the members of the gathering composed themselves, the Chakravarthy spoke first:

'My dear beloved brothers and sisters! I believe that we are still under the spell of the peruntachchar, whose sagacity, wit and powers of articulation stunned us all into silence and spurred us into action. It is after that meeting that we meet today, to further share our visions for our humble offerings to Emperuman and the ways in which we may realize them.'

Vandiyathevan leaned forward eagerly, and the Chakravarthy gestured for him to speak.

'To the esteemed Chakravarthy, the brother to my beloved and respected wife Kundavai Pirattiyar, and by virtue of that, my beloved brother-in-law, and to the genius peruntachchar, I submit a humble procedure. The elders in my clan have often spoken about the power of worshipping the *ashtadikpalaka*s—the guardians of the eight directions. Deities such as Indra, Agni, Ishana, Varuna, Vayu and Kubera were apparently worshipped by our ancestors in the early times, as the Vedas were first recited in the northern reaches of Bharata Kandam, but had not attained great popularity or importance in our native Chola Desa. Indeed, I am informed that the benefits of worshipping them are so profound, they may even alleviate periods of famine and disease with ease.'

Dandanayakan, hitherto someone who spoke minimally, then began speaking: 'Esteemed Chakravarthy and peruntachchar! I completely support and concur with the opinions expressed by my very dear *annan*, the respected Vandiyathevan! In my travels across Chola Nadu, I have observed that towns and temples in dusty pockets of our vast land that worship the ashtadikpalakas have never known a day, nay, even a passing moment, of misery. Their days are happy and bountiful; they have nothing to envy, for they have attained true fulfilment through the worship of, and the consequent benediction showered by, these deities. Imagine what would happen if the entire nation were to worship the feet of these deities!'

The peruntachchar hesitantly made eye contact with the Chakravarthy from across the room, whose eyes seemed to light up with the possibility. Thus ascertaining the mental state of the sovereign, the peruntachchar stepped forward and said:

'Oh Senapathi Dandanayakan and the esteemed Vallavarayan Vandiyathevan! Your words on these hitherto unsung deities have filled the entire room with optimism and hope. Constructing temples for the ashtadikpalakas is a task unfamiliar to me, for I have not constructed a temple which has had altars for those deities....'

The peruntachchar adjusted his angavastram. Suddenly, his face lit up. 'I know what to do! Oh Chakravarthy! Two of my close associates—Maduranthakan Nithavinothan and Lathisadaiyan Gandarathithan—must be known to you. They are also important *tachchar*s, who happen to have done detailed research into the agama shastras regarding the constructions of shrines for esoteric deities—in fact, at the Royal Library in Thanjavur! I believe that if we were to construct the shrines for the ashtadikpalakas, and even in general, their inputs would be enriching. Would you permit me to recruit them into the construction of the temple?'

The Chakravarthy smiled and nodded in assent.

Kundavai Pirattiyar was the next to speak. Brushing aside a tress of silvering hair that had fallen across her face, she said, 'Chakravarthy! My dear brothers and sisters! As you are well aware, constructing a temple is not something that only we in the room can do—despite the brash exploits of some who grace us with their august presence.' Kundavai smiled at the Chakravarthy, who let slip a rare bashful smile, in reference to his volunteering for the construction of a part of the temple at Chidambaram, as penance in service of Emperuman. 'We need to initate a discussion on the variety of workers needed to construct the temple. Oh peruntachchar! Would you, perchance, have any insights?'

The peruntachchar smiled beatifically and began speaking, '*Thaye*! We would require quarrymen to excavate stones from the mines, sawyers to cut the stones into cubes and cuboids suitable for construction, fixer masons to build the temple structure, and *sirpi*s to sculpt. We can train our soldiers to work as quarrymen, sawyers and fixer masons within two months. I request the Chakravarthy to summon the other renowned sculptors and their sishyas in Tamizhagam to work on the site of the Periya Kovil. I will enlist my fifty sishyas. I estimate that around five hundred sirpis in Tamizhagam and fifty thousand soldiers will be adequate. Of course, as the construction of the temple proceeds, there will be more and more workers needed, but in my experience, they may be recruited and hired as and when specific requirements arise.'

It was then that the hitherto silent Rajendra began to speak. First stumbling into the sentence, Rajendra found his footing, saying, 'Respected peruntachchar! Till now, the brave men and women who sally forth in the construction of our temples have lived in temporary accommodations, huts made out of mud and thatch and just off the roads, near a small lake or a pond. This temple is not a project where that can happen. Thanjai and its neighbours will be overburdened with the sudden influx of workers—many of whom are temporary—

and, most importantly, the workers will not be able to live in inhumane conditions for that long. Something needs to be done.'

Dandanayakan smiled and said, 'A well-placed question, Ilavarasey. Fret not. We have secured land for the construction of clean, hygienic and durable workers' dormitories, with all the necessities for a decent and dignified life. The land is centrally located and, as you know, Thanjai abounds with temples whose *madapalli*s may provide food from their kitchens. I have spoken to the dhanadhikari, and he informs us that due to years upon years of good rains compounding the stock of grains in our granary, we have no need to worry. The workers will be well fed, well taken care of, and well-treated. We cannot build a monument for our Lord on foundations of cruelty, can we?'

Bolstered by the fillip of a universally well-approbated point, the ilavarasan continued, 'It is not only the workers in the temple who need our protection, as this august *avai* is well aware. It is also the borders that need protection, isn't that right? Yes, we should protect our nation too, against those who seek to invade us. In a time of peace such as now, when our soldiers wage the war of building this temple, how will we protect our nation if our friendly neighbours cease being so cordial?

Again, it was Dandanayakan who possessed the answer: 'Ilavarasey! We have approximately two lakh soldiers in our mighty army. If we deploy one and a half lakh soldiers at our borders and fifty thousand soldiers at the temple site, we will achieve our twin objectives of national security and construction of the grandest temple in Bharata Kandam. I propose that bell towers be constructed every five *kadham*s. At the sign of any insurrection, we will be able to mobilize our troops and thus protect our borders.'

'We already do have bell towers built along our border villages, don't we, Ayya? Do we need to build or upgrade our existing infrastructure? How many do we need to build anew?' asked Rajendra.

'Dandanayaka!' piped up Kundavai. 'In addition, what will be the financial cost of the new bell towers.'

Dandanayakan responded, 'Excellent questions, Ilavarasey and Thaye! While I have not done the exact calculations, or have the exact number on hand, I can provide some rough estimates. Our system of bell towers dates back to the time of the previous Chakravarthy, Utthama Chola, and the project as envisaged by him was to place bell-towers only in the most sensitive border regions, especially in and around the western regions of our nation where we border the Cheras. Our current Chakravarthy, in the dawn of his glorious reign, expanded the number of bell towers to include the entire border of our nation, in conjunction with a border survey, but at a distance of seven kadhams. However, with the resources of the army mobilized towards the construction of the temple, we need to reduce the distance between the bell towers to ensure better coverage. I estimate that the work will take six months to complete. Materials may be sourced locally, so it doesn't place a burden on the existing highway infrastructure. Labour isn't a problem either; we may ask soldiers and engineers from the army posted locally to work in their respective locations. I can, of course, deliver the exact figures later, upon consultation with the engineers, tachchars and other senapathis, if this exulted avai would so permit me to.'

The Chakravarthy nodded in assent.

The ringing of the temple bell of the Neelamegha Perumal temple, located not far away, signified the end of the Kovil Kattum Kuzhu conclave. A few servants distributed *payasam* in woven cups, in commemoration of the sweet future that awaited the nation.

Subsequent meetings of the Kovil Kattum Kuzhu fell into a predictable pattern. In the next meeting, peruntachchar finalized the designs for the Nandi mandapam, the pillars supporting the temple and the lattice work for the temple windows. The construction of the bell towers began. The demarcation of soldiers for who would be deployed at the border and the temple site was complete. Even the material for the temple—granite, from Senji and Pachaimalai—was finalized, and preparations were made to source it.

And it was thus that the temple was constructed—not only in the mind of the man who dreamt of it but also in the words and actions of those who dreamt alike.

To be very fair, Karpagavalli was never alone. And yet, at every waking moment, every sleeping moment, and at every in-between moment—she consciously felt how alone she was.

Karpagavalli had nothing to complain about. She belonged to a clan of *nakkan*s or dancing girls who were known across Tamizhagam for their felicity in *isai*, *iyal* and *natakam*—the trifecta through which Tamil culture manifested. She too had been a skilled dancer, attached to the magnificent temple at Chidambaram in service to the presiding deity Nataraja, until an unfortunate accident with a bullock-run-amok in her native Vandavasi had ended her service to the Lord. Yet, her God-rendered skills had found other expressions—she began to establish her name as a skilled, knowledgeable and erudite teacher, well-versed in Bharata Muni's Veda and other texts in iyal and isai, who taught many students from the nakkan community she was born into. Eventually, her fame reached Kundavai Pirattiyar, who employed her as a performing arts teacher for the princesses at the Thanjavur palace.

And yet, she felt something was lacking in her life. It was not rational for her to feel discontent—compared to the many women in her community who lived off endowments from villages that were still subject to the tempests of war and drought, she enjoyed the munificent patronage of the royal family, which ensured that she never had to fret about where her next meal would come from. She lived in a large, comfortable mansion within the palace grounds, surrounded by a vast grove of fragrant trees. She lived with her aged mother. She had access to the palace library, stocked with rare manuscripts from across Bharata Kandam. She could speak to any of the scholarly luminaries who adorned Raja Raja's court, gaining insights about Veda, Vedanta, language, and so much more. The court was also cosmopolitan, with visitors from Cheena Desa and Gandhara Desa, and so many other places; she could learn so much, speak so much. She was privy to the latest fashions being exhibited at the court by the royal women, and she didn't even need to raise the issue of payment—if she liked something, the royal family ensured that it was made available to her. Everywhere she turned, people looked upon her with admiration, respect and awe.

She really had nothing to worry about. Nothing to worry about. No reason to feel alone.

And yet, she did.

The feeling hit her first in the mornings, as the birds began chirping at dawn break. As soon as she woke up, her chest began tightening, as though her comfortable cotton saree—a good, well-trusted friend—had suddenly turned into a viper threatening to ensnare her and squeeze out whatever life she dared possess within her frame. She would lay in her wooden cot, waiting for the feeling to pass, and watch as the sun began casting its purplish, bruised hues on the small lily pond outside her window. As she collected herself, ate and readied herself in the *koothambalam* where she would receive her first students for the day, the feeling would not pass. Nor would it through multiple classes, multiple outings to the markets in and around Thanjavur with her patron and disciple, Ilavarasi Kundavai, or the long hours at the library. As she lay in her bed at night, waiting for sleep to envelop her, loneliness hung over every fibre of her being, like a millstone on her back.

On one end, she did not want to feel lonely. And yet, on the other hand, she could not stop feeling lonely. She began to doubt herself—did she enjoy the loneliness? That could not be the case! Eating and sleeping were such chores—all her friends, dancers themselves, envied her waist, which was as slim as the middle of an hourglass-shaped *damaru*, but little did they realize that her figure was not the outcome of her dancing for long hours. Little did they realize how each morsel of food, each grain of rice she consumed, engorged itself as it entered her windpipe, choking her almost, making the delicate kohl that rimmed her eyes askew in thin, black rivulets as she struggled to swallow. The vaidhyars in the court had pronounced nothing was wrong with her physically; it was just in her head. And yet, she was trapped in her head, an oppressive prison of her own making, like she was the Sita in the Ashoka grove as well as the Ravana who entrapped her. She could escape, she thought, but yet she couldn't.

Karpagavalli was stuck.

Things had come to the fore in one class when Karpagavalli was teaching a couple of her students. The Chakravarthy had overseen the unearthing of the Thevaram hymns, written by Appar, Sambandar and Sundarar. Nambi Andar Nambi was working towards organizing these hymns from the tatterdemalion palm-leaf manuscripts recovered in the Chidambaram temple into a series of books to be propagated, and Karpagavalli had seen potential for these hymns to be choreographed for the royal princesses. After working with Kundavai Pirattiyar, a fine danseuse herself, she had arrived at one particular hymn to be choreographed—Paingottu Malar Punnai, a paeon penned by Appar for the lord of Tirusengattankudi, asking Him to not tarry and bless the devotee. Karpagavalli, a skilled musician, managed to coax the lyrics into the Takkesi pann, a grand and old melodic mode appropriate for the grand language and sentiments conveyed by Appar. Having practised it at her home and polished the Thevaram, she readied herself to teach it to her students.

The day dawned, and along with it dawned the standard feelings of loneliness and impending doom. And yet, she steadied herself, wrapped herself in a bright red saree and a coral nose-ring—both bought recently from the markets of Thanjavur. She greeted Kundavai Pirattiyar as the latter entered the koothambalam, the large tile-roofed hall where she taught dance. She sat herself down on the rosewood bench, readied the castanets with which she accompanied the dance, and aligned her husky voice against the sonorous *tambura* played by her long-time aide Sahayam. The students came, and she indicated the tone of the piece and taught them to sing the song. As they began to sing and dance, she stopped occasionally to correct an off-beat move, a misplaced gaze, an askew note.

And yet, in a matter of half a nazhigai, her students had captured the essence of the piece. The banyan-wood pillars of the koothambalam began to resonate with the hues of Takkesi, and somehow, the Thevaram began to come to life. She was taken away from the wooden koothambalam with hints of the midday sun filtering in through the dark wood beams casting languorous shadows on the floor, to a sleepy, verdant Tirusengattankudi. Suddenly, she became the devotee, longing for union with her Lord. The parrots and the sparrows and the koels that were to play messenger began to tarry, looking at her askew upon their failure to communicate with the Lord. They taunted her with the Lord's indifference, His coldness, His lack of concern.

'Karpagavalli! Karpagavalli!'

Karpagavalli was shaken out of her reverie by Kundavai Pirattiyar. The room had cleared, save Kundavai Pirattiyar. Karpagavalli was sitting on the rosewood plank from where she conducted her lessons. A stray fly flitted in and out of her room. By judging how the sun filled the room, Karpagavalli adjudged that she had been in a state of catatonic stasis for some time. Her heart began collapsing yet again, into the indeterminate bottomless pit in her stomach.

Observing her dazed look and stunned silence, Kundavai summoned one of her footmen to bring some water, buttermilk, rice and pickle. A banana leaf was placed in front of Karpagavalli, and Kundavai began assembling the modest meal—mixing the pearl-white rice with the diluted and dimmed liquid buttermilk and placing a not-insubstantial portion of pickle at the centre of it.

Karpagavalli still looked dazed.

'You eat now, Karpagavalli. I have asked all your other students to come another day. You look tired; your eyelids are drooping, and your lips look crusty. What you need now is some food, water and rest. I will come back tomorrow,' said Kundavai.

Karpagavalli demurred.

'And don't worry. You may resume classes once you have recovered,' Kundavai Pirattiyar said with a smile and left.

Karpagavalli forced herself to eat and lay in bed, gazing at the ceiling. She drifted in and out of sleep, hearing the animals around her home slowly go to sleep and waiting for the owls to emerge. She saw the full-moon light dart in through her window, making itself at home, reflecting its splendour upon the polished wood and ivory installations in her room. And soon, the moon too departed, to leave nothing but empty, clawing darkness in its wake.

As the break of dawn seemed to emerge, Karpagavalli felt a stiffness in her lower legs. This was her cue to wake up, that she'd been sleeping too long. And thus she woke up. She brushed her teeth with a neem leaf. She bathed, applying the usual array of powdered herbs and powders. She draped herself in her favourite bright yellow and red saree. She put on her gold earrings, her nose ring, a delicate necklace. She adorned her hair with freshly plucked jasmines, encircling it around her autumnal hair. Emptily, gazelessly, she stepped outside her house and strolled to the large pond on the palace grounds.

Karpagavalli sat on the shores of the pond, on a grassy knoll leading up to the water. She gazed emptily at the water, at the rising sun, at the little kids playing on the opposite banks. She was not blind; she could see how the golden hues of the sun danced upon the water, reflecting upon it, making the entire landscape dance in a bright yellow splendour. And yet, she could not see it either. She perceived it, but she could not *see* it.

Kundavai Pirattiyar approached Karpagavalli, and tapped her shoulder lightly. Karpagavalli rose, and as she began to bend downwards to perform a namaskaram to the Chakravarthy's sister, Kundavai Pirattiyar smiled, held her shoulders and beckoned her to sit. The two women sat on the edge of the pond, watching as small fish seemingly leapt from the water into the sunlight.

'Amma, you must find it within you to forgive me for my indiscretion. It was really not on any part of my physical incapacity for me to be stunned and shell-shocked in that manner, so unbecoming of my status as a guru to this noble clan. I do not know what came over me, Amma, it may have been the splendour of Emperuman that Tirunavukkarasar, the veritable Emperor of Gab, illustrated so grandiloquently in the form of that blessed Thevara *padhigam*. I should have maintained composure. I should have maintained decorum. It was unbecoming of my station, Amma...' Karpagavalli rambled and continued, and Kundavai Pirattiyar smiled serenely.

'Karpagavalli, my dear! If it were merely for your state of catatonia, I would not have seen it befitting that such special care be accorded upon you. In reality, you have been building up to this state that I chanced upon yesterday. And if my reading is right, if my sources are correct, your mind and your body require attention. And it is thus that I ask you to open your heart to me. At this moment, I am not your liege lord but your friend; and I have a good feeling it is a friend you need now. So speak to me, dear Karpagavalli, as you would to a friend,' responded Kundavai.

'Amma, such a great lady you are! How much you've improved the lives of everyone in this blessed Chola Nadu... your hospitals dot the land...how am I to speak to you as a friend, as a mere nakkan, and not even as one fortunate enough to pledge her limited abilities to Emperuman due to an injury borne out of the sins of my past births...How am I to speak to you as a friend? My dharma dictates that I speak to you as a liege lord, for if I cannot serve Emperuman, if I cannot serve you accordingly, of what use am I?'

Karpagavalli began to weep. Kundavai put an arm around her.

'Karpagavalli, service is not merely in the form of how your ancestors have chosen to serve Emperuman, but instead it is in terms of how you are best able to do so. You are not your mothers and your foremothers. You are not your community. You are an individual, with her own abilities that shine as effulgently as Surya Bhagavan himself, but your effulgence is made your own by your demons. If not through dance, your knowledge will enable you to serve Him in another way.

'You are aware that the Chakravarthy has commissioned the construction of a temple dedicated to Emperuman at a scale and grandeur hitherto not witnessed by mankind. The temple requires musicians, dancers and *vagyakara*s to perform at the sanctum everyday and during festivals. The royal family has been selfish thus far by appropriating all your talent for ourselves. You did not cease your service of the Lord when an unfortunate accident rendered you incapable of dancing. Your knowledge of iyal, isai and natakam are second to none.

'The Periya Kovil will require a large retinue of artists. A succession plan also needs to be worked out, so that this artistic service to the Almighty continues uninterrupted for generations. Poetry and music that is suitable to be performed within the temple needs to be collated. The remuneration for artists needs to be decided. A knowledgeable person is required to oversee the accurate inscription of all these details on the temple walls. Will you undertake this task? This way your family will grow to encompass numerous uncles, aunts, brothers, sisters, offspring and who knows, even a loving partner. By codifying the artistic services to be rendered at Periya Kovil and overseeing such activities, loneliness will be banished from your life. Meanwhile, I will ask a vaidhyar to prepare you physically and mentally for this task. The Chola Empire is asking you to share your skills for its greater glory. Will you acquiesce?'

Karpagavalli stopped gazing at the lake and started looking at Kundavai Pirattiyar intently. Her words infused a hitherto unknown energy in Karpagavalli's veins; she felt a weight being lifted off her bony shoulders. The maladies and demons that had haunted her for months seemed to dissipate. Karpagavalli smiled spontaneously after long; she blurted, 'Thaye! Your wish is my command. I am deeply touched by your trust in me despite my condition. I feel a certain lightness of spirit I have not felt thus far. I will certainly attempt to discharge this monumental task to the best of my ability. But will the royal family, the nobles and the denizens allow me, a mere woman and that too a nakkan, to assume such a responsibility?'

Kundavai smilingly replied, 'If a nakkan is worthy of performing in Emperuman's presence, if she is worthy of teaching iyal, isai and natakam to the future queens of Bharata Kandam, if her knowledge of the arts is peerless, then she is indeed worthy of codifying the artistic services the Periya Kovil requires. I will personally accompany you and show you around the temple site. I will also give you a ring that bears the Chola insignia; it will provide you unfettered access to all the gurukulams and patashalas in Bharata Kandam. You only need to inform me if anyone dares to question you after this. Why don't you walk back to the palace with me? I will arrange for a palanquin for you to return home.'

As Karpagavalli accompanied Kundavai Pirattiyar to the palace, she could not help but smile at the realization that it was not just misfortunes that struck humans unexpectedly. Immense fortunes might also be bestowed on humans in the flash of an eye. She had been contemplating to seek refuge in the pond and end her misery permanently. But Kundavai Pirattiyar now assigned her a task—no, a mission—that would perpetuate her legacy for as long as the Periya Kovil stood.

18

As dawn broke, the clacks of horse hooves drawing chariots into the pleasure dome on the banks of the Kaveri echoed a sure, yet sibilant, orchestra within the royal palace complex. As the members of the Kovil Kattum Kuzhu disembarked from the chariots and entered the high-ceilinged complex, they greeted each other with warm words of affection. Seating themselves in the circular chamber, they began to make small talk as a footman served them glasses of fresh buttermilk served in small gold receptacles. As the conversation gradually drew to a close, the focus of their conclave emerged.

It was the Chakravarthy who, as always, spoke first to set the tone. 'Good morning. In the previous session of the Kuzhu, Dandanayakan was instructed to survey the roads and physical infrastructure of our great land, so we may strengthen the spine and networks in preparation for the construction of the temple. What were your findings, Dandanayakan?'

Dandanayakan rose. Looking visibly uncomfortable, he gulped nervously a couple of times and looked around the room hesitantly. His peers looked at him intently. The golden rays of the sun cast a light across his face, revealing a geography of disconcertedness. He inhaled and began to speak.

'Arasey! Piratti! Ilavarasey! Honourable members of

the Kuzhu! I am afraid that, today, I am not the bearer of good news! Our nation's highways leading to Thanjai are, under normal circumstances, perfectly adequate for troop transportation and general commerce. But for the scale of the project that we intend to undertake, the spine of our nation shall buckle under pressure and break apart. The situation is dire. While it is possible to transport some materials down the Golden River, a lot of the materials need to be transported on land. And doing so with the current state of infrastructure will lead to a breakdown of trade and commerce, paralysing our nation and leading to economic ruin.'

'We need to widen our roads, in other words,' piped in Rajendra.

'Yes, Ilavarasey, but not just that—we need to not only widen our roads but also construct new, direct roads, especially between Senji, Pachaimalai and Thanjavur. The current routes are far too circuitous and inefficient to permit a smooth flow of construction materials.'

The Chakravarthy looked at the Kuzhu pensively. Silence pervaded the chamber. After a minute of thinking, the Chakravarthy turned towards the dhanadhikari, Sarangapani. 'Sarangapani! How much may we allocate to the expansion of roads and physical infrastructure, in excess of what we expend annually for the same?'

Sarangapani said, 'We may allocate the tax income of seven villages, arasey.'

Dandanayakan's expression remained concerned. 'That is hardly sufficient, arasey, especially given that the project must be undertaken at the speed we need it to, to prepare for the initial stages of the temple's construction.'

'Is it possible to release more funds, Sarangapani?'

'I would need to check with our books, arasey, but I am

not entirely confident about the matter. Nevertheless, I shall instruct one of my disciples to assess the possibility.'

It was then that Aniruddhan's eyes lit up in realization. 'Arasey! Dandanayakan Ayya! Sarangapani Ayya! I have an idea that might solve all our problems. Why not we borrow money from the Chettys of Nattukottai?'

The Chakravarthy looked intrigued. 'Aniruddhan! Say more!'

'With the restoration of Kadaram, the traditionally wealthy citizens of Nattukottai have become wealthier and wealthier, rich on trade. When I visited the village recently in relation to a matter pertaining to the army, I learnt that they had entered the business of lending money as well. Given their significant wealth and their loyalty to our nation and people, I believe that they'd possess both capacity and inclination to extend loans to us so we may undertake crucial works of infrastructure development.'

The Chakravarthy was puzzled but managed to maintain his composure. He looked first at Sarangapani, whose expression remained inscrutable. Turning to Dandanayakan, the Chakravarthy observed the light of optimism creep in so tentatively across his face. The Chakravarthy then turned to Kundavai, who smiled, nodding her head slightly. Turning finally to Aniruddhan, he said, 'Invite them to the Kuzhu's next conclave. Let's see what they have to say.'

Not to be undone, Rajendra piped in, 'Arasey! Workplace injuries are inevitable when we embark on construction of this scale. We must have a team of one hundred vaidhyars to tend to the injured. We also need to ensure that there is an uninterrupted supply of medicinal herbs and cotton bandages to treat the injured.'

Murmurs of approval spread across the hall. The members

of the Kuzhu nodded in assent, smiling at a perspective unheard of, unthought of, but with a striking sensitivity and originality. And yet, the Chakravarthy demonstrated nothing, remaining impassive. While the Chakravarthy had implicit faith in Rajendra's bravery, valour and astuteness, he was not quite sure whether the crown prince felt empathy for the citizens. This suggestion proved that Rajendra had inherited the concern of his powerful yet compassionate ancestors.

And yet, the Chakravarthy feared that a demonstration would lead to complacency on Rajendra's part—and the Chakravarthy knew for a fact that the greatest enemy to greatness was not a lack of ability but feeling secure in one's own capability. As the murmurs settled down, and the court turned towards the Chakravarthy, he commanded, 'Rajendra, you and Aniruddhan supervise the recruitment of vaidhyars. Ensure they have uninterrupted access to medicines. Contact Sarangapani if you need any assistance.'

Rajendra might have been puzzled in his mind about the lack of verbal approbation from the Chakravarthy, but he did not show it, instead smiling inwardly. As the Kuzhu began to disperse, the Chakravarthy made eye contact with Aniruddha Brahmarayar, who'd been silent through the meeting.

The two men smiled knowingly at each other.

In the Chola realm, the Chakravarthy's word was law. Several soldiers were enlisted to replant the trees that grew by the highways and do the groundwork for the widening of the roads in anticipation of the loans. Farmers along the route, struck by the bravery and the commitment of the brave army, felt an urge to serve the nation. Convening a series of farmers' congresses, they discussed how best to do so and elected village representatives to represent their concerns. These representatives approached the chiefs of the kottams regarding their concerns, which were communicated to Aniruddha Brahmarayar. Aniruddha Brahmarayar instructed the farmers' representatives to present themselves at the next meeting of the Kovil Kattum Kuzhu.

The pleasure dome had new visitors that day for the next session—a group of merchants and a group of farmers. Greeted warmly and offered buttermilk by the footmen, they nervously awaited their summons into the main chamber of the Kovil Kattum Kuzhu.

It was the merchants who were called first. The circular chamber was bathed in the purple, bruised light of twilight. Oil lamps were being lit, as the smell of *sambraani* wafted in from the windows.

Aniruddhan spoke. 'Ayya! Vanakkam! We have invited you here, as we are faced with a dilemma. As you may know, we are building a temple in Thanjai that will be the greatest in all fourteen worlds Emperuman reigns in. Thus, we are in need of expanding the roads of our nation, in order to facilitate the smooth transportation of people and goods across the land. However, we need additional funds so as to complete the work in a rapid, efficient and safe manner. Thus, we would like to borrow money from you in order to—'

The merchant put his hand up, indicating that Aniruddhan should stop. Then he began speaking. 'Ayya! For something to do with the consecration and celebration of Emperuman, you'd like us to extend a *loan*? Engage in usury? While we may be moneylenders, we are humans, and we are all children of Him. For Him, our Father, how can we extend a loan? Will you extend a loan to your father?'

The entire Kuzhu settled into a stunned silence.

'Let it be a donation, Ayya, Chakravarthy, Amma. Tell us how much, and we shall pay it. With the Chakravarthy securing Kadaram for us yet again, our coffers are flush with gold and silver and bronze and every form of wealth imaginable. And what better use for the wealth than this?'

The silence did not dissipate.

Recovering some of his composure, the Chakravarthy instructed Sarangapani and Dandanayakan to confer with the merchants regarding the amount required to be donated.

Having dismissed the merchants, the farmers' representatives entered the hall.

The citizens' representative told the Chakravarthy, 'Arasey! We are humble farmers, but the work of the brave soldiers of Chola Nadu has motivated us. We request you to allow us to work shoulder to shoulder with our soldiers to widen our highways!'

Again, the Chakravarthy was flummoxed.

'My dear people, your patriotism is touching and invigorates me to work harder for Chola Nadu. But if you work on widening the highways, who will tend to the crops? How can we feed those working at the temple site?'

The farmers looked crestfallen. But it was Aniruddha Brahmarayar to the rescue. Interceding on their behalf, he said, 'Arasey! If you permit them to work in the afternoons, not only will the widening of highways be completed earlier, but our harvests will also not suffer!'

The Chakravarthy nodded in assent, and asked Aniruddha Brahmarayar to remain in touch with the farmers. While he revealed nothing physically, the Chakravarthy felt wave upon wave of joy and pride in his mind, his heart awash from being the recipient of such affection.

Indeed, after aeons, the Chakravarthy was happy.

č

The cool Margazhi month invigorated everyone in Chola Nadu to toil harder. The members of the Kuzhu waited expectantly in the royal chambers as the Chakravarthy, Kundavai, Vandiyathevan and Rajendra entered. A content Chakravarthy intimated the Kuzhu of the progress made in the intervening period, 'I would like to thank you for your wise counsel, support and encouragement for this project. Peruntachchar has almost finalized the temple plan. The task of widening the highways and constructing bell towers is proceeding at a furious pace, ably aided by the noble farmers of Chola Nadu. The part of our army not engaged in temple construction is posted at the borders. We have received a lot of donations for the temple construction. I am particularly pleased that both Kundavai Pirattiyar and Ilavarasi Kundavai have donated lands and gold for the construction of the temple. I was pleased to hear from our revered Brahmarayar and the dhanadhikari that we need not levy any additional taxes to fund the temple construction. Rajendra and Aniruddhan have travelled to Thiruvarur, Kudandhai, Nagai and Kanchi, and have recruited the most competent vaidhyars to tend to the injured at the construction site. I now request Aniruddha Brahmarayar to tell us what we need to do next.'

Brahmarayar spoke in a measured tone, 'Arasey and respected members of the Kovil Kattum Kuzhu! We have spent the last three months in planning for the temple. I understand that widening of the highways is not yet complete. But our farmers have constructed bypass roads to facilitate smooth passage of traffic. Vandiyathevan and Dandanayakan inform me that the highway construction will be completed ahead of the monsoons. The harvest month of Thai is approaching. I believe that the time is ripe to embark on the temple construction. I have taken the liberty of summoning the *jothidar*. He is waiting in the antechamber. With the Chakravarthy's consent, may I ask him to come here and suggest an auspicious date for the bhoomi pujai?' The Chakravarthy nodded in assent.

When the jothidar entered the royal chamber, Aniruddha Brahmarayar gestured to him to take his appointed seat. The jothidar bowed first to the Chakravarthy and then to those assembled and sat down. The Chakravarthy then asked him to identify an auspicious date to begin the construction of the Periya Kovil. The jothidar unbundled the almanac that was scribed on a bunch of palm leaves, carefully read its contents, and then made some calculations using his fingers. He pronounced, 'Arasey! Thai Pongal itself is an auspicious day for beginning the temple construction. The temple will bring fame, prosperity and riches to Chola Nadu if the bhoomi pujai is conducted on that day. It will be beneficial for the royal family and the citizens if prayers are conducted at the Thiruvarur Thyagarajaswamy Temple prior to the bhoomi pujai.'

The Chakravarthy gave a reward of ten gold coins to the jothidar, who bowed and took leave of the Chakravarthy. The Kuzhu then had an animated discussion about the bhoomi pujai before dispersing. The Chakravarthy commanded that prayers be conducted not just at the Thiruvarur Thyagarajaswamy Temple but also at all temples in Chola Nadu. He also ordered that the madapallis serve lunch to all citizens on the occasion of the bhoomi pujai.

Thai Pongal finally dawned. The smell of the ripe paddy ready to be harvested wafted across the Land of the Golden River. The Chakravarthy arrived in his golden chariot accompanied by the Queen Consort, Ilavarasan Rajendra, Kundavai Pirattiyar, Vandiyathevan, the other queens Lokamahadevi and Cholamahadevi, and his children. The Chakravarthy looked regal in his white and gold veshti and angavastram, the royal jewels and the Chola crown. Peruntachchar, Aniruddha Brahmarayar, Vellaiappan, the dhanadhikari and Dandanayakan, accompanied by their families, were present at the site. Nobility and civilians alike thronged the roads that led to the temple site. The court musicians started playing the nagaswaram and thavil as the royal family entered the temple site. The herald proclaimed the achievements of Chakravarthy Raja Raja Chola as he disembarked from his chariot and walked to the site of the bhoomi pujai.

The royal priests, Ishana Shivapanditar and Saiva Achariyar Pavana Pidaran, had completed all the preparations for conducting the bhoomi pujai. The temple site was beautifully decorated with plantain trees and kolams. Once the Chakravarthy and the royal family reached the site, the royal priests chanted prayers seeking the blessings and assistance of Mother Nature for the temple construction and seeking forgiveness for all the insects and organisms that would die during the construction process. Everyone was focussed on the prayer ceremony, with two notable exceptions. Needless to say that the two were none other than Rajendra and Kayalvizhi.

A boulder specially transported from Pachaimalai was kept at the site of the prayer ceremony. It was smeared with turmeric, vermilion and sandalwood paste. Flowers and *akshadai* were showered on it. Ishana Shivapanditar gestured to the Chakravarthy, who, along with Rajendra, Aniruddha Brahmarayar, Vellaiappan, Dandanayakan, the dhanadhikari and Vandiyathevan, lowered the boulder into a pit to signify the laying of the temple's foundation.

The sounds of musicians playing the nagaswaram and thavil and people cheering were heard for several kadhams around Thanjai. This was followed by Karpagavalli and other musicians rendering the Thevarams to the accompaniment of the *veenai* and thavil—a performance that left the listeners spellbound. The Chakravarthy and his family then partook of a sumptuous lunch along with the Kuzhu members and those working at the temple site. That the royal family partook of the food prepared for, and along with, those working at the temple site rendered the workers and denizens delirious with joy. It was a tumultuous start to the construction of an iconic monument that would stand the test of time and symbolize the pride of not just the Chola Nadu or Tamizhagam but also the whole of Bharata Kandam.

19

It was thus that the construction of the Periya Kovil began, and changed the course of the lives of every single inhabitant and citizen of Chola Nadu irrevocably. For one, there was the physical metamorphosis—the transformation of the undulating, featureless piece of land in Thanjavur into what seemed to be the centre of the universe. Like ants marching towards a piece of candy cast askew in the ground, the entire nation seemed to march towards the site of the construction. The roads were chock-a-block with bullock carts laden with goods, construction materials and people headed towards Thanjavur, while empty bullock carts galloped freely away from it, in search of goods and people to take back to Thanjavur. The highways were lined with people joyously walking towards Thanjavur, hand in hand, singing *kummi* songs through the paddy fields. It came to the point that local kottams began organizing large bullock carts to ferry many people at once, owing to the large passenger demand and the congestion on large highways. Through night and day, people marched and galloped and hopped towards Thanjavur in joy, ecstasy and excitement.

It seemed like the city of Thanjavur festooned itself with an air of celebration, in anticipation of the construction of the temple. Workers' colonies—the idea of the Ilavarasan Rajendra—were constructed across the city. Thanjavur began to resemble a metropolis of late, with the construction of the temple—visitors to its multiple markets and fairgrounds were confronted by the odd aural smorgasbord born out of overlapping conversations not just in various varieties of Tamil but also other languages such as Kannada, Telugu, Sinhala and Sepangese. Every day, the city seemed to swell with migrants who had just arrived, taking in the grandeur of the imperial Chola capital, looking at awe at its colonnaded mansions, vast public gardens, and the Kaveri which roared past the city, unmindful of what went on amidst its banks. With the construction of the workers' quarters and the meticulous planning of the Kovil Kattum Kuzhu, the incidence of crime went down and was barely perceptible. Indeed, under the reign of the Cholas, residents of Thanjavur—or any city in the land—could leave even their golds and their silks on the *thinnai*s of their house and sleep, rest assured that their brethren would not steal from them.

And now, Thanjavur had the honour of being one of the greatest cities in Bharata Kanda—no, the world. Was it a new Kanchi? Or a neo-Ujjain? Perhaps a Varanasi anew? It wasn't—for it was Thanjavur, a metropolis whose personality and character and grandeur were defined in a vocabulary completely novel, which could not be compared to any other human settlement before or after.

And then, there was the site of the temple's construction— not just did the workers congregate there to work, but the citizenry also gathered there to gawk and watch the work. The flat piece of unornamented land became, seemingly overnight, a place of grandiloquent magnitude—a site of a spectacle, a large carnival which had hitherto not been seen anywhere in the world. People congregated along the fringes of the site, seating themselves on wooden benches. Sitting cross-legged in the harsh afternoon sun, they watched the hustle and bustle, workers scurrying around as their supervisors hurled abuses in a variety of tongues foreign and native, eating peanuts out of *dhonnai*s and *bajji*s made out of plantains. A small market had begun to mushroom at the southern end of the site, selling fruits, elaneer, mor and other refreshments. When any of the workers approached the stalls for mor, however, the shopkeepers refused to accept a single coin. 'You're paying *our* collective debts to Emperuman by working here, Ayya,' they'd say. 'To accept this is to steal from Emperuman. *Sivan Sottu, Kula Naasam.* To steal from Emperuman is to bring misfortune upon my clan.'

But the spectacle continued. It was not that the citizens of Thanjai had not seen a massive construction project before—the city was still young compared to the metropolises that were Madurai and Kanchi, so a lot of the edifices that dominated the city were relatively new constructions which had come up in the past fifty-odd years. Yet, this construction was different. This was far more important. This was far more significant, in a way that no person could possibly articulate. Tamil was a classical language with a rich history, whose literary culture had found fecund ground in the Chola capital. And yet, contemporaneous poets were unable to do anything but express wonder and gape at the wonder that was the construction of the temple.

As the process of transporting the rocks from Senji and Pachaimalai was underway, Vellaiappan, Vandiyathevan and Dandanayakan supervised the mining of sand at Thiruvarur, loading it on to open bullock carts and transporting it to Thanjai. This was a time-consuming and labour-intensive process, so the trio took turns to live in Thiruvarur to oversee the process.

As the construction progressed at a brisk pace, Alagiya

Nayaki watched. She would observe the workers at the temple site every day, bearing heavy loads, erecting monolithic pieces of granite and toiling in the unforgiving sun. Alagiya Nayaki was an ardent devotee of Emperuman and wished to be of some service at the temple site. But alas, she was an elderly woman and knew she would only be an impediment. So, she decided to quench the thirst of the workers at the site. Every morning, when she made buttermilk, she would make double the usual quantity, pour it into separate earthen pots and transport them in a hand-drawn cart to the temple site. At noon, a few nazhigais before lunch, she would distribute the buttermilk to the thirsty workers. The poor woman's act of bounty did not go unnoticed by the ever-observant Aniruddha Brahmarayar.

In most temples dedicated to Lord Shiva, it is the shrine of Vinayakar, the Obliterator of all Obstacles, which is instated first to ensure the smooth completion of the construction. This was the case with Rajarajeswaram too. Once the Vinayaka sanctum had been constructed and the idol sculpted, a consecration ceremony was performed. The Kuzhu decided to keep this ceremony a low-key affair and so it was attended only by the Kuzhu members and the labourers working onsite. As part of the consecration ceremony, *abhishekam*s of water and milk were performed to the idol of Lord Vinayaka.

'You know, Kayal,' Ilavarasi Kundavai whispered into Kayalvizhi's ear as they stood in front of the Vinayaka idol being consecrated, 'I don't know why, but this temple doesn't feel like those old, grand temples our clan has been frequenting. The deity here is no different from those enshrined in Chidambaram, or in Thiruvarur, or in Uraiyur, but standing here just feels different.'

Struck by inspiration, Kayalvizhi responded, 'It is all in the smell, Ilavarasi, all in the smell. Our pandits have called the olfactory sense one of the five "intelligences" for a reason, and that is because a smell tells so much. In Thiruvarur, or in Chidambaram, or in Uraiyur, you don't just smell the smells of a day, or a year, but of centuries upon centuries. The smell seeps through the small crevices, speaking the stories of the millennia. It is the smell of the sweat of the throngs of devotees, intermingled with the burnt camphor, flowers both fresh and wilting side by side at the feet of the lord. It is the sweet aroma of the bananas and the guavas and the mangoes and the jackfruits softening in the heat of the garbagriha in those massive silver plates on which they're offered. This is the smell of the rich with their fine perfumes and silks mingling with the veritable salt of the earth, in front of the Supreme. This, dear Ilavarasi, is the smell of humanity at its most human—the smells of the tears of the happy, the angry, the joyous. And today, we have begun filling the smells of this humanity in this temple. Akin to raw bananas and mangoes that ripen over weeks to become delicious fruits, this temple too will attain the status of Chidambaram or Thiruvarur.'

A smiling Kundavai whispered, 'Maybe, but maybe even greater.'

Kayalvizhi broke into a wide smile, 'Maybe even greater, but maybe for eternity and beyond,' as she looked in the direction of the praying Ilavarasan Rajendra.

Once the ceremony was completed, the Kuzhu members stepped out of the sanctum. They observed that the water and milk used in the abhishekam had formed a messy pool outside Lord Vinayaka's sanctum. The wise Kundavai Pirattiyar pointed out worriedly, 'Thambi! Look how the water has stagnated outside this sanctum! If this is the case for one shrine, then imagine how it will be once the entire temple with several sanctums is completed!'

The Chakravarthy fell silent with worry, as did the entire Kuzhu. Vellaiappan reassured all, stating, 'Arasey! Do not worry! I will design a durable water plumbing system that will filter and transport the fluids used for the abhishekams to irrigate the trees and plants of the temple complex. It would suffice if the temple's drains are periodically cleaned after the consecration.' While the Kuzhu collectively heaved a sigh of relief, the Chakravarthy and Brahmarayar exchanged smiles recollecting the incident that had turned their attention to Vellaiappan almost two decades ago.

The construction of the temple continued. The sculptors, the best in Chola Nadu, worked on the various ornately carved pillars to support the gigantic structure. Workers toiled outside in the courtyard of the temple, arranging stones and making sure they were of the right dimensions. Alagiya Nayaki still unfailingly supplied delicious, frothy buttermilk to the weary labourers. The holy sanctums were being constructed according to the agama shastras and with great precision. Near the Thyagarajaswamy Kovil in Thiruvarur, sand was being excavated and loaded on to the bullock carts. It was then that an unanticipated incident occurred.

Vellaiappan had earmarked a vast area to mine sand, so that the labourers did not have to dig deep. An embankment was built around this area and logs were placed at regular intervals to ensure the labourers could climb to the top once the day's tasks were complete.

The sun beat down relentlessly in Thiruvarur, making the backs of the labourers digging into the field glisten in a vale of luxuriant ebony. Labourers dug sand, transferred it into vats that were hauled up using pulleys. The sand was then loaded into massive bullock carts for transport to Thanjavur. The gentle breeze cascaded over one of the numerous tributaries of the mighty Kaveri which flowed through the town. It caused the dust to rise from the ground and make the air heave and haw with the collective labour of hundreds gasping for breath as they quarried sand for the temple.

And then, suddenly, a labourer heard a rumble from under the ground. As the rumbling intensified, the men and women looked at each other, concernedly. A couple of them were sent to fetch the *anipathi* who was deputed to oversee the quarrying in Thiruvarur. Yet, even he, a man who had seen many a battle to its victorious conclusion, could not begin to fathom the mysteries that were the progressively loudening rumbling of the ground. And then, slowly, the hitherto yellow sand, as blisteringly yellow as the best of marigolds, began to darken.

Coincidentally, the temple bells in the nearby Thiruvarur Thyagarajaswamy temple began to ring loudly and resonantly enough that it could be heard across the town. Matching the steady rhythm of threes in which the bell was being rung, the rumble turned into a gurgle, and water sprung forth. The dust began to settle, and the land began to gradually recede as water confidently flowed from the spout.

One man screamed loudly, 'Look! Water is gushing out!' Everyone was shocked and immobilized, but only for a few moments. Vandiyathevan swung into action and commanded all the workers to scale the logs and reach the top of the embankment.

Dandanayakan quickly scribbled a message on a palm leaf manuscript, affixed the tiger insignia of the Cholas and dispatched a horseman to deliver the message to Brahmarayar. On reaching Aniruddha Brahmarayar's palace at Thanjavur, the horseman informed the guards that he was carrying an urgent message from Dandanayakan and showed them the Chola insignia. As soon as he was ushered in to Brahmarayar's presence, he submitted the manuscript and exclaimed, 'Aiyya, water is flooding the sand mining area!'

20

Brahmarayar was taken aback that the water table at Thiruvarur was so close to the ground surface. But, as always, he maintained his composure and immediately sought an audience with the Chakravarthy. Brahmarayar informed the Chakravarthy, 'Arasey! Water has started sprouting at the Thiruvarur sand-excavation site. The water table there appears to be quite close to the surface. This is something we had not anticipated. I am confident that Vandiyathevan, Dandanayakan and Vellaiappan will ensure the safety of the workers and the citizens of Thiruvarur.' Brahmarayar paused as the Chakravarthy was immersed in thought.

The Chakravarthy recollected that a contradictory feature of the imposing Thyagarajaswamy Kovil was the inconspicuous temple tank. His father, Sundara Chola, had often mentioned towards the end of his life, of his desire to expand the tank at the Thyagarajaswamy Temple. The Chakravarthy interpreted this as an order from Emperuman to fulfill his deceased father's wish. He calmly told the Brahmarayar, 'Aiyya, please summon peruntachchar. A trip to Thiruvarur is in order.'

By the time the trio reached Thiruvarur, work on extracting the sand had ceased and the water level had increased significantly. The Chakravarthy asked peruntachchar, 'Is it possible to enlarge the tank?'

Peruntachchar affirmed, 'Arasey! It is possible. We may

deploy the men engaged in sand excavation in widening and deepening the tank.'

The Chakravarthy ordered, 'Begin expanding the temple tank right away.'

A mammoth tank was constructed in two months. On completion, the water in the expansive tank shimmered in the sun, reflecting the Thiruvarur Kovil gopuram. The Chakravarthy, after consulting his sister, Kundavai Pirattiyar, decided to name the temple pond Kamalalayam after the presiding goddess Kamalambal, an incarnation of Emperuman's consort Parvathi.

The temple site, as always, was abuzz with activity and enterprise. The sounds of the stone masons at work and the raucous rhythm of the boulders being carved into blocks and sculpted thereafter filled the air. Pillars were very important in the temple, as they not only supported the vast ceilings but also added to the aesthetics of the temple. The most talented sculptors of Chola Nadu worked in the blistering sun on pillars of granite, carving exquisite designs of beautiful goddesses and apsaras, scenes from Hindu mythology, and intricate alcoves for the minor deities. The temple, even in its incomplete state, was awe-inspiring.

Alagiya Nayaki didn't refrain even for one day from her self-imposed service to God and humanity. Her equally pious family aided her in making the delicious buttermilk, which she served to the workers. At the temple site, Alagiya Nayaki served copious amounts of buttermilk to everyone, including the royal visitors. The sight of her, carrying the pots of buttermilk, pouring it into the earthen mugs and serving it to the workers, became an integral part of any description of the temple construction.

One day at sunset, the Chakravarthy, having completed all his administrative duties and meeting citizens from various provinces of Chola Nadu, pensively watched the golden orb sink into the western horizon. The construction of the gopuram was to begin the following morning. He recollected the contributions of the Kovil Kattum Kuzhu with pride and happiness. It then occurred to him that while all other members of the Kuzhu were native to Chola Nadu, Vellaiappan though foreign-born had served Chola Nadu and contributed to the temple construction with equal zeal. The Chakravarthy, a devout Saivite, never failed to recognize divinity in humans. He summoned peruntachchar and ordered him to place a boulder with the visage of Vellaiappan carved on it on the temple gopuram.

The massive and imposing gopuram was to be constructed using numerous cube-shaped granite boulders with intricate carvings. When the sculptors had finished carving the boulders and assembling them at one place, the Kuzhu members were perplexed, wondering how these could be transported to the temple ceiling and fashioned into a gopuram. Peruntachchar realized that these sculpted boulders couldn't be hoisted up by conventional means. He secured the Chakravarthy's permission to construct a scaffold from a not-too-distant village to the ceiling of the temple. The Kuzhu decided to transport the sculpted boulders to the temple ceiling by fastening them on to elephants, which would then walk up the inclined plane. Workmen standing at the temple ceiling would untie the boulders and assemble them with great precision in the form of a gopuram. Peruntachchar identified a village, which lay less than a kadham from the Periya Kovil, named Singarakottai as the starting point of the scaffold.

The sculpted boulders and elephants were assembled at Singarakottai and a scaffold that started at Singarakottai and led to the temple ceiling was constructed. It was then that peruntachchar realized that there was a problem: there was no stone of appropriate size and weight to form the base of the gopuram. But the indomitable peruntachchar took the setback in his stride. He sent missives to Senji and Pachaimalai, asking for rocks of the right dimension and density to be transported to Thanjai immediately. He appointed a few of his understudies to inspect the carts coming to Thanjai from Senji and Pachaimalai to identify the right stone. Not stopping with this, peruntachchar deputed Madurandakan Nithavinotha Peruntachchar and Lathisadaiyan Gandarathitha Peruntachchar and a few of his senior disciples to scour the mountainous regions of Tamizhagam for the right rock for the keystone.

One day amidst all this running around, peruntachchar felt very thirsty. He headed to the temple's construction site, hoping to get some buttermilk from Alagiya Nayaki. The workers informed peruntachchar that she had just finished serving buttermilk and had returned home. Peruntachchar's desire for a thirst quencher was so strong that he made his way to Alagiya Nayaki's modest abode.

As peruntachchar entered the courtyard of Alagiya Nayaki's home, he spotted something. At the edge of the courtyard, forming a pseudo-wall, were large, flat and durable stones that would together form the perfect keystone for the temple gopuram. He felt the stones and knocked on them at several places to confirm their durability. He was shocked.

Peruntachchar's thirst disappeared! He rushed to the palace and informed the Chakravarthy, who was discussing important state matters with Brahmarayar, that the keystones had been found at Alagiya Nayaki's house. The duo ceased their discussions and rushed to the home of Alagiya Nayaki, who was taken aback that the Chakravarthy himself and Brahmarayar were visiting her humble abode. People thronged her house within minutes, curious to know what was going on. When peruntachchar informed her that the keystones for the gopuram had been found at her place, Alagiya Nayaki was rendered speechless with shock. She joyously donated the keystones, exuberant that she could make such a tangible contribution to the temple.

When Aniruddha Brahmarayar informed the Chakravarthy of Alagiya Nayaki's services, he was touched. The Chakravarthy rewarded Alagiya Nayaki with ample grants of rich agricultural lands in and around Thanjai.

21

Peruntachchar was lost in thought.

Like any temple architect, he had commissioned the best sculptors in Chola Nadu for the carving of intricate sculptures in the Periya Kovil complex. While doing so, he had hired two sculptors from rival schools—Ekambareswaran, from a northern province in Chola Nadu, and Thyagarajan, the torchbearer of the school of sculpture that flourished in and around Thiruvarur. Ekambareswaran and Thyagarajan, though united in their talent and passion for sculpting, were polar opposites in personality. Peruntachchar hired these two sculptors and their students, who despised each other.

The scale of the project and the Chakravarthy making it clear that he would brook no delays were not the overarching reasons for peruntachchar's seemingly quixotic decision. Peruntachchar engaged in this risky gambit with trepidation and hope. His trepidation was that the egos of the two sculptors may stall the progress of work or cause the artistic quality of the Periya Kovil to deteriorate, or both. Peruntachchar hoped that out of the conflicts of the master sculptors will emerge an edifice of unparalleled beauty. Nevertheless, he braced himself for much rancour and recrimination.

Peruntachchar was not disappointed. From the very first day of work, the air was charged with disharmony. Ekambareswaran and Thyagarajan could not bring themselves to even sit next to each other while discussing the sculptures that needed to be carved in the Periya Kovil complex. Peruntachchar's tact and authority were inadequate to get the duo to collaborate. He was forced, rather sheepishly, to seek Brahmarayar's assistance. The shrewd Brahmarayar fortuitously dropped by peruntachchar's residence when the seventh futile day of discussions were underway. His presence instilled instant civility in both Ekambareswaran and Thyagarajan. The consensus that peruntachchar unsuccessfully tried to bring about during the last week was achieved during the two days Brahmarayar spent at the former's residence, supposedly to understand the overarching theme of the sculptures and to communicate the same to the Chakravarthy.

As it was impossible for Brahmarayar or any other member of the Kuzhu to supervise the activities of the two quarrelling groups of sculptors round the clock, Ekambareswaran and Thyagarajan passed on the baton of their conflict to their understudies. It was not like Ekambareswaran and Thyagarajan wanted to work with each other, but they had to. Peruntachchar had been very insistent on their working together, and said that if they fought or disrupted anything during their work, the matter would be reported to the Chakravarthy himself. This ultimatum resulted in the contrived union of oil and water.

In the beginning, it was an endless volley of arguments between the sculptors, ranging from simple matters of logistics to more important matters, like sculptures to be carved in the various parts of the expansive temple complex. Their fights stopped short of getting physical as they did not want the Chakravarthy to summon them, but there was discord and lack of cooperation between the two groups of sculptors.

It always began innocuously, for example, with a sculptor from Ekambareswaran's school 'accidentally' colliding with a sculptor from Thyagarajan's school. Or when Madurantaka Peruntachchar, a deputy of Peruntachchar, assigned more work to Thyagarajan's coterie than Ekambareswaran's because the latter was overburdened. Accusations, counter-accusations and chaos ensued. It often culminated with a heated exchange of words, and sometimes with a physical tussle between Ekambareswaran and Thyagarajan. A member of the Kuzhu was forced to mediate to maintain order. Hence, the Kuzhu instructed that the duo work on different ends of the temple, and quartered them in different parts in Thanjavur to avoid disruptions but ensured they were paid together and at the same time to minimize conflicts. At least one member of the Kuzhu made it a point to visit the temple construction site daily and converse with both groups to preempt brawls.

With the passage of time, almost all the outer precincts of the temple were built and sculpted, save for one structure—the Maha Mandapam, the grand main hall of the temple. Peruntachchar had been delaying the completion of the Maha Mandapam, for he knew that it would inevitably lead to a fight between the two groups, and asking other sculptors to finish it would lead to unsatisfactory results. Hence, faced with not much of a choice, he sent a messenger to summon Ekambareswaran and Thyagarajan to his quarters and braced himself for a thunderstorm. He also requested Brahmayar to be present.

Ekambareswaran and Thyagarajan walked into peruntachchar's abode expecting Brahmarayar's presence. They had reached an unspoken and unprecedented consensus of requesting that only one of them be handed over the task of sculpting the Maha Mandapam. Both had seemingly undisputed reasons for this ask. The two men and peruntachchar himself were in for a surprise. Within a nazhigai of Ekambareswaran and Thyagarajan reaching peruntachchar's mansion, Brahmarayan walked in, followed by Kundavi Pirattiyar.

The presence of the Chakravarthy's powerful sister transformed the warring sculptors into the very picture of cordiality. It was child's play to convince them that one half of the Maha Mandapam was to be sculpted upon by Thyagarajan's disciples, and the other half by Ekambareswaran's disciples. Peruntachchar's insistence that there be an artistic and stylistic continuity in the sculptures of the Maha Mandapam to present a holistic experience to the viewers, left the duo with nary an option but to collaborate without reservations. Even then, there was uneasiness hanging like Damocles' sword.

The forced collaboration resulted in the discord manifesting differently and had a positive effect. Ekambareswaran and Thyagarajan were competing to carve the most beautiful, imaginative and intricate sculptures. There was no longer a battle of fists and words, but of art, chisels and endurance, which was of utmost importance. Never did the sculptors display such fervour for their craft and a willingness to ignore even food and sleep, for their creativity took precedence over their other needs.

The Maha Mandapam was emerging slowly and steadily based on the design conceived by Ekambareswaran and Thyagarajan, executed to perfection by their disciples. Towards the final stage, after decades, Ekambareswaran and

Thyagarajan stood at opposite ends of the gargantuan room, hunched like all other sculptors, their eyes straining to focus on the most intricate of details.

All the torches of the Periya Kovil were extinguished at the end of the day, but not those in the Maha Mandapam. They blazed on throughout the night—Paranjyoti—an eternal light in a nebulous world.

Competition brings out the best and the worst in humankind, thought peruntachchar again and again as he surveyed the Maha Mandapam every day, inspecting the intricate and soulful carvings on the walls and pillars and ceiling of the Mandapam—the minute details, the symmetry, the perfection devoid of any flaw. *It creates such beauty, such innovation, and revolutionizes the world around u*s, he contemplated as he looked at a carving of a king on a chariot on his way to the battlefield, passing his rough-hewn hands over the tiny spokes of the chariot wheels etched on the walls, all of them distinct despite their size. As he gazed at a damsel on the upper panel of the Maha Mandapam with her face perfectly proportioned as per the Takshashila style of sculpture, even the shimmer of her silk robes replicated in stone, he thought how obsessive art could be and its ability to blind the real world.

Days after the sculpting of the Maha Mandapam ended, at the other end of Thanjavur, in a funeral ground, the smoke from the funeral pyres of both Ekambareswaran and Thyagarajan rose in spires, mingling in the darkness, as their disciples stood around their pyres on opposite ends of the ground.

In death, a consequence of exhaustion for the elderly, they did not fight. The grieving peruntachchar cried softly in the Maha Mandapam, slumped on the floor, beneath a sculpture of the royal family, as the battle-scarred face of Raja Raja Chola gazed down at him, every single one of the scars reproduced to perfection.

22

From the floodplain of the fertile Kaveri delta arose a new Meru.

Meru, a mythical mountain, lay at the centre of the earth, the scriptures say—a bejeweled mountain, so very large and so impossible to measure, it is said by the scriptures. Its faces were made out of gold and lapis lazuli and other gems, it is said. Meru was where the Gods live, it is said.

And yet, the Chola Emperors had brought Mount Meru to the realm of the physical. The discernible. The accessible.

This Meru arose from the heart of the imperial capital, Thanjavur. For most of the Kaveri delta, the Meru could be seen on clear days and cloudy days. Somehow, the Meru of stone had acquired a certain transcendental glow. It shone as a beacon for all those across the land—if they could not see it with their eyes, it remained at the core of their consciousness, the core of their being, the core of the very notion of who they were.

This Stone Meru was a beacon of hope. The citizens of Chola Nadu were no longer simply the subjects of the Chakravarthy; instead, the Chakravarthy too was a subject of this strange new force that this Stone Meru exuded. This Stone Meru made the people in its vicinity, within the geographical boundaries of the Chola Realm, feel a certain indivisible force—a force that strengthened, that nourished, that comforted them.

Despite being a mother that nourished the nation, the Golden-Hued One, Kaveri, was also a very capricious, tempestuous mother. On certain occasions, She would shower Her bounty in abundance, and on other occasions, Her parsimony caused many stomachs across the land to balloon in emptiness. And yet, for some reason, the Stone Meru obviated all those problems.

What else would explain the collective aura of elation that pervaded the nation as the Big Temple neared completion?

All the citizens of Chola Nadu watched the construction of the temple with great pride and excitement and discussed its architecture, construction and the expenses incurred in detail. Several wealthy merchants of Chola Nadu dropped pouches of gold coins in the temple *hundi*s placed at various temples of Chola Nadu. It seemed as if it was not just the stone masons, construction workers and sculptors, but the entire nation was constructing the Periya Kovil. Did any other grand monument across the globe garner as much citizen participation as the Periya Kovil did?

But then again, was the Periya Kovil a mere monument, a transient edifice, a *building*?

The royals emptied their coffers into donating generously into the temple. Raja Raja Chola contributed twenty-four bronze idols, Kundavai Pirattiyar contributed five, the Queen Consort contributed six, and the rest of the royal family contributed ten idols. The cloister mandapam with thirty-six sub-shrines for the ashtadikpalakas and the minor deities was funded by Dandanayakan. Funded not because the rich Chola Empire couldn't afford to use state funds, but funded out of a love for Emperuman.

The Stone Meru galvanized the nation as a whole, in more ways than one. The elephants diligently and doggedly pulled the sculpted blocks from Sarapallam to the temple ceiling. Workers, waiting at the temple ceiling, untied the sculpted blocks and assembled them with great precision to form a vimanam. Despite her age and recently acquired wealth, Alagiya Nayaki did not cease to be of service to Emperuman. She continued to serve the thirst-quenching buttermilk to all those engaged in the temple construction, with immense affection and humility.

Karpagavalli, during the five years of temple construction, was labouring to compile the music, hymns and dances that were to be performed at the *kumabhishegam* for the regular prayers and festivals of the Periya Kovil. She travelled across the length and breath of Dakshina Bharata, recruiting artists as *asthana vidwan*s and *vidushi*s attached to the temple. Karpagavalli's spirited efforts resulted in Thanjavur becoming the destination of choice for exponents of music, *sadir attam,* and numerous musical instruments, including nagaswaram, thavil, *ghatam*, *khanjra*, yazh and *jala tarangam*.

Karpagavalli's long association with Kundavai Pirattiyar taught her the importance of transparency and fairness in dealings and documenting transactions. She ensured that the duties, remunerations and succession plans for all artists were recorded on copper plates and after securing the Chakravarthy's approval, inscribed on the walls of the Periya Kovil.

During her extensive travels, she met a nagaswaram vidwan, Sivanandam, who introduced her to other musicians and helped her set several tevarams to tune. Their professional acquaintance deepened into friendship and the couple, in a few years, started living together. They performed at several places, including Thanjai, Kanchi, Madurai, Hampi, Vatapi,

Tirupathi and Kashi, and donated their earnings to the temple construction corpus.

Karpagavalli continued to visit the pond within the palace complex whenever she was in Thanjavur. But now it was not to seek permanent refuge in the pond, but to enjoy its cool environs in Sivanandam's company. As the Periya Kovil neared consecration, Karpagavalli and Sivanandam too were expecting their first child.

The Stone Meru truly represented the past, the present and the future—not only of Chola Nadu, not only of Tamizhagam, but of humanity as a whole.

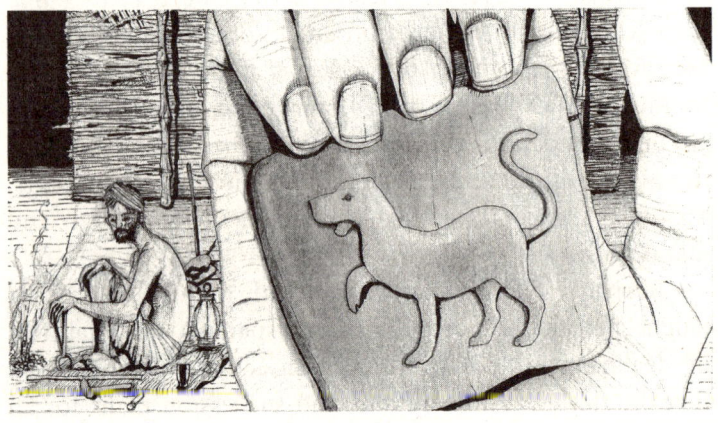

୧

Let us travel back to Sepang to see how far the wheels of revenge had turned since our last visit there. The chief of spies spent a considerable amount of time in the selection of spies for the mission to sabotage the Periya Kovil. He hand-picked twelve half-Tamil spies who not only looked like Tamils and spoke Tamil but were also shrewd, cunning and adept at riding horses, wielding weapons and handling tools. These twelve men interacted with the Tamil prisoners in the dungeons of Sepang, so that they became fluent in Tamil. To gain proficiency in the Chola dialect of Tamil and garner information about the Periya Kovil, they were posted as porters at the Kadarapattinam harbour. The spies interacted with the Tamil traders who regularly made their way to Kadarapattinam.

The Tamil traders who travelled to Kadarapattinam from Chola Nadu were very proud of and excited about the Periya Kovil. They uninhibitedly spoke of the ongoing construction, its grandeur, even in its partially complete state, how the raw materials were sourced, and the immense expenditure incurred on constructing the temple. The spies assimilated this information and passed it on to the chief of spies and Abhinava on a regular basis. Abhinava, as advised by the chief of spies, ordered his naval chief to construct a ship that resembled a ship of the Chola Merchant Navy, in order to transport the spies from Kadarapattinam to the azure shores of Nagapattinam. Three small boats were loaded on to this ship.

The fake Chola vessel carrying the spies sailed the route that was conventional at the time. This route hugged the Sepang coast, touching the northern tip of Sumatra, the small Chola base in the uninhabited isles off the coast of Angkor, before entering the open sea, reaching Nagapattinam two weeks after leaving Kadarapattinam. As the vessel neared the coast of Nagapattinam, the spies finalized their plan of infiltration. They anchored the ship at some distance from the shore and waited until dusk when all traffic had subsided.

The spies then lowered the boats from the ship and sailed to the coast carrying with them a large amount of gold coins Abhinava had granted them. They made their way to *Chattiram* to rest for the night and also to get information about the ironsmiths at Nagapattinam. They identified an aged ironsmith who agreed to make twelve badges bearing the tiger insignia that Chola soldiers fastened on their upper arm. Next, they split up into four groups: one was to work at the sand excavation site of Thiruvarur, another at the temple construction site in Thanjai itself, the third as apprentices to sculptors, and the fourth as cart men, transporting raw materials. This split was to ensure that that they learnt about all aspects of the temple and escaped detection. After agreeing to regularly correspond with each other, they split up in Nagapattinam itself and headed to their new workplaces.

It seemed to be the perfect plan to them; one that would ensure Raja Raja Chola regretted his attack on Kadarapattinam. But even the best of plans has an inherent defect that the conceiver fails to spot or is brought to naught by an unforeseen event. The spies were unaware that Subbiah had spotted them.

After Vellaiappan moved to Thanjai with Angayarkanni and their children, Subbiah continued to live in Nagapattinam, overseeing his business, and visited Thanjai from time to time. One evening as he gazed out onto the ink-blue expanse of sea in front of him, waiting for his men to return from their fishing expedition, he saw three boats reach the shore. Unlike the residents of Nagapattinam who would carry the boats to their houses, these men hid the boats amidst the craggy rocks and left. Subbiah, now an old man, wobbled towards the spot where the three boats had reached the shore. By then, the sprightly spies from Kadaram had disappeared. This incident disturbed Subbiah. He arranged for the boats to be transported to the backyard of his house and sent a message to Vellaiappan informing him of the suspicious incident.

But Subbiah too had committed a potentially drastic blunder. Instead of sending the message to Aniruddha Brahmarayar who lived in Thanjai and was authorized to deal with such developments, he sent the message to Vellaiappan, who was dividing his time between Thanjai and Thiruvarur. The servants at Vellaiappan's household placed Subbiah's message with the rest of his correspondence in his personal chamber. As Vellaiappan was too preoccupied with the construction of the temple, Subbiah's message lay amidst a pile of other messages that required his attention. The message gathered dust at Vellaiappan's residence in Thanjai, and spies successfully gathered momentum and infiltrated the workforce that was engaged in the temple construction.

The fate of the temple hung in the balance.

23

One day, as Vellaiappan sifted through the pile of correspondence accumulated in his chamber, he discovered Subbiah's missive. As he read the epistle, he was gripped by panic and anger. Vellaiappan stormed to the palace, his bronzed face ruddying, gritting his teeth with such force that even the footmen and soldiers began jumping out of his way. After paying his respects to the Chakravarthy, he silently handed over Subbiah's missive to the Chakravarthy. Observing the Chakravarthy's brows knotting up, a vein seemingly springing out of his wrinkling forehead as he read the epistle, a deathly silence descended upon the court.

The Chakravarthy regained his composure, stood up regally and apprised the court of the impending disaster. He then instructed, 'First, we must arrange to check the identities of our workforce and nab the twelve spies. It is highly likely that they are sporting forged army badges. We must also be vigilant and observe suspicious activity at the temple site, throw the miscreants in our dungeons, and ensure that no harm befalls the temple.

'Since there are ten *jaamam*s in a day, I propose that the seven members of the Kovil Kattum Kuzhu, including me, accompanied by fifteen soldiers each, spend approximately one and a half jaamams each in the temple incognito, surveying the Periya Kovil for suspicious activities.'

As the Chakravarthy made the pronouncements,

Aniruddha Brahmarayar, Dandanayakan, Vandiyathevan, Aniruddhan, Rajendra and Vellaiappan grimaced inwardly, bracing themselves for a formless disaster looming large in the horizon.

※

The Cholas became aware of the infiltrants from Sepang barely two months ahead of the *kumbabhishekam* of the Periya Kovil. By then, all twelve spies had congregated at the Periya Kovil to deliver the coup de grace.

A contingent of fifty Chola soldiers rode swiftly to the nearly complete Periya Kovil and ordered all workers to stop working and assemble in the blazing midday sun for a badge inspection. Word was sent from the palace to peruntachchar and his deputies to be present at the site to identify any recently employed labourers. The spies stood in the serpentine line, trying not to reveal their inner turmoil. The Chakravarthy's security guards ordered the labourers to form twenty-five queues, so that two guards may inspect one queue. So immobilized were the panic-stricken dozen spies that they failed to split up and join separate queues. This mistake would work to their advantage.

The spies stood amongst the other labourers, holding their badges between their sweat-soaked hands. Was this their end? Were they so foolish that they could not even forge a badge properly? While their badge mostly resembled the official badges of the labourers of the Periya Kovil, a trained eye could detect the discrepancies. As the guard approached them, their hearts started beating faster. The spies made a brief, futile motion of attempting to search for their badges and a few seconds later handed over the badges to him.

Suddenly, the guard turned around and saw the smiling face of Alagiya Nayaki, holding a mud pot of cool buttermilk for him. He took the pot and gulped the buttermilk in one rapid motion. Not looking at the badges in his hand, he handed them back and proceeded down the line.

Thereafter, the spies merged with the ocean of labourers and moved on. The Kuzhu, however, didn't.

Upon hearing that no one with forged badges was nabbed, the Kuzhu met in the royal palace in Thanjai. There, Kundavai, trying her best to hold back tears, announced, 'While the spies have escaped our grasp for now, we will have to ensure that this is the final time this happens.' Immediately, silence hung over the members of the Kuzhu. 'However', spoke the ilavarasan, 'while it may be difficult to nab the saboteurs directly, we can do so indirectly. We should send our spies to the markets in and around Thanjai to investigate if there were any suspicious purchases recently. Thereafter, we can act upon the information appropriately and protect the home of our Lord, He who protects us.'

The Chakravarthy nodded in agreement.

It was another hot and tedious day at the Periya Kovil

for the labourers. As they continued carrying rocks from the shipments from Senji to the temple, the sun mercilessly bore down on them. Stopping their work for a moment, the spies travelled down from the temple site to a secluded site on the banks of the Kaveri where no one was likely to hear them.

'It has been a long time since we've entered this land, and yet we've done nothing at all,' complained the first spy as he washed his face.

'There is a reason for that. The closer we carry out our plans to the kumbabhishekam, the less time the Chola Emperor has to save his face, and the more humiliated he will be,' responded the other, stretching out his legs on the grass.

'Yes, but we should not get caught in the intervening period and should safeguard our stocks. We must begin planning for the climax,' responded the former, and sat down. The grass behind them ruffled and squeaked. The spies turned around, their heart skipping a beat.

And there stood a tiny child, wearing nothing but a loincloth, blissfully sucking on his thumb, smiling at the spies, eyes glinting with curiosity.

The spies were relieved. As they heaved a sigh of relief, the mother stormed in, and dragged the child back, grasping his shoulder tightly as reprimand.

The spies continued their conversation.

𑀘

'Everyone is required to stand in front of your tents! The soldiers are going to inspect your tents!' boomed the voice of the foreman one evening.

This spelt doom for the spies.

For the past two months, they had been stockpiling a variety of explosives from the markets of Thanjavur, each time from a different merchant from a different part of the market. But little did they know that the sale of explosives was being tracked by the Kuzhu to identify potential saboteurs, and that the merchants had reported the sale of explosives to two labourers working at the temple site.

Immediately, the Kuzhu had swung into action. They now possessed a clue that would help them nab the potential saboteurs. One rainy evening in Thanjai, the Chakravarthy told the Kuzhu, 'Now that we know that the saboteurs possess large quantities of fireworks, we should be able to apprehend them with ease and cull this growing threat to the temple. Our troops led by Vandiyathevan must search the tents of all labourers. However, to ensure they have little time to stash their implements of destruction, we should undertake this search without prior intimation.' The plan was then put in motion.

On hearing the foreman's announcement, one of the spies peeked out of the tent. A Chola soldier was seen nearing the adjacent tent. The next one in line was theirs. Quickly, the spies concocted a plan.

They removed the fireworks from their tent and dumped them in the grassy wasteland behind it. One of the spies began drinking copious amounts of water.

Just as the soldier was escorted in, the spy began shaking like a dead leaf in the breeze. He fell down, his muscles moving involuntarily. A watery froth escaped his mouth as he lay on the floor, his body jerking randomly.

The Chola soldier rushed out and called for a vaidhyar. A couple of other labourers took the writhing spy on their broad shoulders and carried him out as he continued to spew forth gargled water and saliva.

The fireworks rested behind the tent went undetected and

the correspondence between the spies and their controllers in Sepang, unearthed.

The Big Temple teetered closer to obliteration.

The temple had not been consecrated yet. It stood alone, solitary in the skies of Thanjavur, towering over every other building. The idols had just been placed. The final touches were being made. Construction materials were being removed from the piles that they had been dumped in for as long as people could remember. The heat and dust from the construction had subsided, leaving an odd calmness, a solitude that the temple exuded.

And yet, the temple felt inhabited.

Anyone who walked through the precincts—through the three-thousand-odd kuzhis that comprised the campus, the various shrines within the complex to a variety of deities, the cloister mandapam which kept away the sun, the heat, the dust, and the cool, almost ethereal sanctum sanctorum of Brihadeeswara himself—would have unanimously agreed, without a shadow of a doubt that the temple was not empty.

Indeed, the temple inhabited its own historicity—the weight of the future it held, the promise that it conveyed to citizens today and tomorrow.

A visitor would have heard the whispers of the future in the cloisters, in the nooks and the crannies. They would have felt the palpable air of progress, the noticeable way in which the temple seemed to exude a sense of timelessness in it. The stone which had travelled a long way to get there, was here to stay.

This truth was so self-evident, the writing was on the wall. Adorning every single vertical surface of the temple was a web of inscriptions, of letters reaching out not only at each other in a series of squiggly curls but also reaching out into the times that were to come. The inscriptions, at the first glance, seemed very quotidian—detailing mundane things, such as who contributed what, where the dancing girls of the temple lived, the daily accounts of the temple, the villages attached to the temple's upkeep.

And yet, it carried so much import. It was not only a record for administrative purposes, an effort at state transparency to ensure that the citizenry were aware of the wealth of the temple. It signified so much more than that—it signified the temple constructed by the people, for the people, of the people, and something far beyond what mere words could capture. The tendrils of Tamil that stretched across the wall stretched across time, across place, across every concieveable barrier that humanity could put up to create division, to convey a unity of cause, of resolution and of vision.

A temple had been built, whose dimensions would take at least a day to measure, months to plan, years to construct, and which would go on to stand regally for millennia to proclaim the regality of the Chola Empire. The temple showcased the rich artistic and cultural heritage of the Chola Dynasty and its subjects. The temple had been built to honour the gods who blessed and protected the nation during times of trial and tribulation. The temple had been built not only to assuage a troubled conscience but also to employ the vast army of a nation and to motivate the citizens.

And it was built not by one family, or by one person—instead, it had slipped through the vision of its founder and become something unfathomable and beyond one people. It became a temple not only to the deities it propitiated but also to the power of human endeavour.

A nation had contributed and built the temple and built itself up too in the process. To that, Vinayaka, Subramania, the Dakshina Meru Vidanagar Paramaswamy manifested in the form of a perfectly carved cubical Lingam—the presiding deity of Rajarajeswaram, his divine consort Periyanayaki Ambal, and Chandikeswarar at the Peruvudaiyar Kovil—all consecrated in the temple, remained witnesses.

𑀘

Ilavarasan Rajendra Chola's shift, which coincided with dusk, was a blessing in disguise. After he finished his surveillance of the expansive temple complex, he dismissed his retinue and met his dear love, Kayalvizhi, every day. Finally, the two lovers, who communicated more often through their eyes than their words, separated by the vagaries of protocol and the stresses of the impending kumbabhishekam, were able to meet in person and converse. They spoke of their lives, their families, and most importantly, their hopes for the future. The Periya Kovil stood witness to the sincerity and ardour of the lovers. After their daily meeting, Kayalvizhi returned home via the southern gate, and Rajendra returned to the palace after briefing Vellaiappan who led the last surveillance shift for the day.

The Kuzhu frantically tried to nab the elusive spies who were busy finalizing their plan to sabotage the temple. The spies decided that the best method to destroy the temple was to mutilate the vimanam and the main sanctum with crowbars and fireworks. Since one of the spies was an assistant to a stone mason, he stole a dozen crowbars and hid them.

As the finishing touches were given to the Kovil, the

nation was exhilarated that a monument that would stand testimony to their might and splendour was complete. The spies were ebullient for diametrically opposite reasons.

The kumbabhishekam is an essential ritual conducted once a temple is built or renovated and is meant to homogenize, synergize and unite the mystic powers of the deities instated in the temple. It involves the ritual bathing of the temple's crown, which is located at the peak of the vimanam. The royal priests, Ishana Shivapanditar and Saiva Acharya Pavana Pidaran, chose an auspicious date for the temple's kumbabhishekam to ensure the well-being of the Chakravarthy and the entire nation.

The date they had chosen was the two-hundredth-and-fifty-seventh day of the twenty-fifth year of the Chakravarthy's reign, or the thirteenth of Karthikai, 1009 CE. After securing the Chakravarthy's approval, heralds announced this date from the largest of cities to the tiniest of hamlets in Chola Nadu. The citizens of Chola Nadu descended upon Thanjavur on foot, by palanquins, bullock carts and horses to witness the kumbabhishekam of the temple whose vimanam seemed to graze the skies.

The spies realized that the moment for executing their devious scheme was imminent. Meeting discreetly at a market in Thanjai, they decided to execute their plan on the eve of the kumbabhishekam. This would be the perfect day, for the Cholas would have no time to repair the vimanam and the vile Raja Raja Chola would be humiliated in the presence of foreign dignitaries specially invited for this momentous occasion, the citizens of Chola Nadu, and the whole world.

24

Vellaiappan—or Roeland Crape—never liked discussing his past. When asked, when prodded, he would offer the most cryptic of responses, the coldest of stares, the most hostile of repartees. The person who knew the most was his beloved wife, Angayarkanni. But what she knew did not emerge beyond the barest of details—a string of vignettes, slipped out during moments of exceptional vulnerability or nostalgia, that she strung together to construct the life of a man she had married and loved. The past was a subject that Angayarkanni dreaded to tread with her husband. And that she would perhaps not know the full extent of his life before she found him in the sea was a fact that she had gradually made peace with. There was nothing that she could do about this, she had realized, and she'd grown to love the man more.

But seeing those men, seeing that tongue being spoken—that made Vellaiappan realize that his past would never move past him.

Vellaiappan was born as Roeland in the Kingdom of Denmark. His father was a feudal lord, owning a sizeable estate right outside the city of Aarhus, in Jylland. His father had died when Vellaiappan was five. His mother, Ingenborg, remarried another man of her late husband's social station, and he was decidedly unkind to his step-children, an unpleasant reminder of his new wife's past. Vellaiappan's older brothers and sisters—of whom there were six—were more amenable and put up with their lot in life.

Vellaiappan, however, was not his older siblings. His mother had a special affection for him, her youngest-born and the most different from his siblings. Yet, his insouciance towards any form of parental authority provoked resignation and despair from his affectionate mother and beatings from his not-so-kind stepfather. One beating over a minor perceived infraction, however, was too much for Vellaiappan to take. And thus, at the age of eleven, in the dead of night, he stole a sizeable amount of money and ran away from home. He was never to see his mother or his siblings again.

Vellaiappan may have been a decisive child, but he still remained a child. He didn't get far before he was swindled of most of his bounty. It was also a period when a number of unkind men took advantage of his boyish looks and his peripatetic existence, and took advantage of him in more ways than one. And yet, Vellaiappan was determined not to make his way back home—a life of abuse was still a life that he led on his own terms. He may have been miserable, but at least he was free and unencumbered.

Two years passed thus, and Vellaiappan bounced around from market to market, from name to name. As he ended up in Venice, the bustling port on the Adriatic, a certain merchant took a shine to him. The merchant saw that behind the roguish demeanour common amongst many of the young urchins of this metropolis lay a keen mind, a curious mind, and a personage eager to prove himself and stand on his own feet. And thus, the merchant, for all intents and purposes, adopted Vellaiappan and took him under his wing. Vincenzo saw to it that Vellaiappan was trained in the great Latin books that formed the core of the canon in that region, as well as a variety of other disciplines, such as mathematics and construction. Vincenzo taught Vellaiappan the various intricacies of managing a large enterprise, how to maintain a ledger of accounts, how to ensure that personnel were well-trained. Perhaps, most importantly, Vincenzo taught Vellaiappan what it meant to be loved, what it meant to feel safe, what it meant to be a part of a family.

And yet, Vellaiappan's restlessness could not be contained. Five years on, as he completed his education, he began travelling across Europe's ports, ostensibly to expand and supervise Vincenzo's trading empire. And one day in Constantinople, he just left. He travelled eastwards, into Saracenic lands, much like he did in his childhood, bouncing from place to place. He usually worked with some trader or the other, supervising accounts or making sure that the internal dynamics of the business were well-managed.

He never stopped learning, though. In addition to his native Danish and his Latin, he had taught himself Greek, Arabic, Syriac and Persian. In Baghdad, where he spent a happy four years, his evenings would be spent in the House of Wisdom, reading something or the other in the massive treasury of knowledge that overlooked the Eupharates. He was an enthusiastic observer of *kalam*s—the traditional styles of scholarly philosophical debates that took place in the House of Wisdom. Upon knowing that he was proficient in Latin, he was tasked by the scholars of the House of Wisdom to translate their Latin collection into Arabic. When he didn't have to work, Vellaiappan rode his horse across the region, marvelling at the ancient pre-Islamic structures, attempting to understand how they were constructed, the materials used, the dedication that went into their maintenance. He was particularly enraptured by the tale of the Hanging Gardens of Babylon, a mystical structure constructed apparently for the homesick wife of a king—that nature could be defied by human ingenuity never ceased to marvel him.

And yet, Vellaiappan remained restless. Something about even this locale, so distant from the pain of his youth, made him feel restless. But one thing was certain—he did not want to go back home. And thus, he continued travelling. In the great port of Basra, he discovered an expedition of traders and engineers heading east, towards a strange kingdom named Sepang. Vellaiappan had not heard of the place before, but he enthusiastically signed up and set sail.

When he arrived in Kadarapattinam, he was first confronted by its stifling humility, and second by the vast green forests that swaddled the city, enveloping it like a warm, sticky, gooey green blanket. He found the city beautiful. He picked up Sepangese rapidly, and ingratiated himself with the local ruling class. He did a variety of jobs—he helped organize the accounts of the port, he helped supervise the construction of the ramparts, and commissioned a brand new public library, located in the heart of the city and funded by the Shailendra family. Vellaiappan became wealthy too—he was able to buy a large house against the sea, where he was awoken every morning by the sun dazzling across the azure ocean like a sheet of solid gold. He had a large staff. Through the library, he had access to many of the finest texts that money could buy. He was well-known and well-loved by the people of the city.

And yet, Vellaiappan remained restless. Five years in, and his feet began to itch. He sold his property, parted ways with his patrons and boarded a ship heading back to Basra. His future was uncertain.

And then a storm hit. Roland died. Vellaiappan was born in a house in Nagapattinam.

Vellaiappan remained restless. But not once did Vellaiappan think of leaving.

25

With the impending kumbabhishekam, Thanjai had assumed a festive air. People walking around the streets of the Chola capital city could smell the delicacies being cooked in the kitchens of homes to feed those who were visiting the city to witness the kumbabhishekam; the fragrance of jasmines that adorned not just the deities in the temples but also the womenfolk; and the incense at the temples and prayer alcoves of houses alike. People draped themselves in their finest silks, drew elaborate kolams outside their houses and temples, and decorated the streets with plantain trees and flower festoons. Temples and rich merchants in Thanjai set up *thaneer* and mor pandals to quench the thirst of the innumerable visitors who had descended upon Thanjai. *Theru koothu*, *mayil aattam*, *puli aattam* and *poikkal kudhirai aattam* were staged at large street junctions in the evenings.

And yet, the threat was still very imminent. Rajendra started his final shift of reconnaissance. He was both worried and excited—worried that the miscreants were still scot-free and unidentified, and excited about spending time with his dear Kayalvizhi. He was about to complete his shift when his heart skipped a beat. Kayalvizhi had just reached the main entrance of the temple. Signalling to the soldiers to disperse, Rajendra rushed towards Kayalvizhi.

The duo, intending to row down the moat surrounding the temple complex, rushed outside. As they crossed the main entrance, they failed to notice the murmurs of the spies hiding behind the nearby bushes. They got into a boat and started rowing around the temple complex. They also failed to notice Vellaiappan at a distance approaching the main entrance, followed by his contingent of soldiers.

When Vellaiappan inadvertently bumped into the lovers, all three of them were startled. Vellaiappan quickly composed himself and whispered, 'Kayalvizhi! Go home right now and tell Aniruddhan to come to the palace. Immediately! Ilavarasey, please fetch Aniruddha Brahmarayar and Dandanayakan to the palace immediately. There is an emergency.' An unsettled Kayalvizhi rushed back home, while Rajendra headed to Aniruddha Brahmarayar's palace in a mixture of shock and embarrassment after discreetly asking one of the soldiers to fetch Dandanayakan. Vellaiappan hastened to the palace.

When Vellaiappan entered the royal chambers, the Chakravarthy and Vimaladityan were meditating. A month or so after seeking refuge in Thanjai, Vimaladityan had made it a habit to observe the proceedings at the royal court, meditate with the Chakravarthy at dusk, and join him, Rajendra and Brahmarayar in their final deliberations for the day. Vellaiappan stoically announced, 'Arasey! I have discovered the vile spies of Sepang. From what I could gather, they intend to demolish the vimanam and sanctum using crowbars in another jaamam. We must act at once. I have asked ilavarasan to fetch Brahmarayar and Dandanayakan.'

The Chakravarthy's expression of equanimity dissolved into rage. His voice quivering with wrath, he told a waiting guard, 'Summon Vandiyathevan immediately! Tell him that the infiltration has been discovered.'

Vandiyathevan rushed into the royal chamber. By

then, Rajendra, Aniruddha Brahmarayar, Dandanayakan and Aniruddhan had reached the royal chambers. The Chakravarthy, who had decided on the course of action, exclaimed, 'Vandiyathevan! The spies are at the temple complex as we speak. Gather the Kuzhu members and twenty-five of our finest archers and horsemen. I will accompany you. No harm should befall the temple. I want these spies dead.' Vandiyathevan nodded.

Vimaladityan exclaimed, 'I'll accompany you.'

The Chakravarthy vetoed the offer. 'Ilavarasey, you are second in line to the Vengi throne. Your father and the people of your nation have entrusted me with the responsibility of crowning Shaktivarman and anointing you as the senathipathi of the Vengi army. There will be several occasions for you to stand shoulder to shoulder with the Cholas and demonstrate your gallantry. Will my family members ever forgive me if harm befalls you before you and Shaktivarman have retrieved Vengi?'

Despite the looming danger, Vimaladityan felt a moment of joy, elated that he had indeed won the Chakravarthy's approbation. Vandiyathevan, Vellaiappan, Rajendra, Aniruddha Brahmarayar, Raja Raja Chola, Dandanayakan and Aniruddhan, along with the archers and horsemen, left the palace for the Periya Kovil on horseback and at breakneck speed.

The temple precincts were bathed in the milky-white moonlight. A perfect setting for a performance or a feast, rued Rajendra Chola, as the Kuzhu members and other warriors rode near the Periya Kovil. The guards whom Vellaiappan had posted pointed to the miscreants scaling the temple gopuram.

As Rajendra leapt off the horse, the sarapallam caught his attention. As a large contingent of priests and royal family members had to reach the gopuram during the kumbabhishekam, the scaffold was not dismantled. Rajendra gestured to Aniruddhan and a few other soldiers as he silently made his way to the scaffold. Aniruddhan and a few soldiers followed Rajendra. Meanwhile, the rest of the Kuzhu members and soldiers entered the temple complex.

In the dim light cast by the moon and the torches, the Cholas observed the dozen saboteurs steadily scaling the temple gopuram, loaded gunny bags tightly fastened to their backs. As the handful of Chola archers began dipping their cotton-coated arrow tips in oil to set them ablaze, the Chakravarthy stopped them, commanding, 'This is not just any temple. This is a monument to Chola glory and our collective effort over the past years. It is important to stop them; but the temple must not be damaged.'

Immediately, the seemingly effortless task morphed into a Herculean one.

As the contingent with the Chakravarthy paused to think,

the Sepang spies started falling off the gopuram. A volley of arrows pierced the chilly Karthikai air, the twang of bows resonating around the temple with the tonal purity of the yazh. A wet thwap indicated that the arrows had penetrated an object, entering it, destroying it. It was then that the Chakravarthy's contingent realized that there were archers and torch bearers on the scaffold too. They looked around and realized that Aniruddhan, Rajendra and a few soldiers were missing.

The mystery was solved. Ladders flanked the scaffold at periodic intervals to provide access to the scaffold. Using them, Rajendra, accompanied by Aniruddhan and a few soldiers, clambered atop the scaffold. As they stood on the scaffold, they were almost at the same height as the spies, who were presently scaling the gopuram. Shooting arrows at them from the scaffold was much easier than from the ground.

The soldiers accompanying the Chakravarthy hastened to examine the Sepang spies sprawled on the ground.

The saboteurs were dead.

They gestured at the Chakravarthy, who made his way towards the spies.

Raja Raja Chola looked downwards. He saw the faces of the saboteurs. Their eyes remained open, glazed with shock and abjection, piercing the souls of the Cholas who they swore to kill. And Raja Raja Chola repeated an act he had performed almost a lifetime ago; bending down, he closed the glazed eyes of the cold corpses.

By then, Rajendra, Aniruddhan and their coterie had climbed down the scaffold and joined the Chakravarthy's contingent. Raja Raja Chola rushed towards Aniruddhan and hugged him tightly. Rajendra looked on.

Vandiyathevan then ordered the soldiers, 'Remove the corpses now and cremate them before sunrise. Summon Ishana Shivapanditar at once. A cleansing ceremony must be performed before the kumbabhishekam.' Ishana Shivapanditar was sleeping when he was abruptly summoned to the temple site. When he was informed about the incidents that night, he rushed to perform the cleansing ceremony. With the crisis blowing over, everyone was more relaxed and looked forward to going to sleep.

Everyone, except Vellaiappan.

26

Oblivious to the tumult in Thanjavur, Kundavai Pirattiyar and Ilavarasi Kundavai were visiting the Sundara Chola Adhura Salai, one of the several free hospitals the Chakravarthy's sister supported in Chola Nadu. The Sundara Chola Adhura Salai was close to the Pirattiyar's heart; it was amongst the first hospitals she had patronized, in the memory of her beloved father, Sundara Chola.

The visit to the hospital was part of their monthly routine. But this visit was special, for they were donating clothes and money to the needy seeking their good wishes for the successful consecration of the Peruvudaiyar Kovil.

When the duo returned to the palace, the air of muted pandemonium took them by surprise. They extracted bits and pieces of the events of the evening from the overwrought security guards and ladies-in-waiting, but no one could tell her coherently what exactly had transpired. Confused, tired and desperate to understand the threat to the Periya Kovil, the construction of which the Pirattiyar had dedicated six years of her life to, she commanded a coterie of soldiers and her own personal guard to rush to the Peruvudaiyar Kovil to ascertain the situation and to send updates every nazhigai.

While the Ilavarasi sat motionless, the Pirattiyar's footsteps resonated across the hallowed royal chambers in a constant, maddening rhythm. Beads of sweat escaped her hairline and slid down through her now-contorted face on that chilly night. Suddenly, she had aged a decade, seemingly in a second, her face contorted with panic.

The miasma of ignorance was not to prevail around the senior statesperson for long. Even before the first nazhigai would end, they observed the Kuzhu riding into the vast palace grounds. The Kuzhu members' erect postures as they rode into the inner courtyard of the palace and relief and happiness on the faces of the palace guards enthused the duo. The ever-sprightly sister of the Chakravarthy immediately asked her ladies-in-waiting to prepare an arathi. The Pirattiyar and Ilavarasi rushed to the palace entrance to perform the arathi and welcome the Kuzhu members.

The victorious Kuzhu members, after posting archers and horsemen to guard the temple complex, had returned to the palace. After the aunt and niece performed the arathi and welcomed the Kuzhu members, they triumphantly informed the duo that their mission had succeeded. It was Vandiyathevan who broke the good news. He exclaimed, 'Devi! The saboteurs have been killed! Our soldiers have been posted to guard the temple complex. The kumbabhishekam will be performed at the appointed muhurtham tomorrow.'

Kundavai Pirattiyar heaved a deep sigh of relief, while the Ilavarasi's eyes clouded with tears of joy. Vandhiyathevan narrated in detail what happened at the temple precincts. Kundavai Pirattiyar walked up to her beloved brother, the Chakravarthy, and in a rare public display of affection, kissed him on his forehead. She then embraced Rajendra and profusely thanked the Kuzhu members. Meanwhile, the ladies-in-waiting served cool water and warm saffron-flavoured milk to the Kuzhu members.

The royal family then requested the rest of the Kuzhu

members to disperse and catch up on some sleep before the kumbabhishekam began at dawn.

Everyone, except Vellaiappan, started leaving. He approached the Chakravarthy and beseeched, 'Arasey, I humbly request a private audience with you and Kundavai Pirattiyar. I need to discuss a grave matter with you.' The Kuzhu members were puzzled but did not tarry as the Chakravarthy nodded. Once the trio was alone in the hall, Vellaiappan exclaimed, 'Arasey! Thaye! I just discovered that Ilavarasar Rajendra and my daughter Kayalvizhi are in love. I will talk to her and ask her to desist from this inappropriate relationship. I request you to have a word with the Ilavarasar too.'

The Chakravarthy and Kundavai exchanged glances and then burst out laughing.

The Pirattiyar pacified Vellaiappan, 'We have been aware of them being drawn to each other soon after the Kadaram expedition! The Chola dynasty does not frown upon its family members marrying the denizens of Chola Nadu, who have reposed much faith in—and have showered immense affection on—us. The Chakravarthy married Vanathi, a general's daughter, and I married Vandiyathevar, a brave warrior! Further, Kayalvizhi is the daughter of a man who, though not native to Chola Nadu by birth, has tirelessly worked for the betterment of this nation We have no objections to this alliance and were waiting for an opportune moment to discuss this with you.' The Chakravarthy added, 'I have had the good fortune of assisting couples deeply in love getting married, be it Kundavai Pirattiyar and Vandiyathevar or Utthama Chola and Poonkuzhali ammai. I will announce the wedding of Rajendra with Kayalvizhi tomorrow at the kumbabhishekam with your consent!'

Vellaiappan, rendered tongue-tied with ambivalence, nodded in agreement, bowed to the Chakravarthy and Kundavai and left the Royal Chambers.

While Vellaiappan was happy that he did not have to break his dear daughter's heart by asking her to end this morganatic relationship, he was concerned about Kayalvizhi's possessive streak. Will she be happy married to the next Chakravarthy of Chola Nadu? Falling in love was after all much easier than staying in love and forging a happy marriage, especially in the face of the pressures and challenges the ruling family is relentlessly subject to. It also struck Vellaiappan that the Chakravarthy had mentioned that he had assisted couples deeply in love to get married. Had the Chakravarthy, whom not just Chola Nadu but the entire Bharata Kandam was besotted with, never fallen in love?

27

The next day dawned bright as if even Mother Nature had readied herself to celebrate the kumbabhishekam. The palace employees and residents of Thanjai had enthusiastically stood shoulder to shoulder to decorate the Peruvudaiyar Kovil during the last few days. These decorations enhanced the majesty of the newly constructed temple complex. Expansive, intricate and colourful kolams were drawn at all entrances and in front of each of the numerous shrines. The corridors were decorated with festoons. Plantain trees were fastened on both sides of each of the four entrances to the temples. Illuminated, brand-new brass lamps twinkled in the alcoves that flanked the Periya Kovil's multiple sanctums. Two silver *kuthuvilakku*s were placed in front of each of the deities. Heady fragrance emanated from the flowers that decorated the deities along with the incense, sandalwood paste and *thiruneeru*. The moat that surrounded the temple was filled with fresh water that reflected both the clear blue sky and verdant trees that were planted on its banks. It appeared as though Thanjai had been transported from *bhuloka* to *svarga loka*. One could scarcely believe that this very temple could have been obliterated the previous night and was the site of a dozen gory deaths.

The citizens of Chola Nadu, dressed in their finest silks and jewellery, thronged the streets that led to the Peruvudaiyar Kovil. The Kuzhu members and their families;

Alagiya Nayaki; Karpagavalli and Sivanandam; the two royal priests, Ishana Shivapanditar and Saiva Achariyar Pavana Pidaran, and the court musicians were waiting for the royal family at the entrance of the temple complex. The court and temple musicians had started playing the nagaswaram and thavil. The music and the cheering crowds reached a crescendo when the royal family appeared in sight.

The Chakravarthy, his wives, his son Rajendra and his two daughters Kundavai and Rajammai, Kundavai Pirattiyar and brother-in-law Vandiyathevan, arrived in golden chariots drawn by the finest white Arabian stallions. The Chakravarthy had instructed Vimaladityan to remain in the palace in light of the previous night's horrific incident.

Once the royal family reached the temple complex, the crowd turned uproarious. The Chakravarthy greeted everyone with folded hands, headed straight to the Mukhya Mandapam and announced, 'Today, we are here to celebrate the completion of the construction of the Peruvudaiyar Kovil. It is a proud moment for us, the fruit of our nation's six years of hard and dedicated labour. A lone tree cannot be an orchard. I could not have constructed the Kovil by myself. My dream of building this temple was fulfilled by the esteemed Kovil Kattum Kuzhu, comprising Kunjara Mallan Perunthachar, Madurandakan Perunthachar, Lathisadaiyan Perunthachar, Aniruddha Brahmarayar, Kundavai Pirattiyar, Vallavarayan Vandiyathevan, Vellaiappan, Aniruddhan, Ilavarasan Rajendra and Dandanayakan.'

Rajendra lifted his head imperceptibly when the Chakravarthy mentioned Aniruddhan's name.

The Chakravarthy continued, 'Alagiya Nayaki Ammal quenched the thirsts of the numerous labourers working on the site and also donated the cornerstone on which the gopuram stands. Karpagavalli has been toiling during the last five years compiling the music and dance to be performed at the Peruvudaiyar Kovil and recruiting the asthana vidwans. The farmers of Chola Nadu worked side by side with the Chola army to widen the roads to transport the raw materials needed for the temple construction. This grand edifice would not be standing here today without the selfless contribution and tireless toil of these people. The two sirpis—Ekambareswaran and Thyagarajan—may have left their earthly abodes, but their sculptures that adorn the walls and mandapams of the Peruvudaiyar Kovil are immortal. We must pay our obeisance to these immortal artists.

'Kunjara Mallan Peruntachchar's contribution to this temple is immeasurable. He transformed my vision into reality. He is the unparalleled emperor among master sculptors. I confer the title "Raja Raja" on him. Henceforth, he will be known as 'Kunjara Malla Raja Raja Perunthachan".'

The crowd broke into a deafening applause. After it subsided, the Chakravarthy spoke further.

'Numerous hands from different walks of life worked together with those assigned the task of building the temple and contributed their might towards the same. Yet, to me one of the most significant contributors is a man born in an alien land. Strange circumstances brought him to our soil; like a fish that takes to water, willingly he adopted our customs and language, and began to look upon our land as his own and has done his best to enrich it. As the minister of agriculture, this man, with his magical touch, turned the arid areas of Thondaimadalam into lush agricultural land resembling the gardens of Kubera, bringing prosperity to our citizens. This man dedicated himself to the cause of this temple; this man saved the temple from almost imminent destruction; thanks to his alertness and presence of mind. Vellaiappa, the people of Chola Nadu will never forget you; nor will we allow future generations to forget you. Henceforth, Vellaiappa will gaze forth from the northern side of the gopuram, his visage committed to stone, until the arrival of Kalki on his snow-white steed. We thank you, Vellaiappa; and I speak not only on behalf of the devotees of today but also of those of tomorrow, the day after, and from now unto eternity.

'The brave, valiant soldiers of Chola Nadu toiled day and night braving the unforgiving and relentless heat and torrential rains to construct this magnificent Kovil and have made us all proud. Subbiah, Vellaiappan's father-in-law, provided us with crucial, invaluable information about the foreign saboteurs who sought to destroy the temple.

'I am extremely proud that this temple was built lovingly by Chola Nadu's citizens and not grudgingly by prisoners of war. For this, I must thank you, my dear citizens of Chola Nadu, for you have extended your unending support, have contributed large amounts of your time, energy and money, and have prayed to Emperuman and Mahavishnu for the successful completion of the Kovil. Without you, I would not be standing here today.' The assembled people broke into vigorous applause.

The Chakravarthy continued, 'These brave and valiant soldiers and the intelligent, ingenious Kovil Kattum Kuzhu need to be rewarded for their invaluable service to Chola Nadu and Emperuman.' He signalled to the guards who brought massive copper containers filled with gold coins. While the Chakravarthy rewarded the Kuzhu members and Subbiah, the Chola army's anipathis rewarded the soldiers and labourers. Thunderous applause broke out as the Kuzhu members, labourers and soldiers were rewarded. And then the Chakravarthy signalled to his guards, who brought in several plates covered with the finest silks from Kanchi. Regally, he announced, 'By the grace of Lord Emperuman, I am submitting a tribute of fifty-five pieces of the finest gold jewellery to Emperuman and the other deities instated in this temple.' The Chakravarthy handed over the jewellery-filled trays to the two royal priests, who in turn handed the trays to their disciples, instructing them to use these to adorn the deities after the kumbabhishekam and the abhishekams of the individual deities were performed.

'I would like to share some good news with you,' proclaimed the Chakravarthy, 'I have also decided that Kayalvizhi, the daughter of our honourable minister of agriculture, Vellaiappan, will marry my son, the heir apparent to the Tiger Throne, Ilavarasan Rajendra.' The ebullient Kayalvizhi and Rajendra exchanged a quick glance. The crowd cheered loudly for this announcement, which was proof enough of the egalitarian outlook of the Cholas.

Then began the kumbabhishekam of the Peruvudaiyar Kovil. The Chakravarthy, accompanied by royal priests and Kuzhu members, climbed the makeshift stairs leading to the *stupi* of the vimanam. Shivapanditar chanted Vedic hymns invoking Emperuman's blessing for the temple and the Chola nation. The Chakravarthy poured pitchers of water and milk on the vimanam, smeared the stupi with turmeric and vermilion, and showered the vimanam with flowers and akshadai.

The abhishekams of the individual deities were performed. The deities were draped with fine silks and adorned with the ornaments the Chakravarthy had donated. The priests conducted *deeparadhanai* and distributed vibhuti and *kumkumam* to the assembled congregation. The ceremonies ended with a lavish feast of which the royalty, Kuzhu members and citizens partook.

Finally, the kumbabhishekam of the Peruvudaiyar Kovil was complete, and dusk was setting in.

As the royal family returned to their palace in their golden chariots, Rajendra Chola was lost in thought. He promised to himself, 'I will be your worthy successor, Appa. I will hoist the Tiger Flag not only across the whole of Bharata Kandam but also in lands that lie across the ocean. I will build a monument that will be yet another testimony to the greatness of the Cholas and the people of Tamizhagam.'

Epilogue

The Thanjavur Big Temple during the time of Raja Raja Chola didn't exist in the form that it exists today. In a literary fashion, Raja Raja Chola was the author of the Big Temple, and it was merely the first draft of the classic we know of and love today. Rajendra Chola built the Keralakantan Thiruvaasal, the main entrance of the temple. The Pandyas, who ruled Thanjavur for a brief period after the collapse of the Chola Kingdom in 1279 CE, renovated the temple and built the Periyanayaki Ambal (Goddess Parvathi, the consort of Lord Peruvudaiyar) shrine at the corner of the temple compound. Shortly after came the Nayaks, who after overthrowing the Pandyas and assuming power, built the famous monolithic Nandi Mandapam in the Mukhya Mandapam of the temple and the shrine of Murugar. Then came the Marathas from western India, bringing frescoes on the ceiling to overlap with the faded Chola ones, paintings on the wall, the Sikharam (the golden apex atop the vimanam), the stucco sculptures in the front of the arch mandapam and the mighty fort wall. Finally came the British, bringing with them electric lighting to accentuate the beauty of the temple at night.

I have unified the multiple phases of the construction of the Kovil into a single time period in order to give readers a flavour of the entire temple as it exists today. This is not historically accurate; however, I felt that the initial construction of the temple was the most significant event in its lifespan, and thus, liberties have been taken with historical accuracy towards the end, for crafting a more engaging and relevant narrative. To me, the protagonist of the work is not any of the human characters who come and go throughout the story but instead the temple itself that was being constructed. The temple anchors not only the narrative of this work but also the raison d'être of the various characters whose stories are narrated, their voices lost in the quicksand of history. Thus, the temple's narrative has been condensed into a more abbreviated, albeit historically inaccurate form to tell its story better.

Similarly, many of the characters who tell the story of the temple's constructions are, at least in part, fictional. The most interesting of these characters was that of Roeland Crape. He was a historical character, but has been transplanted back six centuries before his birth. The real Roeland Crape was a naval captain in the service of the Danish crown in the seventeenth century, who not only served as an emissary to the Nayaka king Raghunatha Nayaka of Thanjavur, but also was the first governor of Tranquebar the Danish colony which existed in the coast of Tamil Nadu, India. A gold foil from Raghunatha Nayak to Christian IV of Denmark, in the possession of the National Archives of Copenhagen, grants the town of Tranquebar to Denmark, specifically citing Roeland Crape as the resident of the newly created settlement. In both the world of my novel and the world we inhabit, Roeland Crape was a foreigner who did make his home in India and, in a way, became a part of the nation's fabric. It is thus that some scholars opine that the mysterious European face carved upon the north side of the Periya Kovil's gopuram is of Roeland Crape, and was probably made by Raghunatha

Nayak in commemoration of the trade deal made between the two nations.

As I read about Roeland Crape, both in literature about the Thanjavur temple as well as the museum maintained by the Archaeological Survey of India in the erstwhile Danish colony of Tranquebar (now known as Tharangampadi, or 'the place where the waves sing', in Tamil), an image of a man who was inexorably tied to the geographical region of the Chola Empire surfaced. To me, Roeland Crape at that moment ceased to be a person, but rather an idea—the idea that India, and the land once ruled by the Chola Empire amongst other polities in specific, was built as much by people who were its children by birth as by people who adopted this ambrosial nation as their own. Whether it was Roeland Crape on the temple's gopuram, to me, was immaterial, as is the identity of who it may or may not have been. To me, it is a reflection of the fact that the region was—and continues to be—a melting pot. Certain events may be fictional, but they convey an extremely relevant and unspoken truth that needs to be conveyed.

My characterization of events was also predicated on the idea that the truth was more significant than the facts around it. For example, there are, in fact, no historical records of Raja Raja Chola mounting any overseas expedition to Kadaram or of any prosecutions of the Tamil people in that region either. Similarly, while all the characters in the Chola court did exist, and most of the military expeditions depicted in the book such as the conquest of the Kandalur Salai did occur, I have taken creative liberties with the rationale and the individual characterizations of the characters and the events. Information about what these historical characters thought is practically non-existent. So, for all practical intents and purposes, picturizing these characters involved the same process as for picturizing the fictional characters.

The truth remained that Raja Raja Chola was a man deeply committed to enriching his people and taking them to heights hitherto unreached. The universalism that he exhibits is, in my mind, something that is deeply ingrained in the civilizational ethos of the Tamil people. After all, it was the Sangam-era Tamil poet Kaniyan Pungundranar who wrote '*Yaathum ure, yaavarum kelir* (All the world is my village, and all its inhabitants my siblings)'. Again, whether Raja Raja Chola, or anyone in his court, actually read Pungundranar is immaterial to me, but the truth that they collectively embodied his words and put it into action is a truth I narrate in this book.

A visit to the Thanjavur Big Temple today is akin to travelling back in a time machine through the rich and vibrant history of Thanjavur, not only of the temple around which it grew but also of the people of Thanjavur famed for their sharp tongues, quick wit and their epicurean appreciation of all the finer things of life. The Cholas may have been vanquished in 1279 CE, but the spirit of the Cholas, their adventurism, their ambition and their focus, are still deeply ingrained in the DNA of each person who lives in and around Thanjavur. Most significantly, even a millennium after its construction, the Big Temple has remained an indelible part of the family lore of those who live in and around Thanjavur. Families still narrate apocryphal stories about the construction of the temple, its architectural wonders, and the effort that was taken to construct it. Truly, there is a sense of ownership and pride amongst the people of the land about the Big Temple, an edifice constructed by their ancestors. In a way, they are all Cholas.

I bid you, dear readers (and I hope said tribe is in the plurality) for now, to walk the sands of my imagination with Rajendra, Kayalvizhi, Aniruddhan and all the characters I had the pleasure of introducing to you in this book, to catch up to see where they are now, and their plans for the future. When they know for sure, and they tell me, you will be the first to know!

Glossary

This novel's protagonist, the temple (kovil) Raja Raja Chola built in Thanjavur, is known by multiple names including:

Brihadeeswarar Kovil	Brihadeeswarar is another name for Lord Shiva
Peruvudaiyar Kovil	Peruvudaiyar is another name for Lord Shiva. This is the temple's formal name
Rararajeswaram	The Shiva temple built by Raja Raja
Thanjai Periya Kovil	The big (periya) temple at Thanjavur (Thanjai)

Names of gods

Agni	Fire god
Emperuman, Neelakantan, Thyagaraja	Lord Shiva
Ganapathy	The elder son of Lord Shiva, whose face is that of an elephant and body, that of a human
Indra	The king of gods
Ishana	An incarnation of Shiva and the embodiment of learning and knowledge

Kubera	God of wealth
Murugan	Lord Shiva's second son and a warrior god
Nirṛti	Goddess of destruction
Surya Bhagavan	Sun (Surya) god (Bhagavan)
Varuṇa	God of oceans
Vayu	God of air and wind
Yama	God of death

Tamil months

Chittirai	Mid-April to mid-May
Vaikasi	Mid-May to mid-June
Ani	Mid-June to mid-July
Adi	Mid-July to mid-August
Avani	Mid-August to mid-September
Purattasi	Mid-September to mid-October
Aippasi	Mid-October to mid-November
Karthikai	Mid-November to mid-December
Margazhi	Mid-December to mid-January
Thai	Mid-January to mid-February
Masi	Mid-February to mid-March
Panguni	Mid-March to mid-April

Units of time

1 Nazhigai	24 minutes
1 Muhurtham	48 minutes
1 Jaamam	2 hours 24 minutes

10 Jaamams	1 day

Units of measurement

Kadam/Kadu	1 kadam is around 10 miles or 16 kilometres
Kalanju	2.5 kalanju equals 8 grams
Kuzhi	436 kuzhis equal 1 acre
Paagam	625 paagams equal 1.167 kilometres
Palam	1 palam equals 35 grams

Places in a temple, palace and house

Anthapuram	Women's quarters in a palace
Gopuram	The entrance-tower of a temple
Koodam	Hall in a house
Madapalli	Temple kitchen
Mandapam	Hall in a temple or palace
Muttram	An area that is open to the sky in the centre of a hall in a traditional Indian house
Sannadhi	Temple's sanctum sanctorum

Relationships and forms of addressing people

Aiyya	Sir
Akka	Elder sister
Amma	Mother

Ammai	Respectful way of addressing mother and a woman
Anna/Annan	Elder brother
Appa	Father
Arasey	My Lord
Athai	Aunt, father's sister
Bikshu	Buddhist monk
Chakravarthini	Empress
Chakravarthy	Emperor
Devi	Goddess; a respectful way of addressing a goddess, queen and any woman
Ilavarasan	Prince
Kuzhandai	Child
Paati	Grandmother
Sivanadiyar	Saivite monk
Thambi	Younger brother and a manner of addressing a boy/youth
Thatha	Grandfather
Thaye	Mother; a respectful form of addressing any woman

Professions

Anipathi	The historical equivalent of a colonel

Asthana vidwan and vidushi	Artists appointed by the royal court or temple
Bhikshatana	A mendicant, whose garb Shiva takes on
Dhanadhikari	Treasurer
Dubash	Interpreter
Jothidar	Astrologer
Nakkan	Dancing girl
Pathar	Jeweller/jewellery maker
Senacharya	A scholar in the art of war
Senathipathi	General
Sirpi	Sculptor
Tachchar	Architect
Thalapathi	General
Vaidyar	Physician
Vidushi	Female scholar; honorific for a female performing artist
Vidwan	Male scholar; honorific for a male performing artist

Food and beverages

Adhirsam	A deep-fried sweet made of rice, jaggery and ghee
Elaneer	Tender coconut
Ghee	Clarified butter

Karuvadu	Dried fish
Meen kozhambu	Fish (meen) cooked in a tamarind-based gravy (kozhambu)
Neer mor	Diluted yoghurt; buttermilk
Panagam	A beverage made of jaggery, lemon and water
Payasam	A semi-liquid pudding made of rice, milk and jaggery
Thanneer	Water
Thattai	A deep-fried snack made of rice, urad dal and channa dal

The arts

Damaru	An hourglass-shaped drum, traditionally played by Siva
Isai, Iyal, Natakam	The trifecta of music (isai), literature (iyal), and dramaturgy (natakam)
Koothambalam	A traditional dancing hall
Kummi	A dance performed by young women, involving clapping and singing
Mayil aattam	A dance (aattam) in which the dancer fastens a cloak made of peacock (mayil) feathers to his/her waist

Melakkarar	A performer part of the *melam*, a traditional ensemble of musicians attached to a temple
Padhigam	A poem of 10 stanzas in praise of a deity
Poikkal kudhirai aattam	Dummy (poi) leg (kal) horse (kudhirai) dance
Puli aattam	A folk dance in which the dancer is disguised as a tiger
Takkesi pann	A melodic mode (pann), which corresponds to the Carnatic raga Kambhoji
Tambura	Also known as a tanpura, a four-stringed drone instrument
Theru koothu	Street plays
Yazh	A harp, a precursor to the veena

Places

Bharata Kandam	The Indian subcontinent
Bhuloka	Earth
Cheena Desa	China
Eelam	Sri Lanka
Kadaram	The present-day province of Kedah, in Malaysia

Other terms

Agama Shastra	A set of Hindu scriptures

Akshadai	Coloured rice thrown during auspicious occasions
Angavastram	A cloth placed around the upper body by men
Arthi	An act of worship, involving waving lighted camphor in front of a deity
Drishti kazhithidal	Warding off the evil eye
Gurukulam	The residence of a guru, or teacher, where students live and learn
Homam	The Hindu fire ritual
Jamakalam	Floor rug
Kolam	Patterns of rice flour drawn outside homes and temples
Kottam	An administrative subdivision
Kovil Kattum Kuzhu/Kuzhu	A team (Kuzhu) appointed to build (kattum) the temple (kovil)
Kumkumam	Vermilion
Pattabhishegam	Coronation
Pournami	Full moon
Purnakumbham	A decorated pot of water used during auspicious occasions
Rudraksha	Dried stones or beads which symbolize Siva
Sambrani	Frankincense

Samsara	The endless cycle of birth, death and re-birth in Hindu philosophy
Sathurangam	Chess
Sivan Sottu, Kula Nasam	A proverb which says that taking the wealth (sottu) of Siva (Sivan) leads to calamity (nasam) upon one's clan (Kula)
Svarga Loka	Heaven
Tambalam	A large plate on which offerings are placed
Thirumangalyam	A sacred thread worn by women to indicate their married status
Utsava Murthy	The idol of a god (murthy) taken around the town during a temple's utsavam (festival)
Utsavam	Festival
Veshti	A cloth worn around the waist by men
Vibhuti/Thiruneeru	Sacred ash distributed in Shiva temples
Vihara	A Buddhist place of worship

Bibliography

Balambal, V., 'Kundavai—A Chola Princess', *Proceedings of the Indian History Congress* Vol. 39, No. 1, 1978, pp. 77–83.

Chakravarthy, Pradeep, 'On Units of Measurement', *The Hindu*, 24 April 2014, https://tinyurl.com/3tun6u47.

Jayakumar, R., 'Raja Raja Chozhanin Muthal Por (Raja Raja Chola's First War)', *Hindu Tamil Thisai*, 8 March 2014, https://tinyurl.com/2s4xyvhc.

Kulke, Hermann, K. Kesavapany, and Vijay Sakhuja, eds., *Nagapattinam to Suvarnadwipa: Reflections on the Chola Naval Expeditions to Southeast Asia*, ISEAS Publishing, 2009.

Krishnamurthy, Kalki, *Ponniyin Selvan All Volumes*, C.V. Karthik Narayanan (trans.), Pustaka Digital Media, 2014.

Krishnamurthy, Kalki, *Sivakamiyin Sabadham–An English Translation*, Nandini and Vijayaraghavan (trans.), Pothi, 2012.

Pillai, V. Narayana., 'The Chera Empire in the 9th and 10th Centuries A.D.', *Proceedings of the Indian History Congress*, Vol. 9, 1946, pp. 140–44.

Sanyal, Sanjeev, *Land of The Seven Rivers–A Brief History of India's Geography*, Penguin Books Limited, 2012.

Sastri, K. A. Nilakanta, *The Côlas, Second Edition*, Madras University Historical Series, No. 9, University of Madras, 1955, http://archive.org/details/in.gov.ignca.4293.

Satchidanandan, K., 'Reflections: Two Civilizations', *Indian Literature*, Vol. 44, No. 3, (197), June 2000, pp. 7–10.

Sheshadri, M., 'Mysore Under Rāja Rāja', *Proceedings of the Indian*

History Congress, Vol. 21, 1958.

'Tamil Inscription Throws Light on Philanthropy of Chola King's Maid', *The Hindu*, 26 October 2021, https://tinyurl.com/4y7teuk9.

Vanamamalai, N., 'Accumulation of Gold in Tanjore Temple: An Enquiry into Its Sources', *Social Scientist,* Vol. 2, No. 10, May 1974, p. 42, https://tinyurl.com/hwc38aby.

Venkataramanayya, N., 'Jatā Chōda Bhīma', *Proceedings of the Indian History Congress*, Vol. 3, 1939, pp. 605–26.